THE STRANGER WITHIN

Kathryn Croft

First published 2014
Copyright © Kathryn Croft 2014

Kathryn Croft asserts the moral right to be identified as the author of this work in accordance with the Copyright, Designs and Patents Act 1988.

www.kathryncroft.com

ISBN-10: 1502879905
ISBN-13: 978-1502879905

For Steve and Sharon

PROLOGUE

Now

I am a wife. A mother. A friend. But now I am also a murderer.

Sitting across from me, his arms folded as he leans forward, DS Connolly shakes his head. He is a handsome man, but when I look at him, all I see is his label. Police officer. He is here to make sure I pay for what I've done.

Is there sadness in his eyes? He certainly isn't gloating. Does he pity me because I don't look like a murderer? Or talk or act like one? What does a killer look like anyway? Before now I would have been able to produce a description. Someone with a wild or blank expression, something not quite right. But now I know differently.

"Do you understand what's happening?" DS Connolly says. "That you're being charged with murder?"

Murder. It's a strange word. It's probably been used a thousand times in this cold, sterile room, but

1

somehow it feels out of place. As incongruous as I am. I nod, but he doesn't look convinced. Perhaps he thinks I'm not all there, that I'll plead temporary insanity. But he's wrong. My thoughts have never felt more lucid.

From beside him, his female colleague, whose name I have already forgotten, stares at me, but says nothing. I turn away from the judgement on her face – it will scar me if I hold her gaze – and back to DS Connolly.

"Are you sure you don't want a solicitor here with you?" he asks.

This time I nod, but it does nothing to erase his frown. He's being nice to me because I have been cooperative. I haven't fussed or complained. I've seen enough television programmes to know I should ask for legal representation, but what's the point? I must be their ideal suspect. Is that the right word? Well, whatever the case, I will wear the label as I do the others.

He shrugs and pushes my polystyrene cup further towards me. The tea is bound to be cold by now, but I force myself to drink the tepid liquid. It is flavourless, as if my taste buds have numbed, every part of me frozen by what I've done.

I stare into my drink, avoiding DS Connolly's searching eyes. If I look at him, I will lose my defences. It would probably be good to cry, to release the remorse in which I'm drowning, but I refuse. Not until I am alone. There is blood on my hands and I need to suffer the consequences.

The female officer flicks through the papers she is holding and then nods to DS Connolly.

"Okay," he says. "Are you ready to talk? To tell us everything? We'll be recording this." He indicates the tape recorder on the table. It contains three tapes and looks as if it belongs to a past decade, but I try to ignore it, keeping my eyes on him.

Nodding, I push aside my cup. "I'm ready."

CHAPTER ONE

Three Months Earlier

I stand at the front door, holding it open, a clownish smile on my face as I take a deep breath in preparation. How many times have I done this now? Surely it should be getting easier? But the pounding in my chest begins, and the palms of my hands are clammy.

"Where's Dad? He said he'd be home early today." Dillon shoves past me and throws down his school bag. It slides across the floor, reaching my foot.

"Pick that up, Dillon. You know where it goes." And so today's argument starts: me asserting my authority, Dillon ignoring it, the usual shouts of *you can't tell me what to do, you're not my mum!* But still I persist, hoping that if I'm consistent and determined, things will begin to get easier.

Dillon is taller than me, and with no shoes on I feel like a mouse, but I won't be intimidated. I'm not afraid of disciplining him, even if I am on shaky ground here, in this house that is more his than mine. In his eyes I am a usurper, but in my eyes I am his mother.

At least he is speaking to me. Most days, unless James is around, all I'm offered is a grunt, or more often than not, cold silence. I wouldn't mind if I could put his surliness down to normal teenage hormones. But with everyone else, Dillon is the epitome of affability. Even his younger brother – most fifteen-year-old boys' idea of a pain in the arse – gets the real Dillon.

Eventually he picks up his bag, hanging it on the coat hook with a huff and snarl. Ignoring him, I answer his question. "Your dad got called to do a shoot. In Surrey, I think." Somehow I keep the smile on my face, reminding myself my persistence will pay off.

But Dillon is already breezing into the kitchen, where he knows Luke will be, slamming the door behind him. I close the front door and, with a deep breath, follow him, preparing myself to enter a war zone.

The boys are perched on stools at the breakfast bar and fall silent as I enter, eyeing me suspiciously. I don't know what they think I'm going to do, but surely eight months have been enough time to get used to me?

I run through my usual script. Drinks? *Got our own.* Food? *Not hungry.* Any homework I can help with? *Stop nagging.* It has barely altered since I moved in. Since I became their mother.

Luke tugs at his brother's arm. "But Dad said he'd watch me play footy today." Dillon must have already told him the news about James working late, and they are as disappointed as I am.

"I'll come," I say, already guessing Luke's answer. Although with my offer I have deviated slightly from the script, I can still predict the outcome.

Luke looks at me before turning away again.

"It's okay, I'll go with you," Dillon says. And now they are huddled together, speaking in low voices. Even though I can't know for sure if they are whispering about me – it could be something innocent like school or TV – they know what effect their apparent conspiring has.

I walk to the other side of the breakfast bar and flick on the kettle. Do I try again? Some days I don't have the energy, but today I will give it a go. "I'll drop you at the sports centre," I say to Luke. This is a bonding opportunity I can't miss. "Dillon needs to stay at home and revise. He's got exams coming up."

Luke stops whispering and looks up at me. For a moment I think I've made progress, but then he speaks. "No!" I am not surprised by his response, but it still hurts.

"Sorry, but that's final. Dillon, you know your dad wants you home studying in the evenings." I wait for the battle to begin, and the boys turn to each other but neither of them says anything.

Have I really managed to avoid another argument? I put a teabag in a mug and smile at them. "Okay. Well, dinner will be ready at six." I keep my tone perky; otherwise, like rats, they will sense and prey off my fear.

Luke wrinkles his face. "Not spaghetti again?" he says.

Forgetting about my tea, I pick up a J-cloth and dampen it under the tap. "Yes, spaghetti." I will not argue with them about food. I learned that lesson very quickly. Besides, it was only last week that Luke was asking for spaghetti, so I know what game he's playing.

"Whatever," they say in unison. Same words, same thoughts. It might be easier if at least one of them liked me. I can understand Luke's resistance; how can a twelve-year-old be expected to welcome his father's new wife with open arms? But Dillon's attitude surprises me. He's got a full life: friends, school, hobbies, probably even a girlfriend, so I find his resistance harder to fathom. And I know this is not about the accident.

While they resume their whispering, I wipe down the worktops, each swipe of the cloth a stark reminder that this isn't my kitchen. The black granite worktops are beautiful, yes, but they wouldn't have been my choice. Perhaps they are too luxurious, too distinguished for me. And all they do is remind me I am out of place here, in somebody else's home, trying my best to be a mother to somebody else's children.

By the time I've finished cleaning up, the boys have vanished. I hear the front door slam and rush to the living room window, the damp cloth still in my hand.

I watch them race down the road, neither boy daring to turn back to see if I've spotted their trick. I run outside in my bare feet, shouting their names, but it's too late. For now, they have won.

James insists if I give it time, they will grow used to me. Although I am tempted, I never reply that I don't want them to get used to me. I want them to like me. He says they don't even like *him* half the time, but we both know he's just being kind.

The dinner won't take long to prepare, so now I have an hour and a half to myself. I finish making my tea and sink into the sofa. Lauren's sofa. On the coffee table I spot the magazine I bought from the corner shop a few days ago, which I still haven't been able to read. It's not for lack of time. I simply can't relax when things are so wrong.

I should do some extra studying, but I'm frazzled from my seminar this morning and even more exhausted after my encounter with the boys. So I sit back and close my eyes, hugging my mug to my chest, recharging my batteries. I must be ready for another round. It strikes me that I am partly to blame. I wanted motherhood so badly that I didn't even flinch when James told me he had children.

My mobile rings, and in my eagerness to hear a friendly voice, I nearly spill my tea as I reach for the phone. The caller has to be James. Maybe he's letting me know he won't be late after all? Things are always better when he's here; fear of his admonishment forces the boys to be civil. To be normal. But it is not James' name flashing on the screen; it is my friend Bridgette's. I'm not disappointed; she is a welcome tonic.

"Callie? Are you busy? Can you talk?" Her voice is too loud, as it always is, and I am forced to lower the volume.

I tell her I'm not busy, and she bombards me with a flurry of excited words. I'm so happy to hear from her that I don't even take in what she's saying. Instead, I let the sound of her voice wrap itself around me like a blanket, comforting in its warmth and familiarity.

"You're not okay, are you?"

"I'm fine. Really."

She coughs into the phone, a guttural rasp resulting from her ten-year smoking habit. "I can tell, Callie. You didn't hear a word I just said, did you? I don't care – it's fine to switch off when I'm jabbering on – but it means you aren't all right, so stop pretending you are."

Our conversations always end up here. No matter how much time goes by, she will always check up on me. "Really, I'm okay."

"And everything's all right there?"

"James is great. My course is going well. I –"

"Callie, you know I'm not talking about any of that. Are the boys still giving you grief?"

I fall silent. I don't want to have this conversation again. Every time we speak it comes back to the boys. There is rarely a time in the day when they are not messing up my head, whether they are home or not.

"Just the usual. But let's not talk about that now. Please. I'm trying to give my head a break."

Bridgette agrees and I hear the flick of her cigarette lighter, her voice becoming nasal as she inhales smoke. "Let's meet up for a drink this evening. I can leave work early and be in Wimbledon by seven. I'll call Debbie too. When was the last time we were all together?" She will never say it but I know she holds me responsible. Since I married James I have had little time for anything other than studying and being a wife. And trying to be a mother.

I tell her I can't and she tuts. "What is it this time?"

"James is working late and I have to look after the boys. I'm sorry."

"Well, it can't be helped." She exhales, her smoke hissing down the phone. "But we're going out soon, no excuses. You're twenty-eight, you should be having fun. Seeing your friends. Not stuck at home all the time."

"I'm only stuck at home because my course is home-study, Bridgette. Otherwise I'd hardly be here at all."

I've told her this before, but she always forgets my point, so more often than not we fall into a debate about the ten-year age gap between James and me. And the fact that I have taken on his children. I know Bridgette likes James; she is only concerned about me.

"Okay, okay," she says, quickly changing the subject. She tells me she'll call Debbie and arrange for us all to meet next Friday. "We'll have lunch," she suggests. "The boys will be at school then, won't they?"

I tell her I'm looking forward to it, although I already dread their fussing and worrying. I am fine. I am in control.

By six-thirty there is no sign of the boys. They should have been back home no later than six, allowing time for Luke to change and for the inevitable slow saunter back. Why would they rush when they know they are in trouble?

I calculated the time so their food would be ready when they got in, but now the spaghetti sits cooling in the saucepan, and the mince is drying up. I've been hovering by the living room window for nearly half an hour, and now I am beginning to worry. What if they're not just taking their time to annoy me?

In the hallway, I pull my jacket from the coat hook and step outside to see if I can spot them further down the road.

But there is no sign of either boy, and the street is deserted. Mrs Simmons appears next door, her legs wobbling unsteadily beneath her hunched frame as she struggles with a recycling bin.

"Here, let me help you." Our gardens are separated by a flowerbed and I could easily step over it, but she shouted at me the last time I made that mistake. So I rush down our path and back up hers, before taking the bin from her frail, bony hands. "You do know they don't collect the recycling tomorrow, Mrs Simmons? It's the day after."

She scowls. "I know that. I like to have it ready. I like to be organised." She looks me up and down, then rolls her eyes. I have no idea why; I am dressed acceptably enough in jeans and a loose t-shirt so there is nothing for her to judge. Nothing except the accident.

I take her bin to the kerb and ask her if she's seen Dillon and Luke. If they're nearby she will have noticed. In her living room, her armchair is strategically placed by the low bay window so she can peer out without having to move. Nothing escapes her.

She tuts and rolls her eyes again. "I saw them leave a while ago. Have you lost them?" She raises her eyebrows. "Lovely boys, aren't they? So sad about their mother."

I nod, and explain that the boys are late home for dinner. Mrs Simmons frowns; she'd probably been preparing to deliver a monologue about how perfect Lauren was. "That's not like them to be late. Such polite and well-brought-up boys. But..." She looks me up and down again. "I suppose they can be influenced by all sorts. You want to get on to their dad. He'll know where they are."

Leaving me speechless, as she usually does, she turns and shuffles back inside, attempting to shut the door three times before the lock finally clicks into place.

I rush back inside and grab the house phone, dialling Dillon's number first. The voicemail message – his voice shouting over a dance track – threatens to deafen me. I run back out to check the street again and, with still no sign of the boys, try Luke's mobile. His doesn't even ring.

Something isn't right.

I check I've got my keys and pull the door shut, walking up the road towards the sports centre. It has started to drizzle, but I ignore the droplets splashing onto my face. The closer I get, the more convinced I become that something awful has happened. I picture the way the boys' faces light up when they hear James' key turn in the front door, and it is hard to tell the rain from my tears.

By the time I arrive at the sports centre, my legs feel as if they are being weighed down by bricks. Although huge, the reception desk is manned by only one person: a young girl who looks barely older than Dillon. I ask her if the football match is over and she stops tapping on her keyboard, flashing a toothy smile at me. There is a huge gap between her front teeth and I can't help staring at it. "The match finished over an hour ago." She offers nothing more and turns back to her monitor.

"I'm looking for my sons. One of them was playing football and they haven't come home yet. We only live ten minutes away."

The girl's face twists into a frown. "Maybe they're just hanging out in the café?" She resumes tapping on her keyboard, and I am already forgotten. This isn't her concern; I am just an over-protective mother, worrying over nothing.

The café is loud and crammed with tracksuit-clad bodies. I scan every face, but none of them belong to Dillon or Luke. They're not avoiding home for fear of a lecture; they get those often enough from me, but have never disappeared before. My fear increases and I rush outside, wondering how I'm going to tell James I've lost his children. That I didn't stop them going off on their own and now something horrendous must have happened to them.

I see signs for the football pitches and follow them to the back of the building. No Dillon or Luke.

I can't put off calling James any longer. It will only make things worse if he thinks I waited too long to tell him. But my mobile phone is at home so I need to get back before I can call him. Grateful that I'm wearing my ballerina pumps, I begin to jog, convinced that when I get back I will find a police officer on my doorstep.

It is only when I turn the corner onto our road that I see two figures further ahead. Dillon and Luke. I can tell, even from this distance. People are always recognisable by the way they walk. From the boys' casual pace, it is clear no harm has come to them so my panic subsides. And is quickly replaced with anger.

Running faster, until I catch them up, I shout their names and they swivel round, giggling and shovelling chips into their mouths.

"What the hell are you doing?" Even as I say the words, I know I shouldn't use such language, but I am past caring. "Don't you ever do that again, do you hear me?"

They turn to each other and snicker.

"I'll be telling your dad about this. The second he gets home. What do you think he'll have to say?"

Dillon stops walking and faces me. "Please don't say anything. I'm sorry. I just needed some fresh air, to get my head ready for revision. Please."

Beside him, Luke watches him speak, a slight frown on his face. And I am left with a choice. I know Dillon is lying, but how can I burden James with yet another story about the boys' poor behaviour? No, he's got enough to worry about with his business. I need to sort this out my way, stop depending on him to deal with them. I can do this.

"I'll have to think about that one," I say. "Now, hurry up and get inside. Your dinner's cold."

They walk faster, but I lag behind. I wonder if I've made progress this evening; Dillon's begging is a first. Usually he doesn't care one way or the other. But then I notice the empty Seafare fish and chips bag hanging out of his back pocket, and I know with certainty that this is far from over.

CHAPTER TWO

Even before I open my eyes the next morning, anxiety surges through my body, forcing me awake when all I want is five more minutes of peace. Sunlight streams through the thin curtains and I groan, turning onto my side. James isn't beside me, but there is a yellow Post-It note stuck to his pillow. I rub my eyes before reading his words. Two apologies in one: sorry for being late and sorry for leaving early. I comfort myself with the three kisses he's scrawled underneath. He works so hard for us; what kind of wife would I be if I complained about his absences?

I turn over and face the clock, realising with horror that I've overslept. I should have woken the boys half an hour ago. Now they'll be late for school, which is just more ammunition for them to use against me. *Callie made us late, Dad. It's her fault. Everything's her fault. What are you doing with her anyway? She's not like Mum.* With these words, which are mine as much as theirs, circling in my head, I throw on my dressing gown and hurry to Dillon's room.

I knock and wait but there is no answer. Opening the door slowly, in case he is ignoring me, I see he's not there. The duvet is scrunched up at the end of his bed and his pyjamas lie abandoned on the floor, but the curtains are drawn.

It's the same story in Luke's room, although his is tidier. I wonder if James has woken them, but if he'd been here late enough to get them up then surely he would have woken me too?

It's not long before the puzzle is solved. As I creep out of Luke's room, I hear the front door slam. Rushing to the landing window, I see the boys trotting off to the bus stop, their bulging rucksacks slung over their shoulders.

I should be pleased they've got themselves ready. I want to say they did it so I could have a lie-in. But it's not that simple. This is a small victory for them and we all know it.

At least for now I have several hours before they get home from school. I should try to make the most of today; it is a rare day when I have promised myself time off from studying, time off from worrying. At least until the school bell rings.

I decide to visit James at his shop. He will be pleased with my spontaneity; it's something he must think I've been drained of since we got married.

I have a quick shower and wash my hair. It is getting too long and doesn't suit me past my shoulders, but I'll get round to cutting it soon enough. Always one for making the best of herself, Bridgette would joke that I'm on a slippery slope towards letting myself go.

17

And I'm not even thirty. Smiling as I picture her horror at my split ends, I towel it dry, tug through the tangles with a comb and head downstairs.

My stomach cries out for breakfast, but it's already five to ten and I don't want to waste any more of the morning. I could walk to James' shop, but it's drizzling again so I opt for the bus.

Even in the bleakest weather, Wimbledon Village is vibrant, buzzing with possibilities. Stepping off the bus, my walk becomes a confident strut and I feel my age again, almost the person I was when I first met James. Love changes you, doesn't it? Real love, where you know that without the other person you will wither away. Just disappear, as if you never existed.

I reach The Coffee Bean and push through the door, wondering if I'll see any familiar faces. It's only been eight months since I stopped working here, and I know Carlo still runs the place. The aroma of coffee wafts around me as I make my way to the till, and then I hear a familiar voice. "Callie?"

I turn to see Anthony, flapping his arms around to the bemusement of the customer he's just served. "Honey, how are you? Are you coming back to us?"

"No, sorry." I offer a smile. "Just came in for coffee and breakfast."

He shakes his head and looks disappointed. And I feel guilty again, even though everyone knew when I took the job it would only be temporary.

"Oh, well. Worth a try. What can I get you?"

I order two cappuccinos and two bacon and egg baps. James will have had breakfast by now but he never refuses food. I don't know where he puts it – he's as trim as an athlete – but he swears it's the stress of having a younger wife. I wonder how much of that is said in jest.

With the food packed up in a brown paper bag, and the drinks in a tray, I say goodbye to Anthony, step outside and cross the road to James' shop. Vision Photography. Seeing the name always lifts my spirits because I suggested it to him when he wanted a complete change of image. Meeting James here used to make me nervous. The successful man with his own business. Who was I to think he would be interested in me for more than one night?

But even now, as his wife, I feel familiar pangs of insecurity as I head towards the door. Pangs that are only enhanced when I see Tabitha, leaning over him, pointing to something on the window display. As usual she is dressed immaculately in a tight pencil skirt and blazer, not a hair out of place, and even from outside I can see her perfect layer of make-up. I look down at my leggings and denim jacket and wish I'd worn something else. Something to compete with the woman fawning over my husband.

I once made the mistake of telling James, after one of my visits, that it doesn't make a difference how Tabitha dresses. I insisted she could wear jeans and t-shirts and customers would still flock to his shop, but he only smiled at me and said that image is everything. Three words. Straight to the point. But in those three words I understood the message not to be jealous.

For a couple of minutes I watch my husband at work with his receptionist. James says she is more than that. That she is his office manager. But I cannot give her that acknowledgement; she already oozes too much arrogance.

The display of his photography they're creating – an assortment of smiling families, happiness personified – is beautiful, providing customers with a glimpse of who they could be, even if only for a frozen moment in time. The two of them clearly work well together, and James always speaks highly of Tabitha, so I should be happy that he's got someone supporting his business. So why do I feel uneasy?

"Surprise!" I say, pushing through the door and waving the food bag at James. My forced display of confidence is painful to act out, but I have no choice. Although I'm looking directly at him, I notice Tabitha's smile fade.

"Callie! I wasn't expecting you! What's in the bag?" James throws his arms around me, unashamed at his public display of affection. Even after nearly three years together, I still feel butterflies when he touches me. I still want him to see only my best side.

"I brought some breakfast. Probably a second one for you?"

James laughs. His face crinkles when he does so, and I get a glimpse of the man he will be in ten years. Twenty years. He will only get better with age. "Yep. Fried eggs this morning. Surprised you didn't hear me crashing around. You must have been out of it."

I wish he'd woken me. It would have been nice to do it this morning, to feel his solid body on top of me. To distract me from myself.

Tabitha walks over to us and for the first time I notice spidery lines sprouting from the corners of her eyes. I am a bitch for feeling pleased. "Hello, Callie." She says my name as if she's eaten something foul-tasting and needs to spit it out. She turns back to James. "Don't forget your appointment is in ten minutes." She pats him on the shoulder before heading to the back studio, leaving us alone.

"Why didn't you wake me?" I ask, sinking onto the soft leather of one of the window seats. It's almost as comfortable as our sofa at home. Tabitha chose well when she helped him design the shop interior.

James scratches his chin. "Well, I could lie and say something corny like you just looked beautiful and peaceful sleeping so I left you to it." He laughs. "But the truth is you just looked so tired." I can always depend on James for the truth; he doesn't believe in sugar-coating. "Are you feeling okay? It's not like you to sleep that long. I was home by ten last night and you were conked out."

I offer him a faint smile, but don't mention that I'm probably not okay. Perhaps there is a physical reason I'm not feeling myself. I think about Dad, but brush the thought aside. I don't have the space in my head for that at the moment.

"Anyway," James continues. "I knew you'd have your alarm set for the boys." Yes, that's me. Good old dependable Callie, never letting the boys down.

"They're lucky to have you. I keep telling them that." Neither of the boys will have had a chance to tell him they got themselves up for school, that I slept right through it all. Perhaps they will keep quiet, an exchange for my silence about their disappearing act.

I consider telling him but think better of it. He needs a break from the fighting. "No, everything was fine."

James nods, his eyes lighting up. No doubt he is relieved he doesn't have to deal with another argument. "See, that's progress, right?" But quickly his eyes glaze over and I know he's thinking about Lauren. He reaches for my hand and I digest his silent apology. *I'm sorry for thinking about her. That old cliché about time healing? Well, I'm not so sure about it.*

I'm about to change the subject but he does it for me. "So what have you got planned for today?"

Before I can answer, Tabitha strides back in and slides into her chair at the desk. Her nails click-clack on the keyboard, distracting me from James' question.

"I'm guessing you've got coursework to catch up on?" He unwraps his bap and scrunches the wrapper into a ball, hurling it into the bin by Tabitha's desk.

"Great shot!" she says, a bright red smile spreading across her face, her head falling to one side as she eyes James. *If this is how she flirts with my husband when I'm here…*I avoid finishing the thought.

I turn back to James. "I was planning a day off from studying but, actually, I've got an assignment due in next Thursday. I should really make more of a dent in it."

"What's this one about?" James asks, sipping his cappuccino through the lid. He always does this with takeaway cups, even when he is in the shop and not walking around.

"Fear and sadness."

"What's all this?" Tabitha says. I haven't noticed until now that the click-clacking has stopped.

It is tempting to tell her to mind her own business, but I hold my tongue. James answers for me. "Callie's doing an Open University degree. Counselling. We're so proud of her. She'll have her own clients soon. Just think, two entrepreneurs in the family." But I don't hear his praise. All I can focus on is the word he has used. *We.*

Tabitha delivers a fake chuckle. "That's great." Within seconds she is back to her typing, her earlier flirtatiousness wiped out by James' compliment to me.

Standing up, I tell him I need to get going. I still have plenty of time left before I need to be home. Hours of freedom but no idea what to do with it. Then an idea occurs to me. "Shall we go out to eat tonight? Just the two of us? We could get Mrs Simmons to babysit. It's been ages since we…"

James doesn't need much convincing. "Great idea. But not Mrs Simmons. Don't you think she's a bit…I don't know…it would be more like the boys babysitting her. All she ever does is moan and complain. Or get confused. No, I'm sure Emma will do it. I'll leave early this evening and –"

"Oh, sorry, I don't think you can," Tabitha says, standing up. "I've literally just taken a booking for you.

23

Docklands. Seven p.m. Couple want snaps of their engagement party so it could be a late one. Sorry, James."

"Oh." James takes my hand. "Sorry, Callie, how about tomorrow?"

I pull him into a hug and speak into his shoulder to hide my disappointment. "That's fine. Tomorrow. See you later, then."

I add a brusque goodbye to Tabitha and, without waiting for her to respond, step outside. It is no longer drizzling and the sun is trying its best to make an appearance. As I pass the window and head to the bus stop, still unsure what I'll do until the boys get home, I see Tabitha, already leaning over James again at the window display. I give a half-wave but neither of them notices. When I reach a bin, I toss in my bacon and egg bap. Thoughts of leaving Tabitha alone with my husband have destroyed my appetite.

Back at the house, I step through the door and stand in the hallway. For eight months I have been walking into another woman's home. Every day I stand on her mocha carpet, surrounded by her furniture, her choice of paint. Why is the solution only just occurring to me?

In the living room, I drag the sofa to the window. I arrange the two armchairs next to each other, covering the old sofa patch, and then move the TV over to the other side of the room. The piano and cabinet are too heavy for me to move on my own but there is nowhere else they would fit anyway. Instead I will buy some decorative ornaments for them, ornaments of my choosing. I will get a new rug too, one that will cover most of the carpet.

I let out a sigh of relief. This will be good for all of us; a fresh start.

When I've finished, I stand in the middle of the room and study the new layout. I have only moved a few things but already I feel better. I have put my mark on the room and it will do until everything can be replaced.

But it's still not enough.

I race to the car, haphazardly parked outside Mrs Simmons' house. Giving her a wave because I know she must be watching, I screech down the road, excited to be taking action. Doing something positive, to make things better for all of us.

B & Q is only a short drive away so I am back within the hour, weighed down by heavy tins of pale citrus paint. The yellow will be more cheerful than Lauren's sterile white, and it's bound to lift all our spirits. Surely those Feng Shui experts know what they're talking about? As I make trips back and forth from the car, I further convince myself that I'm doing the right thing. Matching what's on the outside to how we should all feel on the inside.

I change into one of James' old t-shirts, then cover the hallway carpet with dustsheets I find in the shed. I have never painted before, but how hard can it be? The words on the tin promise a single coat is enough so, shrugging, I begin. I will just do the hallway for now. I want to surprise the boys, to show them that things are going to change for the better.

With my earphones in and my iPod blasting out summer anthems, I don't notice the time. It's only when my left earphone falls out that I hear breathing behind me. Still on the ladder, I turn around to find Dillon and Luke staring at me, clutching their bags, their eyes wide.

"Does Dad know you're doing this?" Dillon asks, shaking his head.

"No, actually, I wanted to surprise you all. Cheer things up a bit." I climb down but now Dillon towers above me and I feel as small as an insect.

Luke shakes his head, but he doesn't look angry. He starts to stutter. "B..b..but Mum chose that colour. She wanted it all white, she said, because we both loved snow when we were babies."

Suddenly I feel as if I'm sinking. I have made a horrible mistake.

CHAPTER THREE

Now

"I know what you're thinking."

DS Connolly stares at me, his eyes intense, as if searching for signs of who I am. He raises his eyebrows and waits for me to continue, while beside him, the female officer looks on.

"How could I have made such a mistake? How could I not have seen that changing things in the house would upset them? It's clear as day, surely? But, no, it wasn't. Not to me. Not until I saw their faces."

They both frown.

"Do you have children, DS Connolly?"

His eyes widen at my question – this isn't how he has envisioned our interview going – but he humours me and nods. "Two sons," he says. Neither of us smiles at the irony.

"It's not always easy, is it? We don't always get it right. Dillon and Luke had only lost their mum three years ago, and there I was, a stranger in their home. The last thing I wanted was for them to feel I was trying to replace their mum. I wasn't. I wanted to support them in every way I could. But for eight months, nothing I did made any difference. I looked after them, I disciplined them, nothing worked. So what was there left to try?" I stare at my nails, bitten down to my skin. "They'd been through enough losing Lauren so suddenly to a brain haemorrhage, more than any child should have to go through, so there was no way I wanted to make things worse. I was trying to make things better."

The two officers silently digest my words, assessing them, trying to match them up with the crime I've committed.

"How did you meet James Harwell?" the female officer asks. Is this abrupt change of subject part of their game? To throw me off balance, try and trip me up? What would be the point when I am telling them everything?

"I was working in a coffee shop, trying to save up money to do my Open University degree."

DS Connolly shuffles some papers. "Counselling, is that right?" He turns to his colleague and a silent look passes between them.

I focus on my story. This part, at least, is easy to tell. "He runs his own photography business across the road and he'd come in every morning for a large cappuccino." I smile at the memory. James, handsome and kind, always friendly. "Eventually he'd come in the evenings, after my shifts had ended. We'd just sit and talk. He never looked down on me or acted superior, and when I eventually told him about my dream of being a counsellor he was full of encouragement."

I take a pause; talking about James this way is harder than I imagined. "I knew he was a bit older than me and that he'd lost his wife. He used to talk to me about it a lot. And I'd just listen, let him grieve for her. I wasn't trying to…you know…*get* him. It was a while before I even realised I'd fallen for him. And I never dreamed he felt the same about me. But he did. He told me once that I'd saved him. Those were his exact words. I'd *saved* him." I look away from DS Connolly's gaze. "And now look what I've done."

"So you didn't mind that he had children? Lots of people would be put off by that. Would find it too hard to deal with." He ignores my self-pity; there is no room for it here. He only wants the cold, hard facts.

I shake my head. "Not at all. In fact, I loved the fact he had kids. I was desperate to be a mum and it was my only chance."

DS Connolly straightens in his seat, a frown crossing his forehead.

"I can't have my own," I say, saving him the bother of asking. I feel my insides collapse because I have to tell them, I have to relive it and feel the pain afresh. "I…had a stillborn baby. I was twenty-eight weeks pregnant and had to deliver her. She had died inside me. Just like that, no warning. One minute she was there, the next…" I feel my eyes well up and squeeze them shut.

"I'm sorry," DS Connolly says. "I can only imagine what you and your husband went through."

I shake my head. "It…was years ago. With my ex. Before I met James."

And now an image of Max appears in my head. It is a still picture with no words or movement. The only thing I now remember about him is how, despite everything I put him through, he looked out for me. He never went about it the right way – nothing about him was conventional – but he always meant well.

His face disappears and now I am back in the delivery room, giving birth to my silent baby. I reopen my eyes and summon the strength to continue. "And after that I haemorrhaged. They had to do an emergency hysterectomy."

Heavy silence fills the room. They were not expecting this, I'm sure.

"I'm sorry," DS Connolly says. "That must have been hard."

Beside him, his colleague offers me a half-smile, one that says she is also sorry, but she remains silent.

After a moment, DS Connolly resumes his questioning. "So you're saying everything was good between you and your husband?"

Still squeezing back tears, I struggle to get the words out. "No…things were better than good."

Silence fills the room once more and I wonder if it's because they are unsure what to ask next. There will be so many things they want to know and, even for them, it will be a struggle to form a logical order. Logic does not come into this.

"So I take it things got worse after you tried to change everything in the house?" DS Connolly says.

I nod, then remember I need to speak up for the tape recorder. "Yes. Much, much worse."

CHAPTER FOUR

For three days I endure the boys' silence, and somehow it is worse than their snide comments and digs, worse than their refusal to listen or obey. Worse even than their cruel disappearing act. It gives them power over me because there is nothing I can do, no way to force words to leave their mouths.

James and I have a long talk and he apologises for the boys' behaviour. "I should have changed things around the house ages ago. It wasn't fair on you to live here with everything how Lauren had it. I'm sorry, I just didn't think. I've told the boys it's staying how you want it."

As he speaks I see the pain in his eyes. He is caught in the middle and knows he can't please everyone. "They'll come around. It's just hard for them; this house is all they've got left of their mum."

My heart aches for their loss but it can't be good for any of us to live with Lauren's ghost. Even so, I know she will not go anywhere. She will always be in this house, in my head, even in my bed. How can she not be all around when she is so much a part of James?

But there is no way I can vocalise these thoughts; they must stay safely contained in my head.

Each morning, the sight of the bright citrus walls brings a smile to my face. A small victory. Something in this house is finally mine.

But the boys are not content to let things lie. James knows now that I overslept the other morning and didn't wake them up. "Why didn't you tell me?" he asks. "It's no big deal. In fact, it's about time they got themselves up for school." I grab his hand and squeeze it, to let him know he is a good man.

We still haven't gone out for dinner, but James promises we will tonight. "It will be lovely," he says, "just the two of us." So, trying to be positive, I allow myself to look forward to the evening.

I spend the morning working on my assignment. Immersed in learning, I am filled with excitement that soon I will be helping people who have nobody else to turn to. I think of Dad. How he would never consider talking to anyone about anything. Once I am qualified, perhaps I can offer him something, but I know it will have come too late.

At lunchtime I tear myself away from the laptop to make a peanut butter sandwich. I am still eating when James calls to tell me Emma has offered to babysit. I would prefer Mrs Simmons, or anyone else, but at least Emma is not unkind to me. A bit cold, judgemental even, but not cruel. And it is good for the boys to be around her; she was Lauren's best friend and practically an aunt to them so that is all that matters.

By three p.m. I have finished my assignment, and I submit it online. As soon as I've clicked the send button, the familiar panic sets in. What if I've not written an essay at all, but typed the same word over and over until it made up two thousand words? What if that word is obscene? I quickly reopen the document I've just sent and read through it again, checking every line, just to be sure.

Now it is twenty past three: time to go downstairs and greet the boys. All I'll get is silence, of course, but I can't give up. I am the adult, I need to fix this. Wouldn't I feel exactly the same if I were in their position? If Mum had died instead of walking out on Dad, wouldn't I hate any new wife Dad might have found? And I am not Lauren. My stomach twists in knots at this thought. I am so different from her. From everything I've heard, she was calm and poised, while I am panicky and scatty. She made people love her, while all I do is inspire cold silence and arguments. And she would never have accidentally caused the boys harm. How can I hope to live up to her perfection?

But still I stand at the door, holding it open while Dillon and Luke enter, engrossed in conversation, turning blind eyes to me. I clear my throat. "How was school today?"

No reply.

I try again. "Anyone like some orange juice? Smooth with no bits in it."

They dump their bags under the coat rack, instead of hanging them on hooks, and bustle into the kitchen, shutting the door on me. Even though I've been expecting this treatment to continue, it cuts like a blade. I am lost and alone, in a place that's supposed to be my home. I know I have James, and he loves me, but we are not the family I imagined we'd be. I didn't expect it to be easy, but I never thought it would hurt like this.

Tonight I want to look my best. Not just for James, but for me too. I choose the cobalt-blue dress I wore on our first proper date; it's demure, but the high slit at the side hints at possibilities. James' eyes were glued to me all night when I wore it last and I wonder if it will have the same effect tonight? Or perhaps I have changed beyond recognition. Externally I may look the same but it's not just about that. It's about James' deeper feelings for me.

I think of Tabitha's flawless make-up as I apply mine slowly, careful not to smudge my lipstick. With the hair straightener, I iron out the annoying wavy kinks in my hair. I am pleased with the result and I almost feel human again. I am more than a detested, fake mother.

"Wow, look at you!" James appears behind me, grinning from ear to ear. He has probably forgotten I can look half-decent. "You look hot." He kisses me and a layer of lipstick transfers to his mouth. "I need to have a quick shower. Will you let Emma in? She'll be here any minute."

I almost say I'm surprised she doesn't have her own key – this feels more like her home than mine – but I stop myself. Tonight I will be positive. Emma does have more history here than I do and there's nothing I can do about that.

"And can you tell the boys they've had enough TV now? It's homework time."

All day I have been expecting James to cancel our dinner. It would be easy for Tabitha to arrange a last-minute photo shoot and James would never sacrifice a work opportunity. But he is here now and we will soon be alone.

Downstairs, the boys are still playing their hurtful game and don't look up from the television when I appear. "Okay, it's homework time." My voice is firm, completely at odds with how I feel inside.

Neither of them moves. The canned laughter from the comedy programme they are watching feels as if it is directed at me, and I'm sure Luke is smirking. I try again. "Your dad says it's homework time. Now." This time they get up, with exaggerated slowness, but still don't look at me as they leave the room.

"Aunty Emma's here!" Luke suddenly shouts, and they both run to the front door. I haven't heard the bell ring and wonder if they are lying. Another of their pranks. But they can't know I'm uneasy about Emma.

Through the glass I see her shadow, tall and bulky. Dillon flings the door open and she steps inside, ruffling their hair and throwing her arms around them. The scene is a complete contrast from whenever I am the one standing at the door.

After a moment, Emma notices me and nods. "Callie. How are you?"

"Very well, thanks. You?"

"Great. Busy at work. The hospital is so understaffed I feel as if I'm doing three people's work." She shuffles further in and closes the door, Luke clinging to her as if he will never let go.

I admire Emma for being a nurse. I couldn't do what she does, taking care of people's physical needs day after day. It is painfully intimate and I have no stomach for strangers' blood and sickness. She is, ultimately, a good woman. Just as her best friend was.

I decide to try an experiment. "Boys, homework, remember? You can talk to Emma when you've finished."

They both ignore me and turn to Emma, expectant looks on their faces. She looks at them, then back to me, as if trying to identify the struggle taking place. "Okay," she says. "Listen to Callie. Upstairs, finish your homework and then we'll have a session on the PlayStation. Okay?"

The boys grab their bags and rush upstairs, Luke howling with excitement. Part of me wants to believe they are putting on an act for my benefit, but I know it's not that. This is a genuine show of love for Emma.

Once the boys have disappeared, she asks where James is.

"Good," she says, when I tell her he's in the shower. "We've got time for a quick chat then."

In the kitchen, Emma sets about making us coffee as if this is her own house. She knows where everything is, and is unashamed to root through the cupboards. But how can I stop her when she must have done this a thousand times in the past, long before I came along? I sit on one of the stools and chew my lip. There must be a reason she wants to talk to me before James emerges, but I've no idea what it is.

"One sugar, isn't it?"

I nod and she places a mug in front of me before perching on a stool. She sips her coffee, watching me for a moment, then stares at her lap, as if struggling to spit out her words.

"Look, I owe you an apology. I haven't given you a chance and I fully take the blame for that."

I am taken aback by her statement. "I…um…"

"It's my fault. I'm just overprotective of James. But I see how happy you make him, Callie. So, again, I'm sorry."

"Well, let's have a fresh start, then."

"There's just one thing, though. Dillon called me the other day. He claimed you forgot to cook them dinner and said he had to go and buy them some fish and chips with his last bit of pocket money. Now, I know that's rubbish, but I'm worried about their behaviour. About what's happening to all of you."

And then I open up to the woman I have always felt uncomfortable around, telling her things I haven't even told James. Explaining my daily struggle with the boys.

Emma listens patiently until I've finished. "Look, of course it's hard. This happened so quickly for them and they're resisting you at every step. But what you've got to think about is what it's doing to James. All this arguing and tension. He's stuck in the middle with no idea how to keep everyone happy. I just think it's putting a lot of pressure on him."

I watch her mouth moving as she speaks and I know she is right. I shouldn't be running to James every time the boys misbehave. I need to sort it out myself. Keep him out of it as much as I can. For his sake. "You're right." I say. "So does James talk to you about this a lot?" I try to keep my voice casual, to hide the fact my stomach is flipping.

Emma nods. "Yes, he does. But it's only because he doesn't want to upset you. It's not that he's going behind your back or anything."

"I know."

"It's just such a difficult situation. But he knows you're trying your best for Dillon and Luke." Emma takes another sip of coffee and puts down her mug. I still haven't touched mine. "Look, I know Lauren was my best friend, but I just want James to be happy. I was thrilled when he told me he'd met someone, even though it was quite soon. Even the age gap didn't factor in, but then..." She trails off, probably remembering Luke's face that day. The wails that wouldn't stop, even hours afterwards. "The accident, Callie. I just can't get my head around that."

"I –"

"It doesn't matter. I just don't think it's helped things." She stares into her mug and avoids looking at me. Clearly it *does* matter. It matters a lot.

CHAPTER FIVE

My mood is shot by the time we get to the restaurant, but I try my best to focus on James. I am lucky to have him. He is a good man, a good husband. I need to cling to that, and hope the rest will fall into place.

We are at our favourite Indian restaurant, in Wimbledon Village. James wanted us both to have a drink so he suggested we walk here and get a taxi home later. I was happy with this plan because it meant leaving the house earlier, escaping from the boys' hatred, but now my ankles are sore, the skin raw from rubbing against my new shoes.

"We don't do this enough," James says, studying the menu. After a moment he looks up and smiles at me. "D'you remember we came here on our first date? Our first official date, that is. We'd had plenty of coffees together in The Coffee Bean, hadn't we? I was so nervous, Callie, my palms were sweating."

I smile as I remember. Neither of us ate much because we were so engrossed in our conversation.

James leans forward. "I couldn't believe you'd agreed to come out with me. I felt like I'd won the lottery." The cheeky grin I love so much spreads across his face, making me sadder and guiltier about the tension at home. "Do you remember after? We went back to yours. It was amazing, Callie. *You* were amazing. I knew then I couldn't let you go, that even if you kicked me out afterwards I would fight for you."

I reach across the table for his hand and stroke it, letting the familiar feel of his skin comfort me, wash everything else away, letting his words remind me who we are.

"But like I said, we really should do this more often. I know I've been busy but I'll make time, I promise."

"Well, it's difficult, isn't it? We're both so busy and we've got the boys." I want it to be true: for the boys to be mine as much as they are his. Will the void left by my silent baby ever be filled? I don't look at him, but stare at my menu, trying to make my voice sound casual. Unlike James, who always knows what he wants to eat, I need to study each option carefully because I am never sure what to order until I see it. James puts down his menu and watches me, his expression serious. Mentioning Dillon and Luke will have reminded him of the problems we have both left at home.

But then his face relaxes. "Oh, that reminds me. I've got to shoot a wedding in Leeds the Saturday after next. It's a bit far to drive there and back in one day so I'll have to stay overnight. You don't mind, do you? I mean, if you need me for anything –"

"No, no, don't cancel work."

Before he can respond, the waiter comes over to take our order. He is short, and his eyes are more yellow than white, but he has a kind face, and I try to focus on his smile while I tell him what I'd like, because in a few seconds I will have to deal with what James has just told me.

Without hesitation, James orders Tandoori chicken, and because I have been too distracted to make a decision, I ask for the same.

When the waiter has gone, James reaches for my hand. "Look, I know it's the first time you'll be alone with the boys overnight, but maybe it will be a good thing? Without me there you might bond or something?" He flashes a smile, as if he really believes this is possible. That the answer is as simple as the three of us being left alone together. But to me it is the worst possible scenario. The way things are at the moment, a night alone with the boys is my worst nightmare. But James is always optimistic, always wanting to believe things will work out, no matter what evidence there is to the contrary.

The waiter returns with a bottle of red wine, pouring us both a glass. "Cheers!" James says, holding his up and clinking it against mine.

I offer a more subdued cheers. And suddenly I want to tell him that I'm sinking into a pit because nothing is how I thought it would be. None of it is real. I am not a real mother, and how can I be a real wife when I can barely let my husband know me? But then I hear Emma's words in my ear, and know that it is selfish to burden him with this. He has been through enough losing Lauren so he doesn't need to deal with my troubles too; he needs peace, to know that the worst is behind him. So I will keep quiet and put on a face for him that is not my own.

James' phone beeps in his pocket, but he doesn't notice. He is too busy telling me about his and Tabitha's plan for extending the business. I can't see how it is *their* plan because Tabitha is his receptionist, not business partner, but I won't push my negativity onto him. Whatever I feel about her, she does a good job.

"Your phone," I say, pointing to his pocket. "You got a message."

"Oh, right." He fumbles around then eventually pulls out his iPhone and begins pressing buttons. "Tabitha. Asking if she can drive up to Leeds with me." He reads a bit more. "Apparently she's got a cousin up there she wants to visit."

How convenient. "Oh, okay." I sip some wine and try to ignore the fact my insides are sinking. I can trust James. He is not interested in Tabitha. "I hope they hurry up with the food. I'm starving!"

There is often a power struggle in relationships; one person having the upper hand. It can be subtle, unintentional, barely noticeable to the couple, but it's still there. I watch James tapping his reply to Tabitha, feeling the heavy reality of how things have altered. Before we got married, he was the widower who needed to love again. He needed *me*. He needed me to help him enjoy life again because all he did was work and look after the boys. But now I am the one who needs him.

The food arrives, sizzling on silver hotplates, the strong, spicy smell doing little to improve my appetite. James puts away his phone, once again oblivious to the instant beep as Tabitha wastes no time in sending a reply. I can see her message now: flirty with exclamation marks and kisses for a man who does not belong to her.

"You do look great in that dress," James says, and I allow his compliment to fill me up, spread through me and energise me. He doesn't say things he doesn't mean.

We eat in silence, neither of us conscious of it. My silence stems from anxiety, while James' only results from comfort. After eating only half my chicken, I push my plate aside. "We can't let it go to waste," James says as he devours it for me, unashamed of his appetite.

When he's finished and our glasses are empty, he asks the waiter to call us a taxi.

"No, let's walk," I say. Despite having very little skin left on the backs of my ankles, I am not yet ready to go home. James will want me to sit and have a coffee with him and Emma, while they reminisce about days before I was around, things I had nothing to do with, and people I don't know.

Even though James must be surprised by my suggestion – I usually complain about being too full to move after a big meal – he humours me, and I am granted an extra half-hour of time away from the house, and everyone in it. I make the most of each second, linking my arm through his as we walk, clinging to him, letting his laughter comfort me.

I remember that I have forgotten to tell him about my arrangement to meet Bridgette and Debbie for lunch on Friday.

"That's great," he says. "You haven't seen them for ages. It will do you good to get out." He pulls his hand from his pocket, loosening my hold on him, and drapes his arm around my shoulder instead.

It is hard not to overanalyse James' words. Does he think I'm spending too much time in the house? That I have completely changed since he met me, when I was barely out of bars and pubs? Always wanting to drag him off somewhere new. But I realise I am overreacting. Paranoia has a grip on me and it's getting hard to shake off. *Is this where it starts, Dad? Is this how it began for you?*

James stops suddenly and turns to face me. "I'm proud of you, Callie. For everything you're doing. I know it's not easy. The boys…"

"Thank you," I say, saving him from finishing his sentence. He will never know how much his words mean, his faith in me. As long as I have that I will be okay.

We get to the house and his stride increases; he is eager to spend time with Emma before she leaves and I understand this; she is a link to his past. I glance at the house next door but all the lights are off. For once Mrs Simmons is not watching.

Emma is in the kitchen, already boiling the kettle. "Just in time," she calls. "Anyone for coffee?"

I fake a yawn and turn to James. "D'you mind if I go to bed? I'm really tired after all the brain power I've used today." Sleep is the last thing I want, but I can't sit with Emma and pretend our earlier conversation didn't happen.

"Course not." He leans down and kisses the top of my head. "I'll be up soon."

Upstairs, light shines from under Dillon's door so he must still be awake. I consider knocking and calling goodnight, but his silent response would be too humiliating. I whisper a goodnight to both the boys instead and somehow it brings me some peace.

I sit up in bed, letting my food digest. I always feel better once I get into bed, as if I am distanced from everything else in the house, untouchable somehow. This space is just for James and me. Flicking through the magazine I still haven't read, I check my horoscope for the week, but as usual it bears little resemblance to my life. I start reading an article about how to change your life but must fall asleep because the next thing I know, it is past one a.m. and my magazine is beside me on the bed.

The murmur of voices drifts from one of the boys' rooms. I pull off the duvet and slip on my dressing gown, trying not to disturb James. He has an early shoot tomorrow so I will deal with the boys myself.

Trying to avoid the creaks on the landing, I approach Dillon's room, guided by the sound of voices. I prepare the lecture in my head, which will be hard to deliver in a whisper, but then I hear my name and stop in my tracks. The voices are muffled until I step closer to the door and press my ear to the cold wood.

"I hate her. I can't believe she's still here. Dad should have got rid of her by now."

I freeze. I have known Dillon's feelings all along, but hearing him speak these words, and not in front of me, makes my heart ache.

He continues. "It's not working to make Dad kick her out. I think we have to force her to leave. Just keep making her life miserable and she won't last five more minutes."

"But –"

"But nothing. We're doing this for Mum as well, remember? She would have hated her just as much as we do."

"But the accident and everything, I thought –"

"Yeah, sorry you had to do that. I really hoped that would do it."

I can no longer listen. This is worse than I thought.

Forgetting about my lecture, I creep back to our room and sink onto the bed, closing my eyes. I feel as if I am falling, spiralling down an endless hole. But rather than being scary, it is comforting because it is taking me away from here. An image of Dad pops into my head, from the time before he was ill. He is picking me up and spinning me around, and we are both throwing our heads back and laughing. I'm not sure if it's a real memory or something I wish had happened; all I know is that he is not the father I have now.

When James wakes in the morning, I pretend I am still asleep. Otherwise we will start talking and right now I don't know if I can keep from him what I heard the boys say last night. The words are still too raw, like knife cuts on my skin. And I am in a state of shock over the lengths they have gone to, will go to again. Talking to James about it is a bad idea. I can't force him into a corner.

He tiptoes around, pulling on his clothes. When he's dressed he sits on the side of the bed, reaching across to stroke my back. His hands are soft, but I can't feel anything at the moment. I roll onto my side, away from him, still feigning sleep.

I need to do something about this before my marriage comes crashing down around me.

CHAPTER SIX

Over the next few days, I replay the boys' conversation in my mind. It is worse than I suspected and I have taken the blame for the accident, something which was not my fault at all. Their capacity for malice horrifies me, but I cannot go to James; it would only drive a bigger wedge between us. Instead, I keep silent for now, like I have to do with so many things to protect my marriage. When everything is against you there are choices to make: wither away defeated or stand up and fight. I will not be like Dad.

It is only six a.m., but James is already up and dressed, excited because he's just found out by email that an advertising agency has commissioned him to do some work for them. "You know, I wouldn't be able to do any of this without your support," he says, leaning over the bed and kissing me on the cheek.

Despite the early hour, hunger forces me out of bed and into the shower. I keep an eye on the time, conscious that at half seven I need to get the boys up, dressed and fed. I decide I will make bacon and eggs, maybe even fry up some hash browns as a treat. No doubt I will continue to receive the silent treatment, but I will still do my best to look after them.

As I potter around the kitchen, once again their words try to invade my thoughts, but I turn on the radio, as loud as I can have it without disturbing them, and let the music wipe away everything they said. The other night I was deflated, but I won't let this beat me.

Everything is timed to perfection, and at half past seven – with just a few minutes left until the food is ready to be served – I head upstairs and wake the boys. I knock loudly on each of their doors, but don't go inside. Instead, I wait until I can hear them both stirring, grateful for the creaky floors for the first time since I moved in.

Back in the kitchen I dish up, just as Luke pads in, still in his pyjamas, rubbing sleep from his eyes. I look at him and feel sad that he is so easily led by his brother. Dillon follows, half-dressed in his school trousers and white shirt, his tie hanging out of his pocket. Their noses crinkle at the smell of bacon and their eyes drift to the plates laid out on the breakfast bar.

Luke turns to Dillon but neither boy speaks. They edge forward to get a closer look and I notice Luke's smile emerging as he heads towards the food. I feel elated at this small achievement, but my joy is premature.

Before he can get to his stool, Dillon pulls him back. "Remember it's breakfast club at school on Fridays? We'll get a fry-up there."

Luke glances at me and I am sure he looks disappointed, but he follows Dillon out of the room. I had forgotten on Fridays they sometimes have breakfast at school. Alone, I stifle the urge to scream at them and drag them back to the kitchen to demand they eat. It surprises me how good it feels to imagine this scene.

Shaking off these thoughts, I scrape the food from the plates into the bin and load the dishwasher. Anything to distract myself from anger. I was so convinced they would appreciate the breakfast, that it might go a small way to mending things, but they will not be won over so easily.

Fifteen minutes later the boys are back downstairs, fully dressed and sliding their rucksacks onto their backs. I stand in the hallway watching them, summoning the strength for kind words, when all I can hear in my head is Dillon's revelation the other night. *Sorry you had to do that. I really hoped that would do it.* Luke heads out but Dillon stops in the doorway. Keeping his back to me, he speaks the first words he has said to me since the painting incident. "Dad says it's okay if Rhys comes back after school." He doesn't turn around, and is gone before I can answer, banging the door shut behind him.

I stay rooted to the spot, wondering if I heard him correctly. I know Rhys is his best friend but I have never met the boy; in eight months Dillon has not invited a single friend to the house. But after what I heard, I cannot hope this might be progress.

Even in the middle of the day, Oxford Street it is a hive of activity and I force my way through bodies, all moving at different speeds, to cross the road. But despite the bustle, I am relaxed; I am far away from home, far away from the boys. Today I am determined to be the old Callie, the one Bridgette and Debbie will be glad to see has re-emerged. I will not speak of my troubles today, but will listen to my friends; I have no idea what's been going on in their lives lately. I have been slacking as a friend.

Climbing the stairs to the first floor of Costa Coffee, I immediately see them at a table in the corner, smartly dressed and business-like in their work clothes. Not for the first time lately, I feel out of place in my jeans and tunic top, but tell myself it won't be long before I'm dressing smartly for my clients, before I have a life.

Debbie sees me first and lets out a squeal, jumping up and rushing over to wrap me in a hug. Bridgette quickly does the same and I immediately feel stronger. The two of them are proof that I'm not some wicked, evil woman, out to make her stepsons' lives miserable.

"We're not letting you leave it this long again," Debbie says, hugging me a second time. "You look well."

I open my mouth to tell her that I badly need a haircut and threw on the first clothes I found in the wardrobe, but I let it go. It will only set alarm bells ringing.

"We've got you a cappuccino. Is that okay?" Bridgette grabs my hand and leads me to their table. I nod, allowing their kindness to envelope me. It is a far cry from the boys' snubs.

Debbie apologises for meeting here for lunch instead of a restaurant, but she has a work dinner tonight so only wants a cheese sandwich.

"It's fine," I tell her. And it is. Where we are is not important.

Bridgette asks what we want to eat and, once again, I have trouble deciding. "What are you having?"

"Not sure, probably a chicken wrap."

"That sounds good, I'll have one of those." I scramble in my bag for my purse but she grabs it from me. "Don't even think about it."

After she comes back with our food, I bite into my wrap and listen to them both speaking animatedly about their jobs. Bridgette is a human resources manager at Marks and Spencer, and although I have no idea what exactly this involves, I know she thrives on corporate life. Debbie is an estate agent, dealing with high-end sales and I am proud of them both; I never feel inferior around them for being a mature student, which is a credit to them, rather than me.

Once we've caught up on work and my studies, Bridgette announces that she's met someone. *Interesting*, is how she describes him, but I know that means she likes him a lot, as most men she meets – even those she might decide to have a fling with – don't merit a mention. She tells us he's called Aaron and her eyes brighten when she says his name. I am happy for her. She is at the very beginning of something, with all the hope that it will turn out okay.

Debbie also has news. Her boyfriend, Mark, has asked her to move in with him. "I haven't agreed yet, though," she tells us. "Got to keep him hanging a bit." It is always this way when the three of us meet. They deliver all their exciting news, while I unburden myself.

They both turn to me, hoping, I'm sure, that today will be different and I will have some good news of my own. But all I can do is tell them my last assignment went well, that I'm still enjoying my counselling course and can't wait to have my own clients. They smile and nod, trying not to look at each other, but we have all been friends too long to keep up the pretence.

"Talk to us, Callie," Bridgette says, her eyes urging me to be forthcoming. Does she want me to say I've made a huge mistake? That the boys, the house, my life, everything is making me miserable? But I can't betray James. None of this is his fault. I knew where I stood when we made our vows. He is not the problem.

"We're just worried about you," Debbie adds, when I don't answer. "You're not yourself. It's those boys, isn't it?" She looks at Bridgette and I realise they have planned this conversation. That they probably met earlier so they could get it all straight in their heads. But I can't be angry; they are only worried about me.

I've got to put their minds at rest. I attempt a smile but feel my lips quivering. "I'm fine. Really. I'm not saying it's easy, but I'll be okay." I make a joke about being careful what you wish for, but none of us laugh.

Bridgette reaches for my hand. "It's just, you know, you always said you would…get checked out if you felt things were changing. Do you think –"

"Honestly, I'm fine. Things aren't that bad. If they do get worse then I'll tell someone." I stretch my smile, hoping to persuade them they are worrying needlessly.

A look passes between them and I know it is a silent agreement not to push me when Debbie quickly changes the subject, once again apologising that we couldn't eat somewhere else.

When Bridgette checks her watch and says she needs to get going, I am almost relieved. These two women are more than family to me but I can only take so much of their pity and worry.

They walk me to the tube station, despite my insistence that they should get going, and we duck into the doorway of a shop to avoid getting bashed by the herds flocking underground. The hugs they give me now are a complete contrast to their greeting, so I once again reassure them I'll be fine. They make a good show of buying it, but I feel their eyes on me as I walk to the station entrance and head down the steps.

It is only when I get to the platform that I wonder why I didn't open up to them when I can usually tell them anything. It's not as if they don't know I'm struggling with the boys.

It is fear, that's what it is. Fear of even your best friends knowing who you really are.

I am studying in the living room when Luke gets home. I have given up waiting at the front door for them, but when I hear their keys turning in the lock I rush to greet them.

"Where's Dillon?" I ask.

Luke shrugs as he hangs his bag on a coat hook. "Coming."

And then I remember Dillon is bringing his friend home. The last thing he'll want is me hovering by the door, embarrassing him. I wonder what he has told this friend about me. *Just don't call her my mum,* I imagine him saying.

"Come in the kitchen, I'll get you a drink," I tell Luke. He hesitates for a moment, eyeing the front door, but then follows me. He is so much easier to handle without his brother around.

I pour him an orange juice and he glugs it down, putting his glass in the dishwasher when he's finished. He doesn't say thank you but he half-smiles before grabbing a bag of crisps and disappearing upstairs.

Watching him go, it occurs to me that I have been approaching this all wrong. If I am to have any chance of getting through to the boys, I need to work on them separately. But this is easy to say, putting it into practice will be impossible because neither one of them wants to be in my company, especially not without the other.

When I hear the front door open, I throw my remaining tea in the sink and once again boil the kettle. It is pathetic, I know, but I need to be busy when they come in. Perhaps it is like a security shield; I will feel less vulnerable if I'm doing something. I have heard Dillon talking to James about his friend, Rhys, but I have no idea what to expect. Perhaps he will give me an even harder time than Dillon does.

Dillon comes in first, his tie already loosened around his collar. He doesn't look at me, but offers his friend a drink. Behind him, Rhys appears, as tall as Dillon but older-looking. It is only now I remember he is in his final year in the sixth form, so is older than Dillon. I shouldn't feel intimidated – I am the adult here – but I do, almost spilling boiling water on me as I fill my mug.

We all stand for a moment, none of us speaking, but then Rhys walks forward and holds out his hand.

"Nice to meet you, Mrs Harwell. I'm Rhys."

For a moment I wonder if this is another prank, a trick to get my defences down, but behind Rhys, Dillon's frown is unmistakeable.

Despite this, I won't allow my guard down yet, but I respond to the boy's politeness. "Nice to meet you too, Rhys. Would you like a drink? Orange juice? Ribena?" I know I must sound stiff and self-conscious but perhaps he is too young to pick up on it.

He asks for a Ribena but before I can move, Dillon pulls the bottle from the cupboard and starts filling two glasses. Seeing this, Rhys offers me a *thanks anyway* smile, but I still don't know how to take him. Eight months of wariness has flawed my judgement.

It would be normal in this circumstance to make small talk with Dillon's friend. *How's school? What do your parents do? What have you boys got planned for this afternoon?* But riling Dillon will not help my cause. So I tell them I'll leave them to it, feeling both sets of eyes on me as I step into the hallway. "See you, Mrs Harwell," Rhys calls. I hear the muffled sound of their whispers as I close the door.

In the living room, I pick up my textbook and return to my reading on loss and bereavement. I get lost in the words, sucking up new information, excited that soon I will be helping people deal with all kinds of problems. I wonder if this module will enable me to better understand James and the boys and what they went through losing Lauren. But something tells me it won't be quite so easy. It is too close to home.

I have just finished the first chapter when James calls to tell me he'll be late home. "Sorry, Callie, last-minute job." In the background I hear Tabitha talking to someone on the phone. "I'll grab something to eat after so don't worry about dinner." An image of him sitting with Tabitha in a restaurant flashes into my head. "Everything okay there? Boys being okay?"

I lower my voice. "Everything's great. Dillon's friend is here. Rhys."

"That's good. I haven't seen him for a while but he's a good kid. He'll be no trouble." But aren't they always good until they have a reason to dislike someone?

When I hang up, I realise it's almost six o'clock and I need to start dinner. After hunting around in the kitchen, I find some fish cakes, potatoes and green beans. I suspect it won't be anyone's favourite meal but I can hardly win, whatever I do.

I hear movement in the hallway and am not expecting to see Rhys, pulling on his coat. "Oh, aren't you staying for dinner?" As I say this I realise I am disappointed. At least with a friend present, Dillon might put on a display of civility.

Rhys shakes his head. "No, sorry, Mrs Harwell. It's my dad's birthday today. We're going for a meal. I just came over to give Dillon a quick lesson."

"Guitar lesson? I thought he'd given up on that." I feel like I'm prying but can't help asking.

Rhys smiles. "Yeah, he did lose interest for a while but he asked me to start teaching him again. I warned him we'd be starting at the beginning."

I am fully aware that if Dillon appeared at the top of the stairs now and found me talking to his friend, I will have done irreparable damage.

"Anyway, bye Mrs Harwell."

"Bye, Rhys. See you soon."

He hesitates at the door for a moment and I wonder if he's forgotten something, but then he is gone and I am left wishing Dillon were that easy to talk to.

Dinner is an ordeal, and all hopes of Rhys' visit having diluted Dillon's behaviour evaporate the minute I put their plates in front of them. "It's burnt," Luke moans, pushing the perfectly cooked fish around his plate. "And I hate beans. Dad never gives us beans." I wonder how anyone, even a child Luke's age, can look someone directly in the eyes while lying so blatantly; the beans are only in the fridge because Luke insisted they're his favourite vegetable.

Next to him, Dillon clicks away on his BlackBerry, not acknowledging that there is any food in front of him. I don't know what's worse: the silent treatment or the malicious complaining.

I should be used to this by now, my skin should be thickened against anything they throw my way, but this is far from the case. I want to scream at them to eat their food, to stop being ungrateful, to stop causing me this pain. But instead, I take a deep breath and try to keep my voice calm. "Eat your food."

Luke reaches for his fork but Dillon shoves his arm aside, sending it crashing to the floor. "Come on," he says, grabbing his brother and leading him away. "We don't have to listen to her."

Blinking back tears, I watch as they rush upstairs, to whatever it is they do in their bedrooms.

Later, when I am in bed, James still not home, I hear someone foraging around in the kitchen. I should feel sorry that the boys have gone to bed hungry and are resorting to scavenging like thieves. But I'm not. I smile because they have brought this on themselves.

CHAPTER SEVEN

Now

"Do you often have angry thoughts, Callie?"

DS Connolly places his hands together, resting them under his chin, his elbows balanced on the table like the pillars of a goal post.

"No. I mean, not before then, no. But the boys were driving me to despair. Can't you understand that? I just wanted to look after them but they kept pushing me away, testing me, doing everything they could to make my life miserable."

He nods, offering up a half-smile before shuffling through his notes. "Tell us about the accident."

It was inevitable this would come up so I am prepared for it. "There are so many different versions of this story, DS Connolly, so many fabrications, but I'm going to tell you the real one. I have nothing left to lose, do I?"

Both officers lean forward in their chairs, as if I am their entertainment, an actress they're watching in a theatre.

"James and I had only been married a few weeks and the boys were…well, it was difficult for them. You see, I hadn't lived there before the wedding and they hadn't known me as their dad's partner for very long, so it was hard for all of us. But I hadn't lost my spirit then. I was still determined to support them and make things work. And I hadn't seen the worst of the boys yet." My arm begins to itch and I scratch at it, relishing the painful respite my nails scraping my skin gives me.

"I had just driven back from a tutorial. Normally I would have walked to the station or got a bus, but I was running late that day so had to drive. Mrs Simmons was watching the boys. Anyway, we don't have a driveway so I was reversing the car into a space just outside the house when someone appeared from nowhere on a bike. Suddenly I was backing into him, but by the time I slammed on the break, the damage was done. I had reversed into Luke and broken his arm. They said he was lucky it hadn't been worse." I stare at the table, reliving the pain of the memory.

The officers turn to each other once more, a look passing between them. I know without them speaking what it means. They don't believe it was an accident. Yet they will be confused because I have no need to lie now.

Ignoring their disbelief, I continue my story. "Dillon appeared, shouting from the house, and I should have realised he didn't look shocked. He just said calmly that he was calling his dad to tell him what I'd done. You see, that's what's strange, DS Connolly. The fact that Dillon was so relaxed about his brother lying writhing on the road. It only made sense once I'd heard their conversation that night. They planned the whole thing. Or Dillon did. He is always the one in charge, treating Luke like his little lapdog. He didn't even suggest calling the ambulance, I did that myself once I'd checked Luke was conscious."

DS Connolly scribbles something in his notebook. "And your husband believed it was an accident?"

"Yes, he did. Despite Dillon's best efforts to convince everyone I'd done it on purpose. Despite our neighbour saying she saw the whole thing and it looked intentional. I don't know what she thought she saw, but she got it wrong."

That shared look again, officer to officer, a secret language only they can interpret. But I shouldn't worry about this, it is probably for the best.

"Are you on any medication?" DS Connolly asks, his question once again out of the blue.

"No…I…"

He scans a sheet of paper he's pulled from the pile in front of him. "But you should be, shouldn't you? Doctors have been worried about you showing early signs of bipolar disorder. Isn't that right?"

"I've been okay for a while. I've been fine. Until now." I hasten to explain. "I wasn't being reckless, I just wanted to manage it myself, especially as it wasn't so advanced. Isn't. I don't know which."

"You've been without help for the last few years?" DS Connolly says.

I could hold back now, but they already know the worst of what I have done. "Yes, I've been trying.

Being with James helped. Getting married, becoming a mum. But I wasn't always so strong. In fact, with my ex, Max, I fell apart. I drove him away with my…behaviour."

The female officer speaks up and somehow I remember her name is DC Barnes. "And what behaviour was that?"

"I…um…I got into a bit of trouble, spending more than I earned, getting into debt." A memory flashes through my head. Max cutting up seven of my credit cards, his face a picture of despair, telling me I was irrational, that I couldn't see things clearly, insisting he wanted to help me but how could he when I wouldn't help myself? Telling me he didn't know how to handle my mood swings. I shove the thought aside. "But James took all my pain away. Just by loving me, he helped me get healthier."

Glancing at her colleague, DC Barnes frowns. "That doesn't exactly appear to be the case, does it?"

"You help look after your Dad, don't you?" DS Connolly interjects, saving me from answering her hidden accusation. "And I understand he has schizophrenia? Wouldn't you say that's reason enough to take your pills?"

"I'm not my Dad," I say. It comes out in almost a whisper but neither officer asks me to repeat myself.

"Was James supportive?" DS Connolly asks, furiously scribbling again.

"He…until tonight he didn't know about Dad. About me. Any of it."

The detective's eyes widen, judgement pouring out. The kind man I saw glimpses of earlier is slowly disappearing.

"Let me ask you something," I continue. "Do you ever keep secrets from your wife?"

He shakes his head. "No, can't say I do."

"But you would to spare her pain, wouldn't you? To protect your marriage? You'd do it to keep her happy. Well, that's what I was doing. I didn't want James to suffer, to carry my burden for me. So he couldn't know about Dad. I couldn't let him see what I might become."

DS Connolly stops writing and chews his pen. "But didn't you also believe there was a chance he wouldn't, or couldn't, stand by you? You didn't want to take that risk, did you? You were scared of losing him."

"Yes, yes, I was. Terrified."

CHAPTER EIGHT

There is a lump in my throat as I stand outside Dad's door, pressing the buzzer to his flat. No matter how many times I visit, being here in Palmers Green, on the other side of London, always feels odd. It's not like coming home because we never lived here. Dad is Wimbledon born and bred, so I have no clue what made him suddenly decide to cross the river into unfamiliar territory. People who aren't from London may not understand it. London is London, they will say, but that's not true.

I come every week, without fail, when Dad's health worker, Jenny, isn't here to keep him company, and each visit blends into the next. Especially this part, when I am waiting at the door, unsure of what to expect. The four plastic carrier bags I carry are loaded with groceries and their handles cut into my palms.

The blue paint on the door is chipped, the intercom red with rust, and weeds creep up the walls, as if trying to escape from a prison. I used to wonder if that's how Dad felt, but it can't be; he is not aware of his shackles.

I am not surprised that he hasn't noticed the front garden – if you could call it that – declining, but surely his neighbours have? There are five flats in this building so how is it possible nobody cares? The small consolation is the beautiful park on the other side of the road. Dad's front window overlooks it but the view is lost on him.

Finally the intercom hisses with static, followed by Dad's voice, loud and severe. "Yes? Who is it?" It is the same each week, no variation from these four words.

I try to swallow the lump, but it's firmly lodged in my throat. "Dad, it's me. Callie." I should say Caroline. He hates me shortening my name. There is the usual silence that comes after I've announced myself and, as I wait, I look around to check nobody is watching. It doesn't look good to loiter on someone's doorstep. Finally the door groans and clicks and I am inside, heading up the stairs to Dad's flat, wondering what will greet me at the top. It doesn't matter when Jenny was last here; Dad only needs a few hours to get the place in a state.

It is a while before he opens his door so I know today won't be a good day. I always judge what to expect by how long he takes to open up and let me in. "Oh, it is you. I thought it was. Come in, come in." He stands aside and I step into the stale, smoke-filled hallway. I was only here last week, wiping down floors, walls and surfaces, spraying vanilla air freshener in every room. But it's never enough to eradicate years of smoke and neglect. "Be a love and put the kettle on," he says, heading into the living room. "I'm parched. I'll be watching the footy."

I long to hug him but I can already sense he is jittery and unsettled so I don't. It wouldn't be a proper hug anyway, one where it's possible to feel his love, so it's not a great loss. But still I long to hug my dad.

The kitchen is already filthy. Dirty pots and pans are precariously stacked in the sink and there are scattered breadcrumbs and pools of milk on the worktops. It's hard to believe this is a couple of day's worth of mess.

I clean up as best I can and make two cups of tea, trying to ignore the permanent brown stains in the mugs that no amount of bleach will remove.

Mum would have hated to see Dad like this. She couldn't bear the sight of a crumb or speck of dust, so this would have sent her packing even if she hadn't already left. Even now, in my adulthood, Dad won't tell me the truth about why she left. But I know. She couldn't deal with him and the life his illness made them both live. She was a good person, I know she was, but she was pushed to her limit, something I refuse to do to James.

In the living room, Dad sits in his armchair with his feet on the coffee table, and just for a second he is the father I remember. But then he says, "You don't mind if I watch the footy, do you? I can still hear you if you want to talk." I glance at the television and it isn't even switched on, the black screen coated with a thick layer of dust.

We sit in silence for a while, but I tell myself it doesn't matter. What's important is that I'm here with him. I am not scared to be alone with Dad because underneath whatever has taken control of his mind, he is still the father I love.

"So what's new in Caroline's life? he asks, his eyes still fixed on the blank television. He always uses this third person address when he asks me questions, but it is something else I've grown used to.

If we were any other father and daughter I would be able to tell Dad everything I've been struggling with for the last eight months. He would hold my hand and nod along while I explain how Dillon and Luke have frozen me out since the day I married James. That they want to be rid of me. And that I'm holding onto this life by a thread. He would tell me what to do, his advice delivered in clear instructions that, once followed, would solve everything. But even if he was having a clear day, how could I tell him my troubles when neither he nor James knows the other exists?

"Everything's fine, Dad," I say. I have become an expert at feeding this lie to the people I care about, as if it is programmed into me, only requiring the press of a button.

He lifts his mug and takes a long sip, still staring at the television. For the first time I notice a red stain on the front of his shirt and I stand up, moving towards him to get a closer look, preparing myself to see blood. But it's only ketchup or something else Dad has eaten. It saddens me to see him in this state; he was a dignified man when I was a child, or at least that's how I remember him. I make a note to try and get him into a clean shirt before I leave, but I don't fancy my chances.

"They've been here again, you know," he says, turning to me. "All night, they talk and whisper about me. I can't make out what they're saying but I know it's not good."

This is what I fear the most. If I humour him it feeds his paranoia, but what choice do I have? Telling him he's mistaken only ends up in an argument.

"I'll talk to them," I say, falling back onto the worn sofa. "I'll tell them to stop."

Dad frowns and places his mug back on the coffee table. "Don't be ridiculous, Caroline, they won't listen to you. They don't listen to anyone. They just keep on and on." He turns back to the television. "They better not interrupt my football game."

Now that his focus is back on the invisible match, I tell him I'm going to clean the flat, and begin my search for cleaning products. I only brought a few today and no matter how many I buy, they have always disappeared by the following week. "You can't trust them," Dad says when I question him. "They take all kinds of things."

For the next hour I scrub, dust and vacuum, taking out my anger on the filthy surfaces of the flat. I wonder how Dad fills his days when I'm not here. Does he just stare at his reflection in the television all day? What kind of life is this? By the time I start on the bathroom I have convinced myself that the only peace he will ever get is when he's asleep.

Wiping down the cabinet mirror, I am startled when the door springs open and several white packets drop to the floor. I don't know what I'm most shocked about: the fact that I've caused this mess or the fact that Dad's cabinet is unlocked. He always locks it, claiming that *they* will snoop through his personal items if he doesn't. I scoop up one of the packets and study the label. They are Dad's pills. But he shouldn't have so many packets. I check one and it's from three months ago.

"Dad? What's going on?" I stand in front of the television, waving one of the packets in front of him. "Why haven't you been taking your pills?" Dumping the other packs on the coffee table, I wait for him to explain himself.

But he doesn't even flinch, continuing to stare ahead as if I'm invisible. I try a different approach and kneel in front of him. "Please, Dad, you need to take them. Just take a couple now. I'll get you some water." I stroke his hand, his rough, calloused skin feeling like sandpaper. I will need to speak to Jenny about this; clearly Dad's been fooling us both.

He turns to me and his eyes seem to soften. I begin to stand again but then he opens his mouth and bellows, louder than I've ever heard him, his voice shattering the silence of the flat.

"Get out! Get the fuck out of my house!"

When I get home, I am surprised to find James is already home from work, sitting on the sofa with his laptop perched on his knees. The house is quiet – too quiet – and I can hear the whirr of the laptop fan. "Where are the boys?" I ask.

James taps on the keyboard but doesn't look up. "Emma's taken them to the cinema. I thought you could do with a break." He looks up at me and his frown lines show me he is struggling with something. "You've been gone a long time."

I hold out the Sainsbury's carrier bags I'm still holding. "Traffic was bad and I forgot the list. Had to try and remember everything. I stopped for a coffee as well." This is not exactly a lie, more of an omission.

He nods and turns back to his laptop. "Why don't we get a takeaway tonight? It will save you cooking, and Emma said she'd take the boys out for food after their film."

"Sounds good," I say, wishing it was me taking them to the cinema, me with whom they want to spend time.

Sometimes it is easier to ignore things. Push them under the carpet, out of view, and hope they won't trip you up. This is what I think as I sit cuddled up to James on the sofa, stealing Peking duck from his plate because I've already finished my own and I'm still hungry. He playfully nudges me away and shoves the last forkful in his mouth before putting his plate on the floor. I make a grab for him but he wrestles me away and we collapse in a heap. I can't remember the last time I laughed so hard but am sure it was more than eight months ago. At this moment I am grateful James doesn't know the extent of my problems with Dillon and Luke.

So what he says next surprises me. "You know all you had to do yesterday evening was call me. I would have made them eat."

I freeze, my mouth half-open because I am still in the middle of a laughing fit.

He continues without waiting for an answer. "I've been thinking about it all day and I just don't know what to do. I've talked to them till I'm blue in the face but they're still giving you trouble. Aren't they?"

I remember the boys late last night, scurrying around in the kitchen when they thought I was asleep. "I, um…" I trail off when I see James' expression. This is harder for him than it is for me. He is stuck in the middle.

"I'll talk to them again, tell them we won't tolerate any more nonsense. We've got to keep trying, haven't we?"

Hearing this, something inside me snaps. "I *am* trying, James. Every day I try to make this work, try to be a mother to them. It's impossible! Whenever I ask them to do anything, they either ignore me or try to argue. But that's not the worst of it. They lie and play nasty tricks, they just want me out!" I am too angry to hold back, to keep James from hearing the truth I've tried to protect him from, so I tell him everything. And when I get to the part about the overheard conversation, James' face pales and his eyes drop to the floor.

The silence in the room is torture, until he eventually speaks. "Are you sure? I need you to be sure about this. There can't be any doubt if I bring this up with them."

I nod, but am suddenly unsure of myself. What if I have got it all wrong? What if my mind is playing tricks and I only thought I heard Dillon admitting they planned the accident. Come to think of it, did I even hear him say that? Or have I just jumped to conclusions? I stare at James, already regretting that I've brought this up.

"Right, I'll speak to them as soon as they get back." His frail voice betrays his shock.

"James, let's think about this. Surely confronting them won't help? We need to think about this carefully. Besides, they'll just deny it, of course."

"Callie, I don't understand. I'm trying to help but now you're saying I shouldn't? You've told me now so I can't just pretend I don't know. If they planned the accident…well… I won't have that kind of appalling behaviour. Let me talk to them, okay?"

"But don't you realise that does no good? You've spoken to them already, several times, and they still make life impossible!" My voice gets louder, and even to my own ears I sound unreasonable.

James grabs my hand. "I told you, I'll sort this and they will be punished. I've had enough, and this is the worst of it. I know they've been through hell but it's no excuse. Lauren would…" He trails off.

And then, without thinking, I ask him the question I don't want to know the answer to, don't want him to think about. "But what if it never changes? What then?"

Our eyes meet and there is something different in the way he looks at me. I have opened a floodgate and will not be able to avoid what comes through it. I also realise something else: the boys have a permanent position in James' life, whereas mine is not so secure.

CHAPTER NINE

Days pass and the house is shrouded in a frosty atmosphere. There is tension between James and the boys, and I feel responsible, even though James would never say so. He grounded them for a few days and took away their PlayStation but I should have kept my mouth shut, like I'd planned to, and sorted it out for myself, instead of making the situation worse. Things just aren't right, and I am certain we both feel it.

Even sex between us has become strained. Both of us go through the motions with our bodies, but we are disconnected somehow. It's as if we hope to fill a gap with an act that leaves us feeling even emptier afterwards. Perhaps we are both scared that if we leave it too long our desire will fade. And where would that leave us? But I am not without hope that this fog will lift. For all of us.

I am stir-crazy today, full of energy I need to expend. The boys leave for school and for a few hours my time is my own. I've been working tirelessly on my new module and need to give myself a day off. I don't want to burn out and begin questioning what I'm doing.

This course is the one thing in my life that is going well at the moment.

But standing in the hallway to gather up the letters the postman has shoved through the door, it occurs to me that there is something I could do to make things better. It doesn't matter whether or not Dillon and Luke appreciate my gesture, it only matters that I don't give up.

So I change into some old clothes, already splattered with paint, and spend the morning replacing my yellow walls with Lauren's snow-white shade. With every brush stroke, I imagine what these walls have seen: James, Lauren and the boys, happy together. A real family. There will have been laughter and all the noise a family should make, none of the tense silences now characterising our home.

It should be enough that James is happy, that he made the choice to be with me, to marry me. But it's not. Not when his first choice will always be Lauren. It is strange to think it but I probably would have liked her. From everything I've heard people say about her – and there is no shortage of participants eager to share their stories – she sounds like a woman it would have been impossible to hate. James insists she was far from perfect and her need for control exasperated him, but she was just *right* for him. I can tell from their family pictures that what lies beneath the surface of smiles and poses is something pure. How can I compete with that? No photos of the four of us exist; the boys would rather be skinned alive than stand in such proximity to me.

But you are here now. That's all that matters. Isn't it?

The afternoon is almost over by the time I've finished painting and clearing up, but I have done the right thing. Dillon is taking Luke straight to football after school so I'll have even more time to myself. James insists the boys aren't coming home first because they want to go to homework club but he is just trying to see the best in them. I suppose that's what any father would do.

I have worked up an appetite and crave chocolate and crisps so I head to the shop, pretending I can't see Mrs Simmons pulling her net curtain aside and watching me from her window.

As desperate as I am for junk food, I now have no idea what I want to eat. I walk aimlessly up and down the aisles, picking items up before putting them down again when they don't feel right. The cashier eyes me from behind the counter and doesn't smile when I look up at him. I know he just wants me to hurry up and make a purchase, but once again I'm finding it difficult to make a decision. About something as insignificant as food. I sigh at my stupidity.

Finally I give up and head to the bakery next door. But the same thing happens and with even more choice in front of me, I still cannot make a decision. I look at the young woman behind the counter; she is busy taking some pasties out of the small oven by the back wall, but it won't be long before she's exasperated like the man in the shop.

"I'll have a sausage roll, cheese pastry, ham salad roll and pork pie," I say to her back. She spins around and begins gathering up what I have asked for, probably assuming I am collecting an order for family or work colleagues. "Oh, and an apple turnover and chocolate doughnut," I add, fishing in my purse for some change.

When I reach home, Mrs Simmons is still at her window, this time holding the curtains as far back as she can manage and waving frantically to get my attention. I wave back and she points to her right, jabbing her finger towards my house.

There is someone on the front doorstep. I take a step closer and am surprised to see it is Dillon's friend, Rhys. Seeing me, he stands up, pulling his headphones from his ears and stuffing them in his pocket.

"Hi, Mrs Harwell. Sorry, I was just waiting for Dillon but he's not home yet."

Feeling apprehensive, I walk towards the door and fumble in my bag for my keys. "He's gone with Luke to football practice today. Didn't he tell you?"

Rhys steps aside to let me pass, heaving his rucksack onto his back. "Oh, yeah. But I thought that was later? I was going to give him a quick lesson before then."

He seems genuinely disappointed and I begin to relax. I am so used to the boys' tricks that I am always on edge, but there is something about Rhys I trust. He is different to Dillon. More mature and calm. Maybe being a little older helps. I can't imagine this kind-looking boy being cruel or malicious, but I still won't let down my guard.

"He won't be back for a while," I say. I have forgotten till now that Rhys is teaching Dillon to play the guitar. It might not make sense but perhaps this is another reason I believe he is being genuinely nice.

"Okay." He nods but makes no move to leave. "What's in the bag?"

I hold it up, laughing as I remember my impulsiveness in the bakery. "Too much food!"

He chuckles. "Would it be okay if I wait for Dillon out here? I won't be any trouble."

I turn to Mrs Simmons' window and see she is still holding up the curtain, watching us. What would she think if I left him sitting out here? "No, come in and wait. I hope you're hungry because I'll need help finishing off this lot." I hold up the bag again and he grins. A wide smile that stretches across his face. A smile I can trust.

It feels strange to be alone in the house with Dillon's friend. My guard is still up, part of me expecting any moment that Rhys will tell me I'm the worst mother in the world and I need to stop ruining his friend's life. Or worse.

But there seems to be nothing cold about him, and if I can't trust my instincts, what else do I have?

Rhys asks if he can help with anything, but I tell him to take a seat. He sits at the kitchen table, rather than on a stool at the breakfast bar, and watches as I plate the food and pour two glasses of orange juice. I wonder what he's thinking.

"Are you sure it's okay for me to have some?" he asks. "Isn't all this for Dillon and Luke?"

I shake my head and tell him about my indecision in the bakery, expecting him to conclude that I must be crazy. But his eyes don't glaze over, so perhaps he is not writing me off altogether. "Well, I'm glad you went because this sausage roll tastes good."

His compliment lifts my spirits, even if it comes from a teenage boy. Even if he is the friend of a stepson who loathes me. I am almost tempted to ask him whether Dillon ever talks about me, but it's not fair to put that burden on Rhys. Instead I will wait and see if he brings up the subject.

"What's your mum like, Rhys?" I am certain he has loving parents. He wouldn't be so grounded if he didn't.

He shrugs. "She's nice. A bit strict sometimes. Dad too. But I guess I understand why."

As Rhys continues to talk about his parents, it crosses my mind that this is all an act. I have no idea what kind of act, or what Dillon could hope to achieve if he has set this up, but I file the thought away, ready at any second to say I knew it, that I wasn't fooled.

"Well, it sounds like you're all quite close. That's good." I have put it out there. An opening for him to mention Dillon. But he doesn't.

Instead, he tells me about his band and how he wants to study music at university once he's finished his A levels.

"That's right, you're older than Dillon, aren't you?" Will throwing Dillon's name out again compel Rhys to talk about him?

He nods, looking pleased with himself. "Yeah, I'm eighteen. Well, I will be soon."

"So you're seventeen?" I smile to let him know I'm teasing him. I remember being his age, when years are added on rather than taken off.

"Yeah, but not for much longer, Mrs Harwell." Perhaps he didn't get that I was teasing him, after all. He dusts some pastry flakes from the table onto his plate. Neither Dillon nor Luke would have bothered.

I clear away the plates and ask him if he wants a hot drink, but he shakes his head. "Unless you've got hot chocolate? I wouldn't mind one of those, thanks, Mrs Harwell."

I almost tell him to call me Callie but something stops me. Dillon would not appreciate his friend referring to me so warmly. And if it's done once, it cannot be taken back, and I can't tell him to call me Callie only when Dillon is out of earshot.

While I make our drinks, I check the time on the clock above the window. It's four-thirty, so Luke will only just be starting his game. How am I going to entertain Dillon's friend for over an hour? He's nice enough, but eventually I will run out of things to say. And I wanted to relax today while I've got the chance.

"Do you want to take this up to Dillon's room and wait for him there?" I ask, handing Rhys his mug.

He appears to consider my suggestion, scratching his cheek and looking around the kitchen. "Um, if it's okay with you could I just stay here?"

I am so used to the boys running off at every opportunity that Rhys' request comes as a shock. "Oh…I suppose —"

"But don't worry if you've got stuff to do…" I sense his disappointment and it convinces me that it won't do any harm to keep him company while he waits.

"No, it's fine. But let's go in the living room. I've got some reading to do for my course, but maybe you could watch TV or something?"

He jumps up, his chair sliding back with a screech. "That's okay, I've got some homework to do anyway."

As soon as Rhys follows me into the living room, he heads for the piano and runs his hand over the top of it. At first I think this is strange, but then I remember he is studying music, so of course he will be interested in James' piano.

"This is great," he says, putting his mug on a coaster someone's left on top.

Feeling foolish because I know nothing about pianos, I sit on the sofa and make the only comment I can. "It's very old and none of us really play it. James' grandparents left it to him and I suppose he doesn't have the heart to get rid of it." I don't mention that Lauren played. Or that this is more likely the reason James wants to hang on to it, even though it takes up too much space.

Rhys' eyes widen. "What? You can't get rid of it! This is like…a work of art!"

His enthusiasm brightens his face and I smile because it is contagious. This is what having kids around is supposed to be like, although I have to remind myself again that Rhys is older than Dillon. Perhaps, in a year or two, Dillon will be more like his friend.

"Mrs Harwell? Can I…I mean…would it be okay if I played it?" He looks at me and I shrug. What harm can it do? It would be difficult to break a piano and I can still get on with my reading.

"Maybe just a quick go," I tell him, hoping he won't play too loudly. The piano is right next to Mrs Simmons' wall, and she'd surely have something to say about any disturbance.

I settle back and open my textbook, but within seconds it is closed on my lap and I am staring at Rhys as beautiful classical music floats around me. It is a strange sight: this teenager with his shirt hanging out and hair flopping over his face playing with such skill and confidence, and I am immediately mesmerised by his performance. I have no idea what piece he's playing, but I close my eyes and let the sound drift over me. I have my moment to relax after all.

Even though I've told him to have a quick go, I am disappointed when he stops after only a few minutes. He turns to me and I can't hide my excitement. "Wow, you're really good. That was…" But I don't have the words to describe his talent.

Rhys flushes. "Thanks, Mrs Harwell."

I want to tell him to keep playing but instead I ask what other instruments he plays.

"Oh, not many," he says, picking up his mug and taking a sip. "Just the drums, flute and saxophone. And I sing a bit too. But I'm not that great."

"Well, your parents must be really proud," I say. If only I had a chance to feel the same about Dillon.

Rhys shrugs. "Ah, they're used to it. I've been playing since I was a kid."

I open my mouth to remind him he still is one, but think better of it. He doesn't deserve to be patronised. "You can play some more if you like," I say, trying my best to sound nonchalant.

"I might just listen to my iPod, if you don't mind." He stays on the piano stool and draws his knees up so he is sitting cross-legged. Pushing his headphones into each ear, the tinny sound of rock music blasts from them and he nods his head to the rhythm. I don't mention that he is supposed to be doing homework.

I flip over my book and resume reading, happy to have some company, even if the boy sitting across from me is not the teenager who should be.

At half past five, I ask Rhys if he wants to stay for dinner and am relieved when he says he will.

"How were the boys today?" James asks, climbing into bed. "Any trouble?"

I turn on my side and smooth the duvet over us. "Fine," I say, which, for the most part, is true. I don't add that it's only because Rhys was there that they bothered to sit down.

"Thanks for repainting the hall. It means a lot to them. I know it's difficult, but they miss her, Callie…"

I reach for his hand. It is my way of comforting him because I know he isn't only speaking for the boys. We are silent for a few seconds, and then James reaches over and strokes my arm. I know what he wants and I want it too because, somehow, today has been a better day. I know it was for Rhys' benefit, but I got a few civil words out of the boys this evening at dinner and it feels as if we may be able to turn a corner.

Afterwards, I lie across James and listen to his slow, deep breaths. He is already halfway towards sleep, but I am happy just to rest on his chest.

I have almost drifted off when a pounding on the bedroom door shatters the silence. I sit up and shake James, who is still half-asleep so hasn't realised what's going on. Rushing to the door, I throw it open and Dillon stands in front of me, his arm around Luke, who is bending over, clutching his stomach, his face almost yellow.

Dillon looks straight past me. "Dad, quick, Luke's been sick. He's really ill."

I step forward and try to touch Luke's forehead but Dillon stands between us, like a bodyguard. "Dad? I think it's something he ate."

James clambers out of bed, looking at me as he passes but saying nothing. For a second something flashes in his eyes, but I won't allow myself to dwell on what it is. "Don't worry, I'll deal with this," he says, rushing to Luke and ushering the boys out of the room. The door clicks shut behind them.

How quickly things change. Only moments ago I was convinced there was hope that it would get better, but now I know I was foolish to believe that. The boys will not stop playing their game.

CHAPTER TEN

Saturday arrives and with it the reality that my husband will be going to Leeds with Tabitha. I know they work together almost daily but this is different. They will be away from home, away from me. That would be bad enough on its own, but the distance I thought was narrowing between James and me is now wider than ever. I don't want to believe he thinks I am responsible for Luke's sickness the other day, but with the way the boys have built me up to be a monster, anything is possible.

"Emma will be here to pick them up in a minute," James says, throwing clothes into his weekend bag. He has arranged for the boys to spend the weekend with her, and I am relieved I won't be left alone with them. I am beginning to doubt whether I can trust my own perspective, so having some space will give me a chance to try and make sense of things.

But the minute they have gone, I feel as if the ground is falling from beneath me. I wanted this peace, the silence an empty house brings, but now it feels oppressive. The thought of being alone here once night arrives begins to worry me. It's not that I'm afraid of intruders and I don't believe in ghosts or anything like that; what I fear is worse than that. It's myself. I don't want to be alone with myself.

Eager to distance myself from the house, I decide to drive to Kingston. I doubt shopping will ease my anxiety but it is worth a try, and there is no way I can concentrate on coursework.

Walking in and out of shops, I half-heartedly flick through clothes rails, not interested in anything that's on display. Even in the middle of the Saturday morning swarm, I have never felt lonelier and the mid-morning sun does little to lift my mood. Eventually I give up and decide to have a coffee, but as I cross the road to Starbucks, I notice a computer game shop next door.

Thinking of Luke's paper-white face the other night, I decide I will get the boys a new game for their PlayStation. I will give it to them if they do some chores around the house, that way they won't think they're being rewarded for poor behaviour. They will probably still see it as a futile attempt at bribery, but I don't let that deter me. This feels like the right thing to do. Isn't a mother's love meant to be unconditional? No matter how the boys have behaved in the past – and regardless of whether they change in the future – I have to forgive. I have to try to love them.

The inside of the shop is a maze of games and I have no idea where to begin. I think about asking one of the cashiers for help but I would only look stupid. *Hi, I'm looking for a game for my sons but I have no idea what they might like. Can you help me?*

Turning around, I am about to admit defeat and leave when someone taps my shoulder. "Hi, Mrs Harwell. What are you doing here?"

Rhys stands before me, grinning as if he's caught me somewhere I shouldn't be. He looks different dressed in jeans and a hooded top; I have only ever seen him in his smart school clothes.

I confess I've been looking for a game for Dillon and Luke but have no clue what to get. I don't feel ashamed or idiotic admitting this to Rhys, although I still wonder if Dillon has roped him into toying with me.

He smiles and leads me to a section by the counter. "They'll love this," he says, handing me a case.

I study the cover and immediately notice the sixteen rating plastered across the front. "*Call of Duty*? Are you sure?" It crosses my mind again that my judgement has lapsed and this is all a trick.

Rhys nods. "Yep. Dillon's been saving up to get this. Everyone at school loves it."

I am not convinced. The game is fine for Dillon, as he'll be sixteen this summer, but Luke is only twelve. But after some hesitation, Rhys' smile convinces me to give in. If James asks I will tell him I didn't notice the rating, and by then it will be too late. I'm sure he wouldn't take a gift from his sons, not when it's obvious that I'm trying to do something nice.

"Okay, then. I'll get it. Thanks, Rhys. See you soon," I say, heading to the till.

I don't notice where Rhys wanders off to, but I am not expecting to find him standing outside, leaning

90

against the window, tapping something into his phone. I ask him if he is waiting for someone but he shakes his head. "No…I just wondered…I'm supposed to me meeting my friends but they're late and I've got nothing to do. Could I get you a coffee or something? To say thanks for all that food the other day. You know, the sausage roll and dinner…" He looks directly at me, seemingly not embarrassed by his unusual request.

My shock soon disappears as I search for an excuse. The last thing I want is to go for a coffee with a seventeen-year-old boy who isn't my son. And I am not good company today. But before I can speak, Rhys continues.

"Come on, Mrs Harwell, just a few minutes. My friends won't be long." His tone and determined expression exude a confidence beyond his age.

I am about to say no when I realise I can use the opportunity to get him to talk about Dillon. Maybe I can find out where I am going so wrong. But I will have to be direct this time because so far Rhys has not taken any of my hints. "Okay, a quick coffee, then. But you're not paying."

Rhys laughs. "I've got a job, you know, Mrs Harwell. Helping my uncle out in his shop on Sundays." And I smile at his determination to be treated as an adult.

Starbucks is crowded, so it is a while before we get a table, our takeaway cups almost empty before we sit down. I feel guilty for letting Rhys pay, but he practically shoved the money at the cashier and I didn't want to make a scene.

"Don't worry, Mrs Harwell, they won't think you've made your son pay for drinks. You're nowhere near old enough. My mum's much older than you."

I'm about to thank him for the compliment but then realise something: if people don't think I'm his mother then who *do* they think I am? Not wanting to explore the idea further, I ask him about school.

"I've got a gig in two weeks in the sixth form hall. Loads of people are coming, I can't wait." He doesn't ask if Dillon has told me about it. He must already know how unlikely that is.

"That's great. Hope it goes well."

"Come if you like," he says, taking a sip of his hot chocolate, even though it must be cold, as mine is, by now. "I mean, it will be nice if you can. Everyone's welcome. Students, parents. It doesn't matter."

Nodding slowly, I tell him I'll try, but there is no way Dillon will want me there. I decide now is the time to ask him about it. When will I have the opportunity again? "Rhys, can I ask you something?"

He leans forward in his chair, an expectant look on his face. "Course."

To distract myself, I lift my coffee to my mouth, but put it back again. I can't stomach cold coffee, not even as a defence mechanism. "I, um, was wondering…I know this will sound strange, but does Dillon ever mention me?"

Rhys shakes his head. "I was thinking you might ask me about that." He hesitates for a moment, moving his cup around the table in small circles. His defence mechanism. And at that moment I know with certainty that he is trying to decide whether to lie or tell the harsh truth. He's probably wondering how he can soften the blow if he is honest, but his lack of years might not have prepared him for that.

When he speaks, I am horrified to hear his words are soaked in pity. "I'm really sorry, Mrs Harwell, but he…kind of seems to hate you. I don't understand it. I keep telling him you're really nice but he doesn't want to listen."

I am not surprised but it still hurts, like a punch to my gut.

"Don't worry, though. It's just because of his Mum dying and everything, that's all. He'll grow up eventually. I mean, I know he's my best friend but sometimes he drives me mad."

But I don't want Rhys to try and ease the blow. It is out there now. Of course I've known all along, but hearing that Dillon tells other people how he feels about me makes it a hundred times worse.

"I know this, I just don't know exactly *why* he hates me," I say, to stop him trying to make me feel better. And then before I can hold them back, tears are streaming down my cheeks. For months I have held it together, dealt with whatever the boys throw my way, stayed strong for James, but now I am falling apart in front of a teenage boy. I try to swipe my tears away with the sleeve of my jacket but it's too late; Rhys has noticed.

His eyes widen as he takes in what is happening, but then he leans forward and says, "I'm so sorry, I didn't mean to upset you. Come on, let's get out of here. Where are you parked?"

Outside, it is much brighter and I am not prepared for the glare. Squinting, I follow Rhys as he weaves in between shoppers, expertly avoiding being bashed by huge bags. I am not so skilled at this and get knocked into several times before we get to the multi-storey car park. I can feel the mix of mascara and tears pooling under my eyes and hate to think what a state I must look.

We get to my car and I dig around in my bag for my keys. There are some tissues in the glove compartment and the sooner I get one the better. I give no thought to what will happen now, but Rhys is standing right next to me so I've got to say something. "Thanks, I'll be okay."

But he doesn't move. "I can't just leave you upset like this. How about you give me a lift back and I'll walk home from yours?"

My instinct screams at me that this is a bad idea, but I'm too upset to argue. Pointing out all the flaws in his plan will take energy I don't have. "Your friends will be waiting for you," I say. It is a feeble attempt when he's already standing by the passenger door.

"Nah, that's fine. I'll text them. I kind of feel like it's my fault you're upset."

Can he really be so kind? So different from Dillon and Luke, who would both bask in my tears?

"Okay." I click the key fob and we both get in. Rhys is being so thoughtful, the least I can do is drive him home.

As soon as we are in the car and heading out of the car park, I expect him to mention Dillon again but he doesn't. Instead he tells me all the tracks his band are planning to play at their gig, laughing when I admit I haven't heard of some of them. "But you must have!" he insists. "You're not old."

"Rhys, I'm twenty-eight. Almost twenty-nine. To you, that's old."

He shakes his head. "No, it's not. But isn't Mr Harwell much older than you?"

I only forgive his question because he is distracting me from the thought of going back to the house. I should be looking forward to it. No Dillon or Luke. Nothing to worry about until tomorrow. So why aren't I? "He's not that much older," I say. "Thirty-nine."

Rhys seems to work this out for a moment before coming to a conclusion. "You're right, it's not that bad."

"Well, I'm glad you approve," I say, pretending to be serious.

I put on the radio and let him choose a station so that he won't ask me any more questions. It feels wrong discussing James with him, even a matter as insignificant as our ages.

We reach Wimbledon and are almost at the house before either of us speaks again. Then Rhys lowers the volume on the radio and turns to me. "Mrs Harwell?"

"D'you know what? Maybe you should call me Callie. I mean, you've bloody seen me cry now, so I think you've earned the right." I cover my mouth with my hand. "Sorry for swearing."

"Oh, come off it. I'm not a bloody baby." We both laugh and it feels good, as if I am releasing some of the tension that seems to be a constant companion.

I pull up outside the house and Rhys continues smiling as if he's just won a prize. "Okay, so…Callie." He says it slowly, as if he is testing it out to see how it sounds.

"Thanks for today, Rhys. You shouldn't have had to see me like that."

He unclicks his seatbelt and grins. "You make it sound like I've seen someone get stabbed or something. I keep telling you, I'm nearly eighteen. I can handle stuff."

I hold my hands up. "Sorry, didn't mean to patronise you."

"I'm not like Dillon," he says, jumping out of the car and shutting the door.

As I get out, I see Mrs Simmons' curtains move. The woman never gives it a rest. I know I can't take her snooping personally – James says it has always been a hobby of hers – but it's hard not to feel that she is keeping tabs on me. What will she think of me bringing Dillon's friend back in my car? I will tell the truth if she asks. I bumped into him and have given him a lift back to Wimbledon.

Rhys insists on waiting until I get the front door open and seems offended when I laugh. "Look, honestly, I'm fine. Thanks for everything, but you'd better get home now."

"Okay, see you soon…Callie." He turns around but then changes his mind. "You might need this," he says,

96

thrusting something into my hand before striding off down the road.

The curtains next door twitch again so I head inside and close the door before I dare to open my clenched fist. I already know what I will see when I bring myself to look, and I am right. I am staring at a piece of paper, Rhys' phone number scrawled across it in slanted handwriting.

There are only two things I can read into his action. The first is that he just wants to make sure I've got someone to talk to about Dillon. The second I will not allow myself to consider.

Later, when I've relaxed a little at the inevitability of being alone all night, I make myself a sandwich and cup of tea and settle on the sofa to try and do some reading. I get lost in the words, and they offer me temporary respite. My mood has lifted, but I'm not sure why, other than the fact I don't have to deal with the boys until Sunday night. And even then, I will have the game to give them, although that will bring a different set of problems if James sees the rating.

I text Emma to check on them and she takes a while to reply, but when she does it is a curt message of three words: *They are fine.*

Refusing to let her get to me, I call James to see how his drive to Leeds went. He takes a while to answer but I convince myself this is only because he will be busy setting up equipment and preparing for the photo shoot. "Drive was fine," he says. "Are you okay?"

I tell him I've had a good morning but don't mention going shopping in Kingston or bumping into Rhys. Then I hear Tabitha in the background, her throaty voice unmistakable.

"Is Tabitha with you?"

He coughs. "Oh, yeah. Her cousin had to go into hospital so she's just hanging around with me." It is a strange choice of words, but I tell myself not to panic. "Anyway, better go, the bride's shooting daggers at me. Talk later."

Still clutching the phone, I think about Dad. How his paranoia and suspicion drove Mum away. I can't let that happen. I can't let his life become mine. I repeat this in my head, like a mantra. But as soon as I stop, something else takes its place. *What if it's not paranoia?*

CHAPTER ELEVEN

James comes home earlier than I expect on Sunday. It is not even midday and he hasn't texted to say he will be setting off, so when I hear a key turn in the door, I stay seated at the kitchen table, expecting it to be Emma bringing the boys back early.

"Oh, you're back!" I want to rush over and hug him but something stops me. Nevertheless, I am pleased we have a bit of time to ourselves before the boys get home. "Is Emma still planning to take the boys for lunch?" I ask, trying to sound casual.

Paused in the kitchen doorway, James nods. "Think so. She doesn't know I'm back yet."

This is good news. It means I have at least a couple of hours alone with him. I make us both tea and he joins me at the table. I move my course books and the laptop out of the way of our mugs and smile at my husband, hoping he will reciprocate. But his forehead creases and he stares at his hands. I have never realised how nice his hands are. Large and gentle. Comforting.

"We should talk," he says. He still doesn't look at me so I know whatever he is about to say will not be easy for him. But I watch him now, clearly uncomfortable, searching for the right words. This must be bad.

As I wait for him to speak, I study his face. There is something different about him. He hasn't shaved for a couple of days, but it's not that. I am used to seeing him unshaven. On some men stubble suggests laziness, but on James it's attractive. I've known him for nearly three years, yet today he feels like a stranger.

Paranoia, that's what it is. Fear that his feelings for you are reflected in his face.

Watching him now, I can hear the words he is about to speak. It's not working. I've caused too much trouble. The boys will never be able to accept me and he has to put them first. Then, because he has started he will add all the things he's wanted to say for too long. *I shouldn't have married you. You are not Lauren.*

"It's about the boys," he says, forcing me to focus. I don't know if I can sit and hear this now but I stifle my urge to run from the room. To leave this house without letting him say the words. But then he surprises me. "It's my fault. I should have introduced you to them sooner. Given them more time to get used to you."

It doesn't sound like he's about to end our marriage after all, but I'm still unsure. Is he apologising? Blaming himself for the state we're in? *Wait a year*, he said, when I first asked if I could meet his sons. It was too early. He wanted to be sure. My pleas for us to be introduced fell on deaf ears.

"And now it's just a huge…mess." Finally he looks at me, a signal that it's my turn to speak, but what am I supposed to say?

"I'm trying, James," I tell him. He doesn't look convinced.

Nodding, he stares into his mug. "I know you are. I know. The thing is, I can't see how to make things better."

His words hit me and my breath catches in my throat. He *is* going to end this, he has no choice. He can't choose me over his sons, so if there is no way to fix things, I am the one who will have to go. "I'll try harder," I say. "I promise. We can work this out."

He reaches for my hand and squeezes it. "Oh, Callie, nobody could try harder than you. This isn't your fault. I hate seeing you like this. Stressed. Not yourself. I hate seeing us all like this."

"James, I –"

"I just don't know what to do. This is awful."

"I know. But we'll work it out. We can get through this, James."

"I love you," he says, but his eyes are tinged with sadness. He pushes his mug aside and stands up. "I just need to drop something off at the shop. I'll be back before the boys get home."

And then he is gone. I clear away our unfinished mugs of tea, numb to what's just happened. James didn't say it was over, but why does it feel that way? When the front door closes, the numbness evaporates and I break down for the second time this weekend, hating myself for my weakness. Hating that I don't know anymore whether I love or hate the boys.

When James gets back, I give him space and stay upstairs, telling him I need to study. Lying on the bed with my textbook, I can hear him rattling around downstairs and wonder what he's doing. Perhaps he is just distracting himself.

It's not long before I hear Emma arriving with the boys, and they all bustle in, probably excited to share stories of the weekend with James. I force myself out of the bedroom, with each step feeling as if I am walking the plank.

It falls silent when I appear at the top of the stairs, everyone turning to look at me. "Welcome home, boys," I manage to say, the words sticking in my throat and my legs as heavy as cement. I notice James smile but, again, there is sadness behind it. "I'll put the kettle on. What would you both like?"

Luke looks at Dillon, then James, then back to me. "Apple juice, please." Beside him, James ruffles his hair.

Dillon fixes his eyes on me. "Thanks. I'll have apple juice too, please, Callie." To Emma and James, the boys are being polite and friendly, but I know what game they are playing. There is no apple juice in the fridge and all three of us know it.

But I won't let them win. "No problem. I think it ran out, though, so I'll just nip to the shop and get some. Back in a minute." I brush past them and open the front door, noticing Dillon's scowl as I step outside. Round two to me.

Outside, Mrs Simmons stands by her door, talking to a DHL delivery man. She stops mid-sentence when she sees me but says nothing. "Afternoon, Mrs Simmons," I call as I walk past. She mumbles an incoherent reply, and I increase my pace to escape her heavy gaze.

Back at the house, everyone is gathered around the kitchen table, as if they are having a meeting.

"The boys were thirsty so they're having orange instead," Emma says, "and I've made tea for us."

I take one of the three mugs on the table while James, Emma and the boys resume their conversation: something about Luke's friend Harry, who I have met only briefly, when I've ferried Luke to or from his house. James tries to bring me into the conversation, but I struggle to contribute much.

"So you must have loads of coursework to do," Emma says, peering over her glasses at me. She only needs them for driving so I'm not sure why they're still perched on her nose. "I hope we're not disturbing you."

I shake my head and force a smile. "Not at all."

"So what are you up to this evening?" James asks Emma.

Finally removing her glasses, she leans forward, closer to him. "Actually, do you fancy a quick pint? I wouldn't mind talking to you about something. But don't worry if you're busy. It's nothing urgent."

James looks from me to the boys. "Okay," he says after a moment, "maybe just a quick one. I don't think

I'm up for going into the village but why don't we try The Dog and Fox round the corner?"

Emma rises to her feet. "No time like the present, eh?"

While the boys hug her goodbye, James comes over to me. "You don't mind, do you? I won't be long. The boys can do their homework."

"Of course not. We'll be fine."

He looks uncertain, but follows Emma into the hallway. "Homework," he says to Dillon and Luke. "And I'll be checking it."

"Aw, Dad!" Luke moans, but he follows his brother upstairs, not even glancing in my direction.

I hear nothing from the boys over the next hour, but their silence is disquieting. I have no idea what they're doing: homework? Planning my demise? I walk past both their rooms several times, and although they must hear the floorboards creaking, there is no sound from either room.

Deciding to make the most of it – whatever they're up to – I take my course book to the living room and settle down to study. It takes me a while to get into it this afternoon, and just as I finally begin to take in the words, Dillon appears in front of me, Luke standing behind him. "Oh, is everything okay?"

Dillon stares at the floor. "Um…we've done our homework now. And, er, Rhys said he bumped into you yesterday and asked if we're enjoying our present. What's he talking about?"

The PlayStation game. I had forgotten all about it. "Oh, well, yeah, I did get you something."

Luke steps forward. "Really? What is it?"

I try not to feel angry. This is the most effort they've made to speak to me since I moved in. This is progress. Even if it's involved bribery. "Let me go and get it," I say, leaving my book open on the sofa and ignoring my original plan to make them earn the game through chores.

It takes me a while to remember I've left the shopping bag in the car so by the time I get back to the living room, the boys are standing up, about to give up and retreat to their rooms. "Here!" I say, pulling the game from behind my back. "What do you think?"

Dillon's eyes widen and he steps forward, but Luke is already trying to prise the case from my hand. "Thanks!" he says, when I let go. "This is awesome! None of my friends have it yet!"

"Let me look," Dillon says, grabbing it from his brother.

It is hard to believe these are the same boys who an hour ago wouldn't give me the time of day. I want to be hopeful, but I know better.

"Can we play now?" Dillon asks. Somehow his stubborn refusal to meet my eyes is reassuring. Familiar ground.

"That's fine. I'll study upstairs." I grab my book from the sofa and notice that it's closed, my place lost because I never remember to use bookmarks. I am sure I left it open, but I shrug off my suspicion. Closing the door behind me, I am comforted by the boys' shouts of delight as they load up their new game, debating who will be the better player.

Upstairs, I sit cross-legged on the bed, hunting for the page I was on. Nothing I read sounds familiar, even when I go back to a chapter I know I've read, and I question how much I'm taking in. I grow frustrated. I can't mess this up. It's my one shot at independence.

My mobile beeps and I feel for it in my pockets before spotting it on the chest of drawers. I can't remember leaving it there, but scoop it up and check who has texted me. Tabitha. Very strange. I don't remember ever storing her number in my phone, but I must have, because her name is staring me in the face. Intrigued, I click the message.

So sorry about last night. Couldn't help myself. But it was good, wasn't it?

Puzzled, I read it twice before I realise what's happened. That I am holding James' mobile in my hand, not my own. We both have iPhones and he has taken mine to the pub by mistake. He must have come upstairs while I was at the shop.

For several moments I'm frozen, clutching the phone, unable to absorb Tabitha's words. I read the text again, just in case I have misunderstood it, but the meaning is unambiguous. Something has happened between her and James, and now I know my marriage is dead. The boys will have what they want.

I don't cry, but nausea sweeps through me. I mark the message as unread, place the phone back on the chest of drawers and sit back on the bed, drawing my knees to my chin.

I don't know how long I stay in this position, silent and dry-eyed. The bedroom darkens but I make no move to switch on a light or draw the curtains. Even when I hear James returning and the muffled sound of voices downstairs, I stay where I am.

But then I hear my name and footsteps bounding up the stairs. I switch on the lamp and an instant later James flings open the door.

"Callie, what is this?" He waves the PlayStation game in front of me.

"It's a present for the boys. I wanted to do something nice for them." I tell him about my trip to Kingston.

James sighs, his shoulders drooping slightly. "But I've just spent days telling them off for their behaviour. Why have you rewarded them? Plus, it's got a sixteen certificate. Luke's only twelve, Callie. I don't think –"

"This is all about the accident, isn't it? You don't trust me." My exhaustion turns to anger. "Why don't you give me some credit? I would never give the boys anything that could be harmful to them. It's just a bloody game! That's all! I'll take it back."

James' eyes widen. "What are you talking about? I'm just saying –"

"What?" I am shouting and no doubt the boys will hear.

He shakes his head. "I don't know what's going on but I can't talk to you when you're like this."

His heavy sigh just makes me feel worse, because I know I am being unreasonable. Like Dad. But I am powerless to stop my anger and am ready to tell James that I don't care what he thinks, and that I should be the one criticising *him*.

But before I can open my mouth, James drops another grenade. "The boys said you told them they should hide the game from me and it would be your secret. I know they're lying, but, Callie, this is just getting worse."

Shaking my head, I feel strangely immune to yet another malicious lie.

I stare at James' back as he walks away. For a moment I consider calling him back to confront him about Tabitha's text, but what good would it do? I don't have the energy for a different fight and I need to carefully consider what approach to take. I need to be sure there is no way I have misinterpreted anything. I copy Tabitha's words in the back of my course book, knowing it is not necessary; I am unlikely to forget them.

At the top of the stairs, I lean over the banister, listening. I wait until I hear voices and saucepans clanging in the kitchen, then sneak downstairs and check the pockets of James' jacket. With the way things have turned out today – and for the last few weeks and months – I don't expect to have any luck, but I am wrong. My phone is here. Normally frustrated with the lack of attention James pays to his belongings, I am grateful for it now. I swap his for mine, then tiptoe back upstairs.

Lying on the bed, I think about Tabitha's text again. The words run through my head, tormenting me, giving me something else I have to fight. Isn't it enough that I have the boys to deal with? But I will keep this to myself for now. It is knowledge belonging only to me, ammunition against what is to come.

CHAPTER TWELVE

Now

In this police interview room, I am becoming used to judgement. I have sat on this hard chair for hours now, reliving the last few months, while DS Connolly and DC Barnes try to work me out. What they don't realise is that I also want to make sense of my actions. What seemed rational at the time – being dishonest with James by refusing to confront him – I now know has only led me here. But still I must try to help them understand. And that way maybe I will too.

"Most people would confront their spouse if they had evidence of an affair, wouldn't they?" I throw it out there before they can ask.

Pity crosses DS Connolly's face, and he smiles weakly. "Well, I can only speak for myself but, yeah, I would confront my wife. Course I would. What's the point of living a lie?" His thin smile disappears then; he has probably realised by now that my whole marriage has been based on lies.

"For the last few months," I continue, "I had slowly been losing control of everything. The boys hated me and I felt nobody trusted me after the accident with Luke. And now I could feel James slipping away. The boys were getting what they wanted, driving a wedge between us with all the tension and lies." I let out a sigh and think how strange it is to say things aloud when for months they have been trapped in my head, gnawing away at me. "At first I was afraid of losing James. I thought if I spoke out, that would be it. Our marriage would be over. But the text made me realise I could take some control back. I could determine when to bring it up and how to deal with it."

"I see," DS Connolly says. "Do you think it was your illness clouding your judgement?"

"Now I do," I say, meeting his heavy gaze. I don't add that this knowledge has come far too late. "But back then I just didn't want to end up like Dad. I thought I had control. I couldn't have been more wrong."

CHAPTER THIRTEEN

How quickly things fall apart. Just over a week ago the boys were my biggest problem, but now I've got something even worse to contend with. Tabitha. And James. Tabitha and James. What does this mean for my marriage? I can't end up like Dad.

I sit on the information, fighting the temptation to hurl accusations at James. He tries his best to hide the tension between us from the boys, and I'm grateful to him for that. But nothing can defrost the atmosphere in the house.

While James is on a shoot, I take the opportunity to visit his shop. I have no plan; all I know is I need to see Tabitha. I have been so distracted lately that I am getting behind in my coursework, but this is something I need to do. It is still early, so if I hurry I will have plenty of time to study later.

Walking seems the best option. Adrenalin floods through my body and I need to be moving; I don't have the patience to sit still on the bus. I glance at Mrs Simmons' house as I pass, but for once there is no twitch of the curtains.

Before I've made it to the end of our road, Bridgette calls. I have been expecting her to ring because I emailed her yesterday, breaking my vow to myself by telling her about the text. Now she will be convinced I'm about to have a breakdown. That this is the beginning of something. But I had to tell her because if I hadn't then I wouldn't have been able to hold back from telling James. And now where would I be?

"Callie? I'm so sorry it's taken me this long to call, I've been snowed under for days. Work stuff. Are you okay?"

I thought I was handling it well, but now the tears I've been holding back flood out. I wipe them away with my jacket sleeve and try to keep my voice steady. It won't do any good to let Bridgette know I'm bawling my eyes out in the middle of the street. "I don't know what to think. Or do. It's a nightmare."

"Right, let's think rationally about this. What she wrote doesn't necessarily mean something has happened —"

"What do you mean?" I can't help but spit my words into the phone. "What other explanation is there?"

She sighs. "Callie, you need to calm down. Getting worked up isn't going to help."

I think of Dad when she says this. How I used to say exactly the same thing when he was in a state, before I realised I was patronising him. My ignorance of what I was doing was no defence. A man approaches, struggling with an unruly dog on a lead, and I turn away, staying silent until he's passed.

"I'm on my way to the shop now to see Tabitha," I tell Bridgette, ignoring her last comment.

She sighs into the phone. "Oh no, Callie, I don't think that's a good idea. Is James there? You don't even know for sure anything's happened."

I quote the text to her and she falls silent. She has probably realised, finally, that there is no innocent way to interpret Tabitha's words.

She tries another approach. "Look, why don't we meet up and talk about it first? It will have to be Friday, I've got a training course all week in Birmingham, but I really don't think you should do anything rash. Your situation is tricky enough with the boys and you don't want to make it any worse."

Calmly, I remind her that it has already been eight days since I found the text so I am not behaving rashly at all. I add that I don't even know if I'm going to say or do anything yet. She seems slightly appeased by this, but that may have more to do with the colleague I can hear calling to her in the background, telling her they're wanted back in the training room.

"I'd better go, Callie. But please don't speak to Tabitha…It's James you should be confronting. Debbie and I had a chat the other day and –"

I say goodbye and hang up, not giving her a chance to finish her sentence. I am not a charity case. I am not my dad.

Feeling guilty, I switch off my phone. It would be just like Bridgette to text Debbie and ask her to give me a call, to see if she has more time to snap me out of this. I know they're looking out for me, but they're not here, living through this as I am. And I don't want their pity.

But then it occurs to me that keeping my phone off is a bad idea. What if something happens to Dillon or Luke and the school tries to get hold of me? I can't take that chance. So I switch it back on, doubting my true motivation for doing so. It is not just worry over the boys – that is becoming harder every day – but what would James say if the school couldn't reach me? It would be a final nail in my coffin, forcing him closer to Tabitha.

It truly feels like May today, and I try to pretend I'm just out to enjoy the sun. But as soon as the shop is in view, my attempt at subterfuge fades. I am here to confront the woman who is sleeping with my husband.

From the pavement across the road, outside The Coffee Bean, I freeze, suddenly unsure of what I'm doing. It is one thing having a vague idea of what to say running through my mind, but in reality things are different. I can't just barge in there and accuse her of sleeping with James, at least not without the text as evidence. I need to be calm and composed, like her.

There are chairs and tables set up outside the coffee shop today, inviting people to make the most of the mild weather. I decide to stop for a cappuccino. I need more time to plan what to say. And from here, I'll also have a clear view of Tabitha.

Neither Carlo nor Anthony is around and I don't recognise the young girl serving at the till. She smiles as she keys in my order, then struggles to work the machine. Frustrated, she looks around for help, but no other staff are within sight.

"You have to hold down that round button," I say, and she frowns at me. "I used to work here."

The smile returns to her face. "Oh, thanks. I keep forgetting that! Thanks! Do you want to take a seat and I'll bring it over?"

I tell her I'll be outside and head out into the warmth. Across the road, there is no sign of Tabitha, but I know she won't be out of sight for long. James hates the reception area being unmanned.

The girl comes out with my cappuccino and places it on the table, some of it sloshing over the side as she does so. "I'm so sorry," she says, but I brush it off. Spilt coffee is the least of my worries.

Once she has gone back inside, I glance again at the shop. Tabitha is visible now. Tall and elegant, even in flat shoes. And even from this distance I can tell that her make-up, as usual, is immaculate. I lift my spoon and study my reflection. Even without the distortion, I am a mess compared to her. I have barely touched my hair today and it hangs in dark, tangled waves. It has been weeks since I've bothered to tame it straight like Tabitha's.

Sometimes men stray for a reason, and you have given James his. It's bad enough that you can't be a mother to his sons, but now you are letting yourself go. Just like Dad. I can't argue with myself about this because it is true. And it has to stop now.

Finishing my drink, I head past several more shops and stop outside John Carne. Inside, there are only two people having their hair done and an unoccupied stylist with bleached blonde hair hovers by the front desk, chatting to the receptionist. Within seconds I am seated before a mirror, pulling at my hair, explaining that I want it all chopped off.

The stylist stares at me as if I've just asked to be shaved bald. "What, you mean like a pixie crop?"

I nod. "Yes, short. But stylish. I just want it all off." I am already excited at the thought, desperate to shed what is weighing me down. I know it will take more than a haircut but it's a good place to start. And once it's cut I can step into the shop and face Tabitha.

"But…are you sure? It's nice and long and thick. Most people need extensions to get it looking like that."

I try not to show my frustration. "I just really need a change."

Afterwards, even I am surprised by how good my hair looks. The blonde stylist holds the mirror up to show me the back and from both angles, I don't look like myself. I have never had my hair this short before, but, surprisingly, it suits me. I am now someone glamorous and confident. Someone in control.

Now I can stand tall in front of the woman who is sleeping with my husband.

I pay with my credit card then slip a twenty-pound note into the hairdresser's hand. She stares at it and holds it out as if she's about to tell me I've made a mistake, but I turn and head for the door.

Outside, I pat down my hair, take a deep breath and prepare myself for what is to come.

"Callie?" Tabitha looks up from her computer and stares at me. "You've changed your hair." It is a statement not a compliment and she scrunches her nose but I don't let it bother me. "James isn't here. Didn't he tell you he's on a shoot this morning?"

Her smile is a smirk and I feel myself heating up. I have never considered myself easily riled, but within seconds of being in Tabitha's presence I feel my insides boiling.

"What time will he be back?" I ask, a plan occurring to me.

She shakes her head and her mouth curls up at the corner. "Not for ages. Probably late afternoon."

She is clearly pleased to deliver this news, but I won't let her win. "That's fine. I think I'll just hang around and wait." I shrug to convince her I am unruffled. "I suppose, in a way, it's my shop too. Funny to think of it that way, isn't it?"

Her smirk disappears and she makes a show of dusting something from her skirt, but I know there will be no fluff, crumbs or even a hair on any of her clothes. She is buying time so she can work out what to say. "Well, I…I'm really busy actually, so –"

"That's fine," I tell her, heading to the kitchen at the back of the shop. "I'll make myself a cup of tea. You won't even know I'm here."

Once I am out of her view, I lean against the narrow worktop and breathe deeply. If I've succeeded so far in appearing calm and confident, it's taken everything out of me. If I had eaten anything this morning I would have lost it by now. But Tabitha will never know this.

When I've got myself together, I root around in the cupboards. There's plenty of coffee, even decaf, but all I can find are Earl Grey tea bags. Tabitha's choice. But this will have to do as I've told her I'm making a drink now and I don't feel like more coffee.

I take my time in the kitchen because my legs don't want to move. Despite my bravado a few minutes ago, I am dreading going back out there and facing that woman again. I still don't know how I'm going to confront her. Perhaps it will just be enough to sit in reception and silently drink my tea. It is sure to unnerve her, despite her confidence. She will wonder if I know the truth about her and James.

Back in reception, I sit opposite her, watching her through sips of tea. She pretends not to be perturbed by my presence, but I imagine her mind ticking away. I have never noticed before how long and thin she is; she must be almost James' height. The sound of her manicured nails clicking on the keyboard starts to irritate me, and when she answers the phone, her voice deep and falsely soothing at the same time, it is almost the final straw. I imagine grabbing her and throwing her out of the door, just to see her clothes ruffled and her hair fly out of place. To shatter the perfection. But that picture is slowly replaced with one of her and James together, naked and sweating, laughing at my ignorance.

Tabitha stops typing and looks up. "He won't be back for ages," she says, making no attempt to hide her annoyance. "Why don't you come back later?"

I offer her a smile. "No, I'll wait. I'm fine sitting here." Perhaps she thinks I am crazy. First the extreme haircut and now this. But she *should* wonder about me and what I am capable of. That is a small price to pay for what she has done.

When she pulls her mobile from the desk drawer and starts pressing buttons, I know with certainty that she is texting James. I can almost see the words: *Get your crazy wife out of here* and I can no longer hold back.

Leaving my cup on a side table, I stand up. Tabitha looks relieved but frowns when I don't head towards the glass doors. I walk towards her and she slips her phone back in the drawer.

I perch on the side of her desk and lean forwards. "I think you need to explain the text you sent James last Sunday afternoon."

She takes a moment to react – this is clearly not what she was expecting – and for the first time since I've known her, the smug façade slips away. She avoids my eye, staring at the computer screen, twisting her ridiculously large ring around her finger. It is green and vulgar and doesn't match her clothes. When she remains speechless, I quote the text to her, word for word, letting it hang in the air between us and set in motion what it will. She will have to respond now; she has no way out.

But then everything changes. Tabitha pushes her chair back and stands up. Now she towers over me and

I am the one at a disadvantage. There is no point in me standing up. My five-foot-five frame is no match for her giant body. The smirk returns to her face and her eyes bore into me. "Shouldn't you be asking James about this?" She raises her eyebrows, challenging me to deliver an effective retort.

But I don't have one. I was not expecting her to answer. Despite my certainty, part of me hoped that she would deny sending the text, or maybe offer a plausible explanation for it. Anything other than admit she is sleeping with James. But now I know without a doubt it's true.

Everything is suddenly wrong. My confidence has evaporated and I feel foolish perched on her desk with my ridiculously short hair.

Stammering, I tell her I want to hear her side of it.

With that nasty smirk on her face, Tabitha picks up the shop phone. "I'm not going to talk to you about this, Callie. Talk to James." She holds the receiver to her ear and dials a number. I hear the muffled voice of a man and then Tabitha speaks, loud and confident, "Yes, James will be free tomorrow at eleven a.m. Okay? No problem."

Stunned, I slowly turn and leave the shop, removing my denim jacket as soon as I'm outside because I am coated in sweat. My legs feel weak and I don't know how I'll find the energy to walk home.

My phone vibrates in my pocket. It is James calling and I wonder if Tabitha has already warned him that I know. I don't answer, but stare at his name on the screen until he gives up. Seconds later I receive a voicemail, but I'm in no mood for hearing his voice.

I don't think I've ever hated anyone in my life. Hatred is such a strong word, bandied about too casually, but as I find my way to the bus stop, I'm sure this is what I feel for Tabitha. Not only for what she's done, but for her indifference and contempt. And the injustice of me feeling that I am the one in the wrong.

When I get home, I can't bear the thought of going inside so I jump in the car instead. I don't know where I'll go, but driving should help clear my head. I don't bother to check whether Mrs Simmons is watching; it is for the best because in my current mood, I'm likely to pound on her window and tell her what a nosey, interfering bitch she is.

Before I start the engine, I relent and check James' voicemail, just in case it is something to do with the boys. When it's finished I am glad I've listened because it *is* about them. James says that Luke will be going to Harry's after school and Dillon is also having dinner at a friend's house. This is good news for me; it means I will get a longer break than I thought. He ends the message saying he'll be back late tonight.

It crosses my mind that he might be with Tabitha, but would they really be so indiscreet when I've practically told her I know? I will deal with it later, for now I need to drive as far from Wimbledon as possible.

As I turn into the next road, I notice Rhys walking in the opposite direction, towards the house. Until now I haven't given a second thought to the crumpled piece of paper with his phone number on it. I continue driving but see him turn around, his eyes following the car. I should keep going, there is no need for me to stop, even though I am baffled that he's here in the middle of a school day. But then I remember his kindness in the coffee shop, and how I found it easier to talk to him than even my own friends.

Every instinct screams at me to keep going, but I screech to a stop and wait. I need the comfort of a kind face today. No matter who it belongs to.

CHAPTER FOURTEEN

In my rear-view mirror I watch Rhys approach the car. His long strides are purposeful and confident so he can't be embarrassed about giving me his phone number the other week. I haven't seen him at the house since then as Dillon has spent more time at Rhys' than he has at home over the last few days.

He reaches my window and taps it with his knuckles. "Hey…Callie. Wow, your hair! It looks good."

My hands automatically reach for my hair and I smooth it down, shrugging and trying to pretend I don't feel self-conscious. "Needed a change. Anyway, what were you doing? You can't be looking for Dillon, he's at school. And don't *you* have any lessons?"

Rhys shifts from left to right, clutching the strap of his rucksack. "I have a study day today. Actually, I was hoping to see you. You know, to check you're okay after the other day. I thought you might call or something."

I search his face for signs of sincerity, but have no idea what I'm looking for. "Listen, Rhys, I don't know what you think is happening here, but I'm your friend's...mother." The last word sticks in my throat.

Rhys waves his hand. "Oh, no, no...I didn't mean...I just wanted to check you're okay. You were kind of upset. And you're always so nice to me."

"Well, I'm fine. No need to worry." I tap my fingers on the steering wheel, a nervous gesture I hope he won't notice.

He backs away from the window. "Okay, well, I'll get going then."

Sensing his disappointment, I speak without thinking. Again. "Can I give you a lift home? Or wherever you're going now?"

His face brightens. "Are you sure? Yeah, that would be great!"

Before I can change my mind he rushes to the passenger side of the car, flings open the door, and climbs in. "Do you know Lancaster Gardens? Just off the high street?"

"Not really, but you can direct me when we get close."

"I love Golfs," he says, as we pull away. He runs his hand over the dashboard, seemingly unfazed by the thin layer of dust coating it. "I'm learning to drive now. Maybe you could give me some extra lessons?"

Turning to him for a second, I catch his playful wink and shake my head. But I am not annoyed; he is helping me to forget my encounter with Tabitha.

For the whole drive Rhys talks constantly; I barely register what about but I am content just to listen to his voice. It is surprisingly deep for someone his age. He is so far-removed from everything that's bringing me down, so it is a pleasure to get lost in his idle chatter.

I still have suspicions about why he gave me his number, but I am confident I have put a stop to any inappropriate intentions. The idea of it makes me chuckle, and Rhys stops mid-flow to ask what I'm laughing at.

"Nothing. Carry on, I'm listening."

"I really like your hair, Callie. It suits you. Even Dillon must think so."

"I've only had it done today. Nobody's seen it yet." Hearing my stepson's name reminds me of James' voicemail. "Actually, isn't Dillon supposed to be seeing you after school? His dad said he would be at a friend's house so I assumed it was you."

Rhys shakes his head. "Not today. I invited him but think he's got plans with someone else. It's the next right," he says, almost too late for me to make the turn.

Lancaster Gardens is a tree-lined road of detached houses. It crosses my mind that Rhys' parents must be doing all right for themselves if they can afford to live here.

"Number nine. Just there on the left." Rhys unclicks his seatbelt before I've pulled up. "Thanks, Callie." I know I told him to call me by my first name, but it still sounds strange coming from his mouth. "D'you want to come in for a coffee? I think I can just about make one, although I can't say it will be as good as yours."

At any other time I would refuse his offer. There's no reason I should be alone in the house of my stepson's friend, even with innocent intentions. But my life is a mess and perhaps he can help me with at least one of my problems. Dillon. We only scratched the surface the last time we spoke. It is ludicrous that I have to turn to a teenage boy for help, but I am out of options. So I nod and undo my seatbelt, while Rhys grins beside me.

The inside of his house is impressive. The décor is modern and minimalist and I wonder how they manage to keep everything beige and white with a teenager in the house. But perhaps Rhys has already passed that phase where cleaning up after yourself is not on your radar.

I hover at the door, wondering whether I should take my shoes off because the shiny wooden floors look brand-new, but Rhys strides in, his trainers still on. "Come in, come in," he says. "Just through here."

"Are your parents home?" I ask, following him into an enormous kitchen. I'm hoping he and I will have a chance to talk alone. Besides, what would his mum and dad think if they found me here without Dillon?

He shakes his head. "No, they both work. Mum's a private music teacher and Dad's in advertising. He's never here, really, and Mum works at different schools so she's always travelling around. She's a peri…something teacher. Can't remember the name for it."

"Peripatetic?"

He nods. "Yeah, that's it. Anyway, they might not be here a lot but they always find a way to keep an eye on me. Make sure I'm not up to no good." He winks at me again and I roll my eyes. "Right, let me sort this coffee business," he continues. "Don't know how you can drink the stuff." He urges me to sit down and I pull out a brown leather dining chair.

"Well, when you're all grown up you might just drink it too." As soon as I've spoken I wonder how he will take my joke. His back is turned so I can't see his face but I hope I haven't offended him.

Thankfully, when he spins around he is grinning again. "So that will be in a few weeks then, I reckon. I'll be sure to celebrate with a huge, nasty cup of coffee!"

We both laugh, and I realise for the first time today I have forgotten what I'm trying to escape from.

As it turns out, Rhys' coffee tastes fine. I tell him he's done a good job and he seems pleased at my compliment. "Do you want to go in the living room? Or anywhere, it's up to you."

"Here is fine," I say, sweeping my hand across the shiny mahogany dining table, just as Rhys did to my dashboard earlier. Only my hands aren't now covered in dust.

He joins me at the table with a can of Red Bull and pulls the opener, letting a sharp hiss escape into the air. "Callie, are you okay? Really? I'm just asking because Dillon's been round here a lot lately and from the way he talks, it doesn't sound like anything's better. And with your crying and everything…I'm just worried."

Shifting in my chair, I wonder how much to tell him. I shouldn't be socialising with him at all, not like this. One, he's Dillon's best friend. Two, he's a teenager. And three, it's unfair to make him my confidante. But when I look at his kind face, a face that's far beyond its years, I let my guard down, all the time knowing I am a desperate woman.

Rhys listens with patience as I tell him what's happened over the last eight months. He shakes his head when I recount all the things the boys have done to make my life miserable. From his expressions, I am sure Dillon hasn't told him half of what I'm revealing. When I get to the part about Luke's accident, he falls quiet. Perhaps he is struggling to believe his friend capable of such a thing.

I don't mention James and how strained our relationship has become. Nor do I speak of Tabitha. These are not things Rhys should know about. But I am candid about everything else, and when I've finished I wait to see what he will say.

"I had no idea," he says, running his fingers around the top of his can. "I think I should speak to him. He's being really out of order. He'll listen to me. Can I be honest?" I nod, convinced I won't like what he's about to say. "At first, before I met you, I thought you were…kind of awful…you know, from everything Dillon had said. And I thought it had a lot to do with him missing his real mum. Which I could understand. But now I've met you…" He trails off, lifting the can to his mouth, throwing his head back as he takes a sip. He swallows and looks up. "I just think you're really nice."

I feel a tear in the corner of my eye and rub it away with my knuckle. Why can't Dillon and Luke feel this way about me? It doesn't even matter if Rhys has some other kind of feeling for me; he has still seen the real me, something the people closest to me seem unable to do. "Thanks," I say. It is all I can manage.

"I'll talk to him, Callie. Let me try, at least." He stands up and throws his can into the bin.

"Okay, but be careful what you say. I don't want things to get even worse."

He comes back to the table and smiles. "Well, I'd say they're about as bad as they can get, wouldn't you?"

He only knows the half of it. Everything is falling down around me so I have to do whatever I can to fix things, or at least make sure they can't get any worse.

"Come and see upstairs," Rhys says suddenly. "We've just redecorated and, well, I don't know if you're interested in stuff like that, but it's been done up really nice. New bathroom and everything."

I can't help but laugh at his notion of what interests adults. And the effort he's putting into entertaining me. "Another time," I say, deciding to go easy on him. He doesn't need to know that, as much as I think he's a good kid, there is no way I will ever go upstairs with him. "I'd better get going. I only meant to stay for a quick coffee."

Rhys' face falls. "Stay a bit longer. I can play you our new track. We're showcasing it at the gig on Friday."

I look at my watch and am surprised to see it's nearly three p.m. Although I don't have to rush back, I still want to go for a drive and I need to eat. But Rhys' eyes silently plead with me, weakening me. "Okay. Just quickly, though. I really have to go soon."

In the living room, he slots his iPod into his parents' stereo system. Within seconds, an upbeat guitar riff fills the room and I am once again impressed by the enormity of his talent.

"Rhys, this is great. I –"

He lifts a finger to his lips. "Shhhh, just listen."

Put in my place, I sit on one of the huge leather sofas and let Rhys' talent blow me away.

"So what do you think?" he asks, once the song ends. "Be honest." He sits on the sofa opposite me, his leg twitching. I bet he doesn't even notice this nervous tic.

"Rhys, it's great. I mean, I don't know much about rock music but, well…wow."

Nodding, his eyes flick to the floor. "Thanks, Callie. Really, thank you." He looks up at me again. "You know, I get compliments all the time from kids at school. Yeah, you're great, Rhys, yeah, you're wonderful. But it doesn't mean as much coming from them. Only words. But when you say it –"

"Well, I mean it," I say, before he can finish his sentence.

While I wonder what to say next, Rhys' mobile rings and he raises his eyebrows. "Mum. Checking up on me. Won't be a sec."

I watch him while he offers one- and two-word grunts to his mother. Silently waiting for him to finish, I begin to feel uncomfortable. But I am doing nothing wrong, so why do I feel like a naughty teenager who has been smuggled into someone's house?

As soon as he hangs up, I stand up and tell him I have to go. He doesn't protest this time and shows me to the door, promising he won't forget to talk to Dillon. As I step through the door, he grabs my hand.

Unprepared for the feeling that surges through me, I pull away and almost stumble backwards. I look to my right, expecting to see Mrs Simmons's curtains move, but then I remember where I am.

"Sorry, are you okay?" Rhys takes a step back, as if he has hurt me.

"Yeah, I'm fine. Got to run. See you."

I hurry to the car, racing across the road without checking for traffic. And even without looking back, I know Rhys is still standing in his doorway, watching me go and wondering what just happened.

I drive to Wimbledon Common, too shaken up to go any further. I need a walk, some fresh air to clear my head. Everything is a muddle and it's some time before I can force myself to address what just occurred.

By the time I've circled the common once, barely aware of people out for afternoon strolls, I have managed to convince myself it was the shock of Rhys grabbing my hand so suddenly that confused me, and sent strange signals to my brain. I am *not* attracted to him. There is no way. Even if I didn't love James, even if things were even worse than they are, Rhys is a *boy*.

Back in the car, I turn up the radio until it is far too loud; anything to stop myself thinking. The rush hour traffic has begun early today and by the time I pull up outside the house it is past four.

132

Mrs Simmons appears at her door and calls me over. "It's not right," she says, shaking her head. "Lauren's heart would break if she could see what's going on."

I cross my arms – a subconscious reaction – and ask what she's talking about.

"I'm talking about Dillon. Alone in there with a girl." She jabs her finger at the house. "Does his dad know? I'm sure he wouldn't allow it. Who knows what they're getting up to in there?" She shakes her head again.

"Sorry, Mrs Simmons, but I really don't know what you're talking about. Dillon is meant to be at a friend's house."

Something passes across her face and for a moment she is silent. "I think I'll need to talk to James about *his* sons," she says at last. Then she shuffles back inside, the slam of her front door echoing around me.

Once inside, the anger hits me. Dillon has given Mrs Simmons yet another opportunity to judge me. I'm ready to scream at him. He has done this on purpose. He knows James would never let him be alone in the house with a girl. He knows that I will have to address this.

The living room door is shut but I hear voices. I take a deep breath and open the door. They are sitting together on the sofa, not close enough to touch, and it doesn't look as if they've been doing anything wrong, but I am so furious I don't even bother to say hello.

"Dillon, a word. In the kitchen."

"This is Esme," he says, but I have already walked off.

It takes him a few minutes to follow me, but eventually he strolls in, his hands in his pockets. "What?" he says. "What have I done now?"

I try to speak calmly. I can't let this get out of hand. "Dillon, you know you're not supposed to have girls over when nobody's home. You know that."

He ignores me. "Why did you have to be so rude to her? You're out of order. We weren't doing anything."

I try to tell him this isn't the point, but he doesn't listen. Instead he hurls accusations at me. I'm trying to ruin his life. He's going to tell his dad. He hates me. *Hates me.*

It's something we've both known for some time, but he's never said the words before. At least not directly to me. If this is all a show, part of Dillon's attempt to discredit me even further, he is doing a good job of acting hurt. And when he storms out of the room, I wonder if I have handled this all wrong. Have I dug an even deeper hole for myself?

Seconds later, the front door slams, and when I rush to the window I see Dillon and Esme heading towards the bus stop. Dillon is already on his mobile phone and I know who he's calling.

CHAPTER FIFTEEN

Things have got worse. How is it that when you've sunk as low as you think it's possible to go, there is always more room to fall? I gave Dillon exactly what he wanted when I confronted him five days ago. He clearly planned the whole thing, to provide James with yet more evidence that our arrangement is not working.

It is Saturday, but I have slept in longer than I wanted. I don't feel like I've slept at all, but I drag myself out of bed. James is not beside me and I wonder if he's left without saying a word.

A few nights ago, he told me he is taking the boys to Center Parcs for a few days. "It will be half-term and they need a break. Dillon's been doing so much revision lately and I don't want him to burn out before he sits his GCSEs," he said. I wonder if he would be so quick to reward Dillon if he knew about the Esme incident.

When I told him I couldn't go with them because I had an exam, he asked if I'd mind if they went anyway. "Perhaps we could all do with a break from each other," he said. He has never spoken this way before. Things couldn't be much worse.

I put on my dressing gown and head downstairs, hearing voices as I descend. So they haven't left yet.

The three of them are sitting at the table and when I appear James says good morning, while the boys mumble something incoherent. "We'll be leaving in about half an hour," he says. "After we eat."

Somehow I manage a smile. "Okay. I hope you all have a good time."

I make myself a cup of tea and watch James slicing into his fried eggs on toast. I still haven't decided what to say or do about Tabitha's text, but even if I had, there's been no opportunity to bring it up. And I am scared. Once it's out there, then what happens to us? There is already enough tension in this house so if I mentioned the text now, he will ask me to leave, tell me our marriage is not worth saving. I suspect Tabitha has told him I confronted her, but I'm both perplexed and relieved that he hasn't mentioned it. If he does know, what does his silence say about our marriage?

I don't feel hungry and can't bear the thought of sitting here to drink my tea, suffocating in this atmosphere. "I'd better go and have a shower," I tell James.

He stands and clears his plate away. "Okay. Well, we'll probably be gone by the time you're finished so I'll say goodbye now." He leans towards me and pulls me into a hug, and even though I can't see his face, I know he is watching the boys the whole time. Is this all for show? Have we both become actors?

By the time I've had my shower and dressed I can tell they've gone. Houses have a different feel when you are alone in them. Silent and cold, no matter what time of the day or month it is.

After breakfast I am about to sit in the garden when a horrible suspicion hits me.

You don't believe James is taking the boys away. You think he's asked Emma to do it so he can be alone with Tabitha. They've got a freelancer in to cover the shop.

I don't want to believe this. I try not to. But the thought won't go away. And the more I think about it, the more convinced I am of its truth.

My mobile phone sits on the kitchen table, and slowly I pick it up, still trying to give myself time to change my mind. But then I am dialling, as if my hands are beyond the control of my head.

"Good morning, Vision Photography, how can I help?"

The deep female voice is unmistakably Tabitha's so I hang up, my breaths coming hard and fast. I'm relieved to be wrong, but I still don't feel better. *This is how it starts. Standing on the edge of something, peering over, about to cross over. How much longer can you keep ignoring it?*

Outside in the garden, I study for my exam until two o'clock and then make myself chicken salad for lunch. The chicken is dry and I drench the salad in too much French dressing, but I eat it anyway. Bad food is the least of my worries.

As evening draws in I begin to feel cloaked in loneliness. I can't face any more studying and there is nothing on TV to distract me. I try to call Bridgette but get her voicemail; she is probably busy with Aaron.

Debbie answers her mobile but sounds rushed. She tells me she moved in with Mark today and seems surprised that I don't know this.

"I did mention it," she says, and I sense she is concerned that I haven't listened. We don't talk long as she's still in the middle of unpacking and Mark is calling out in the background. "Moving's a bloody nightmare," she adds. "What were you saying?"

I tell her it's nothing important and I'll call her in a few days when she's settled in. Hanging up, it occurs to me how different her moving day must be from mine. She will have a real home with Mark. The day I moved in, James' excitement was diminished by the boys' cold sulking. I had met them several times before, and although they had never been thrilled about our relationship, they were tolerant. But something changed when I married their dad and moved in. "It won't last," James told me. "Soon they'll love you as much as I do."

I should not think of these things now. I should use this time of peace to recharge, to prepare myself to finally confront James. There is no doubt in my mind now that is what I need to do.

But this is easier said than done, and it's not long before I am picturing James with Tabitha, his hands exploring every inch of her body. Does he do the same things to her that he does to me? Does he enjoy seeing her messy and sweaty afterwards?

There is only one thing I can do to dispel these thoughts.

In the kitchen cupboard, I find a bottle of red wine and pour myself a glass. It's not my favourite, too strong and dry, but it does the trick and by the time I'm on my second glass I have come to quite like it. But what I like more is that I'm starting to forget what a mess my life is.

I try several more times to call Bridgette, but there is still no answer. I leave a message – hoping I don't sound too tipsy – and ask her to call me when she can. When my mobile beeps in my pocket a few minutes later, I assume it's her and pull it out, hoping she's telling me she's free to talk. A small piece of paper falls to the floor, but I ignore it and hurriedly scroll to my message. But it's not Bridgette. It's my mobile phone provider reminding me they'll be taking my monthly payment soon.

The fallen piece of paper catches my eye and I scoop it up and unfold it. Rhys' phone number. I had forgotten about it; I've been trying my best not to think about Rhys at all, which has been easy over the last few days, considering what's going on. But now I wonder if he meant what he said about talking to Dillon.

Before I have a chance to talk myself out of it, I am sitting on the rug, my half-empty glass of wine in front of me and my mobile pressed to my ear.

"Hello?" Rhys' voice sounds even deeper on the phone, more adult, and at first I think I've dialled the wrong number. "Hello?" he says again, this time sounding more like himself.

"Rhys? Hi, it's Mrs…It's Callie. How are you?"

I hear the intake of his breath. "Callie! Are you okay? Has something happened?"

His concern softens me and once again I am comforted by him. "I was wondering if you've had a chance to speak to Dillon yet? Remember you said you would?" Picking up my glass, I take a long sip of wine.

"Course I remember. I did try after the gig last night but he was too angry about the Esme thing to listen. He's away now, isn't he? When he gets back I'll try again."

"Thanks. I really appreciate it." I try not to slur my words, and wonder if he can tell I've been drinking.

"You know, Esme's a nice girl. I'm not taking sides or anything, but she was kind of upset about what happened."

His statement hits me hard because it is another reminder of how I have messed up. If she really is as nice as Rhys says, and if I'd taken the time to talk to her, got her on my side perhaps, then things might be looking up right now. And I wouldn't be sitting here alone, drinking myself into oblivion. A parody of Dad. I don't want to hear any more. "Okay, thanks, Rhys. I'm going now."

"No, no, wait –"

But I have already hung up.

After another two glasses of wine, the bottle is empty and there is no more alcohol in the cupboard or fridge. I will have to go to the shop if I want to knock myself out.

I walk past Mrs Simmons' house, trying to walk in a straight line but not sure I'm pulling it off. It's dark outside now, but her curtains are open and the flickering images from her television light up her front room. I can't see her but am sure she is watching me. I give her a wave, an exaggerated gesture I am sure she won't be able to misinterpret. What I really want to do is stick two fingers up at her.

On my way back home, with two bottles of wine swinging in a plastic bag from my arm, I see that Mrs Simmons' curtains are still open. This time I can see her, but for once her back is turned.

I have barely had time to go inside and pour another glass of wine before the doorbell rings.

Rhys is standing on the front step, his shoulders hunched and his hands in his pockets. "Sorry," he says. "I had to come and see if you were okay. You hung up on me so I thought I must have upset you." He looks up from under his fringe and bites his lip, waiting for me to say something.

"Rhys, you shouldn't be here. Go home." I am leaning on the door but try to straighten myself up.

But instead of backing away, he takes a step forward. Instantly, I inch back, clutching the doorknob even tighter. "Not until I know you're okay." He stares at me, showing me he is serious and wants to control this situation. I would laugh, but I'm touched by his determination.

"Look at me, I'm fine! I'm not slashing my wrists, am I?" I hold up both arms to show him my unharmed skin, and the door bangs back against the wall.

"That's not funny, Callie."

141

He is right. I shouldn't be speaking this way to him. But I don't apologise. "Just go, get out of here. Go and do whatever it is people your age bloody do…" I fall back against the wall but he leaps forward to steady me.

"No way, not when you're like this. Come on." Grabbing my arm, he leads me inside and shuts the door. He takes me through to the kitchen and guides me into a chair. I'm the adult, I should be taking care of *him*, but my brain is too foggy to care. All I can do is rest my head in my hands and flop onto the table.

"I'm making you some coffee," Rhys says, and I hear him rooting around in the cupboards. He soon works out where everything is and after some pottering around, places a steaming mug in front of me. "I promise it will be even better than the last one," he says. "I've been practicing. Even tried some of it myself. Not bad, but I still prefer Red Bull."

I reach up and stroke his cheek with my hand. Somehow, even in my state, I notice how soft his skin is. "You're a good kid, Rhys. Your parents are bloody lucky."

And then I black out.

When I come round I am in my bed, on James's side, wrapped tightly in the duvet. I push myself up against his pillow and in the darkness see Rhys' silhouette. He is sitting in the chair by the window, the screen of his mobile illuminating his face.

"How are you feeling?" he asks, looking across at me. Even in this sparse light I can see concern etched on his face.

"What's going on, Rhys?" I sit up further and then something occurs to me. Sucking in my breath, I lift the duvet and, with a flood of relief, find I am still dressed in my jeans and vest top, and even my cardigan half hangs my shoulders. But my shoes are neatly arranged by the side of the bed.

Rhys notices my alarm. "I'm so sorry, Callie. I didn't know what to do so I put you to bed. You were in…a bit of a state. I stayed to make sure you weren't sick or anything. I mean, you hear all this stuff about people choking on their own –"

"I get the idea. Thanks. I think."

"Please don't worry, I swear I didn't see anything I shouldn't have. Except maybe your feet because I had to take your shoes off." He grins and I immediately relax.

Shifting over to my own side of the bed, I glance at the clock and see it's nearly midnight. "Rhys, shit! Won't your parents be worried?"

"It's okay. They're away for the weekend. It's their anniversary so Dad's treating Mum to a spa weekend. He's even joining in with whatever it is people do at those things."

This doesn't make me feel much better. "You still shouldn't be out this late. And you shouldn't be here. Especially without Dillon."

"But you're here," he says, and I can't help but smile.

"That's exactly my point."

A wave of nausea sweeps through me and I roll onto my side. Somehow this helps, at least for the moment.

"I'll get you some water," Rhys says, jumping up before I can protest.

He seems to take forever and I wonder if he's changed his mind and gone home. But eventually I hear his heavy footsteps on the stairs and force myself to sit up. He hands me a glass of water and I down the whole thing, but rather than helping, it makes me queasy, my mind unable to distinguish between water and wine.

"Are you okay?" Rhys asks.

"Sorry…" I throw the covers back and rush to the bathroom, turning the tap on so Rhys won't hear the terrible sounds of me retching.

When I get back to the bedroom, he is sitting on the edge of the bed, playing with his phone again. "Are you okay?" he asks, as I get back into bed. "You were gone ages."

"Let's just say I feel better now." And I do. Although the thought of drinking anything else – even water – repulses me. "I hope you never have to know what that feels like," I say, knowing he will one day.

"Callie, I'm not a kid. No, I haven't really been drunk before, but does that make me immature?"

He is right. He is not immature and not like any other nearly-eighteen-year-old I have met. Not like I was at his age. "Sorry, I –"

"Do I even look my age? I bet if you didn't know me you'd think I was at least twenty. Wouldn't you?"

I look at him and try to work out if this is true. He is partly right; because he is tall and quite muscular, he could easily lie about his age. "Maybe nineteen," I say, and he seems pleased with my concession.

"Callie, I'm sorry if I upset you on the phone earlier. I will talk to Dillon again, I promise."

His words are so tender and comforting that when he reaches for my hand, I let him take it. His touch sends a shiver through me but I ignore it; the feeling is wrong, but also right. He shifts closer to me, his face leaning towards me and his leg resting against mine, sending a frisson of excitement through my body.

Lurching backwards, I nearly smack my head against the headboard. "You need to go. Now."

CHAPTER SIXTEEN

For days I am riddled with guilt over what I nearly did with Rhys. What I wanted to do. I may have prevented it from going further, but it should never have got as far as it did. I acted irresponsibly by allowing him into the house when I was alone, especially as I suspected how he felt. Even now, four days later, I can still picture the disappointment on his face as I called him a cab and pushed him out of the door.

"I really like you, Callie," were the last words he said before I shut the door on him. I couldn't even bring myself to thank him for looking out for me.

I am also a hypocrite. I was ready to confront James about Tabitha but how can I do that when I am almost as guilty as he is? The fact that I wanted Rhys, got excited when he touched me, makes me nearly as culpable.

It is a miracle that I could focus on my exam, but thoughts of Rhys still edged their way in so I am sure I have not done well.

With Dillon still away, it has been easy to avoid Rhys, and I cut off his calls without answering. But today James and the boys are back, so how long before I'll have to face him again?

"Happy birthday," James says, the minute they're through the door. Dillon and Luke follow him into the living room and repeat *happy birthday* in unison, neither boy looking at me. James pats them each on the back, unwittingly revealing that he has prompted this show of good wishes. But I don't care that it's my birthday and I don't want special treatment; I just want things to be different.

"We're having a special dinner for you this evening," James says, and I wonder why he wants to do this with everything that's going on. But it will be nice to have at least one day when everyone is on their best behaviour. A pretence at normality.

"Can Harry still come?" Luke asks, tugging at James' shirt. James nods and then looks at me with a shrug. So this is how he has convinced the boys to sit down to a civil birthday meal with me.

Dillon smirks before turning to James. "And Rhys. That's still okay, isn't it, Dad?"

A heavy panic forms in my chest. I knew it was only a matter of time before I'd have to face him, but I didn't expect it to be so soon. But there is nothing I can do. The dinner is arranged and I have no control over the guests coming to my own birthday meal.

I offer to make lunch, but James tells me they stopped off to eat on the way home. I make myself some soup while they all unpack upstairs and have just finished eating when Bridgette calls my mobile. It's never occurred to me before, but she never calls the

147

home phone. Even when I don't answer my mobile she always leaves a message instead of trying to reach me here. Have my reports of Dillon and Luke made her so angry that she's afraid to hear their voices, for fear of lashing out? But whatever the case, I am happy to hear from her and wonder if James has invited her and Debbie over tonight.

"Happy birthday! So what are your plans for today?" she asks. In the background I can hear a man's voice. Aaron. Things must be getting serious if she's meeting him on her lunch breaks.

"James is cooking a birthday dinner for me. Are you and Debbie coming?"

"Oh, Callie, I'm so sorry. James did invite me but Aaron's booked us theatre tickets for tonight. It was a surprise and he didn't realise it was your birthday. Maybe Debbie's free, though?"

"It's okay. Don't worry."

"But I want you to meet Aaron. Soon. Are things any better?"

I can't bring myself to tell her they're even worse. She will want details and I can't risk being overheard. "About the same," I say. "But I'm sorting it."

She lowers her voice. "And have you confronted James yet? About the text?"

"No, but I will. Soon."

"Okay. Well, I'm here if you need me. Anyway, got to go. Aaron's looking at me impatiently and I need to be back at work in ten minutes."

Afterwards I call Debbie. Tonight I will need all the allies I can get. But I have no luck there either because

Mark's parents are visiting. We say goodbye, with promises to meet up soon, but I wonder just when that will be. Both she and Bridgette are moving forwards in their lives, thriving, while I'm undergoing a rapid decline.

James joins me in the kitchen and fills a glass with tap water. "I have to pop to the shop for a bit. I want to check in with Tabitha and see if the freelancer has been okay."

Hearing her name makes me shudder, despite what I myself have done. The thought of her and James together ties my stomach in knots. "Okay," I manage to say.

He comes closer to me and I long for his hug, anything to show we are still connected. But when he does hold me it is a stranger's hug. "Sorry I haven't had a chance to get you a present yet. But I will, Callie."

I want to tell him not to bother, but nod instead, forcing myself to smile. "Thank you. That sounds lovely."

He turns to leave but I grab his arm, pulling him back. "James, we need to talk, don't we?"

"Yes, we do." His sighs. "But can we do it another day? I've just got no space in my head. The boys have exhausted me and...Is that okay?"

There is no point pushing him. I will wait; I need more time to get my thoughts in order anyway. Right now they are a jumbled, confusing mixture of James, Rhys, the boys, Tabitha, Dad, Mrs Simmons and even Bridgette and Debbie. It will do no good if I can't get things straight before I talk to James.

"Will everything be all right while I'm gone?" he asks. He doesn't have to spell out what he means; he thinks war will break out, or worse. The thought makes me seethe with rage.

"Of course."

His eyes convey the words he can't say. That he wants to believe me but can't. "Oh, I nearly forgot, I better pop next door before I go."

He has changed the subject so abruptly that it takes me a moment to catch up. "To Mrs Simmons'? Why?"

"She popped her head out the door as we pulled up and asked if I had time for a quick chat. I told her I'd just be a moment but I completely forgot."

I almost forget to breathe. "Oh? What do you think it's about?" But there is only one explanation. She saw Rhys the other night. My stomach sinks to the floor. It might be easy to make an excuse for why he came over, but it would be much harder to explain why he left after midnight in a cab.

"No idea," James says.

"Well, how about I go and see her? Find out what she wants."

James looks at me strangely. "Are you sure? I think I should do it. I don't want her having a go at you again. You know what she's like."

"Honestly, it's fine. I wanted to ask her about the flowers in her back garden anyway."

It is a desperate thing to have said and James doesn't look convinced. I have never before shown an interest in gardening and he knows Mrs Simmons is not so easily won over. But eventually he nods. "Okay.

Thanks. Just don't let her get to you. And let me know what she says."

But I have no intention of doing that.

Later I sit at the garden table trying to get my head around my next assignment. It is due in a week and I haven't written a word or taken in much of what I have read since Saturday.

I have been next door three times to see Mrs Simmons but she isn't answering her door. She rarely goes out so I can only assume she is ignoring me. But I will try her again tomorrow; I am bound to spot her at her window so she can't avoid me forever, and hopefully I will get to her before she has a chance to grab James.

My wooden chair is uncomfortable and I am certain it couldn't have been Lauren's choice. She would at least have got seat cushions. How funny that all this time I thought Lauren was the only threat to my marriage, but now I know Tabitha is a far greater one.

So what does that make Rhys, then?

I look up at Dillon's window and see him watching me. There is no smile on his face and he doesn't turn away when our eyes meet. I won't look away either. I won't let him see that he unnerves me.

When I first met Dillon and Luke, they thought James and I were just friends. That's the lie James told them to help them get used to me. "They need to get to know you without thinking you're taking their Mum's place," he had said, and although I was sceptical, it made sense. And it worked for a time. Both boys were okay towards me and I caught glimpses of their warmer personalities. I never anticipated their hatred. Now I know misleading them was a grave error. Perhaps that is a huge part of why they resent me so much? We lied. They trusted us and we lied. They can forgive their father, but I have to pay for our lie.

I look away from Dillon to take a sip of lemonade and when I glance up again he has disappeared. Back to whatever he is doing up there. It crosses my mind how different this house would be – and my life for that matter – if Dillon didn't live here. Luke would still cause problems but I'm convinced he wouldn't be half as bad without his older brother's influence. But there are at least three years to go before he's old enough to leave home, and who's to say he'll even go to university? Even if he does, there are plenty of good ones in London, so the chances of him going to live away are slim.

As I pick up my book, I hear something rustling behind me. On my guard, I spin around, expecting Luke to be up to something. But a skinny black cat sits staring at me. I have never seen him before and he is such a wretched-looking thing that he must be a stray. His fur is dull, and there are patches of bare skin scattered over his body. I don't even know if he *is* male, but somehow he doesn't seem female.

"Hey, fella," I call, holding out my fingers. He trots towards me and rubs his mangy head against my hand. "You look just how I feel."

I go inside to look for some food for him, but the only suitable thing I find is some cheese. I have never owned a cat so have no idea if they like it, but he scoffs it down and doesn't leave my side for the next hour.

Sometime later, I look up at Dillon's window and wonder if the boys would like to keep him. Perhaps a pet will give us something to bond over? I know he looks bedraggled but with a bit of care he'll be healthy in no time.

"I think your name should be Jazzy," I say to him. "Because you're so far from jazzy, aren't you?"

Excited by my idea, I let him into the house and call the boys down. Slowly they appear, both eyeing me suspiciously. "Look what I've found! Shall we keep him?"

As if sensing it is time for his appearance, Jazzy pads to the bottom of the stairs and peers up at Dillon and Luke.

The boys stare at him and then Dillon says, "What is *that* doing in here?"

Appalled by his response, I try to keep my voice calm. "I thought we could keep him. What do you think?"

Dillon looks at Luke, forcing the half-smile from his younger brother's face. "I don't like cats. Mum didn't either. That thing is filthy and it's probably got fleas! Dad won't let him in here."

He turns and heads back to his room, while Luke's eyes remain glued to the cat. I am about to ask what he thinks, but then he too disappears.

Scooping Jazzy up, I take him back outside. But I am not ready to give up on this poor creature. Nobody uses the shed in the corner of the garden, and all that's in it is an old lawnmower and some junk, so I fetch a spare duvet from upstairs and make a bed for him.

"This can be your new home," I tell him, as I fold it into a comfortable bed. "But I'll come and visit."

Seeing the cat's pitiful expression makes me loathe the boys even more. It is all I can do not to drag them out and throw them in the shed to see how *they* like sleeping in there.

We are all seated around the table and I can feel Rhys' eyes burning into me, all the while he is chatting away to Dillon. Every now and again Dillon also looks over at me, and I wonder if Rhys has told him anything about what happened on Saturday. I have ignored his calls and texts so how can I expect any loyalty? But this can't be the case. If it were, we would not all be sitting down to dinner.

James has ordered an Indian takeaway. It's tasty enough, but there is too much noise at the table and I struggle to make out any strands of conversation. I am the only one who is silent. I lift my glass of wine to my lips but put it down again. It is a disturbing reminder of Saturday night.

Somehow I make it through the meal, even though I have barely touched the food on my plate, and begin clearing away the dishes. Rhys asks if I need any help but I assure him I'm fine. I wonder if he notices the look he gets from Dillon.

When I've finished I linger a moment longer in the kitchen. Hopefully when I go back into the lounge, the boys will all have disappeared.

But then James appears at my side, Dillon and Luke following him. He nudges them forward and Luke holds out a plastic bag.

"This is for you." He stares at the floor. "Sorry we didn't wrap it."

I take the bag and thank them, reaching inside to find what feels like a bottle. Pulling it out, I see it is eau de toilette. I smile and lean forward to hug them both, all of us rigid. As I draw back, I notice Dillon smirking as he and Luke hurry out of the room. He knows that I have never worn perfume in my life.

"And I got you this." James hands me an envelope.

It is a gift card for my favourite clothes shop. "Thank you," I say, moving forward to hug him. Something still doesn't feel right. He no longer feels like mine.

"Better get back and check what they're doing in there," he says, oblivious to my sadness. "By the way, Rhys and Harry are staying the night."

This is all I need. I have been counting the minutes until it is time for Rhys to go, but now we will be under the same roof for several hours more. How will I be able to sleep knowing he is just metres away?

Once James has left, I go outside to check on Jazzy. I don't know if the boys have told him about the cat but he hasn't mentioned it. Perhaps they are saving it up to use as ammunition against me. If only they knew that they already have the best weapon they could possibly ask for to end my marriage to their father for good.

Rhys.

It is nearly two a.m. but I am still awake. Even though I got through the evening, and Rhys left me alone, I am worried about Mrs Simmons. I will have to get to her first thing in the morning, before James leaves for work, or she might flag him down on his way out.

James is as far across the bed as it's possible to get, a physical manifestation of the state of our marriage. It would be easier to handle if I thought only the boys are responsible for our problems. But my knowledge of his affair with Tabitha makes our distance a hundred times worse.

Sickened again by the thought of James and Tabitha together, I lift the duvet and slide out of bed. I need to use the bathroom and then I will make myself a chamomile tea. I doubt it will help me sleep, but it's better than lying on my back, staring at the ceiling.

When I open the bathroom door, Rhys is standing before me in the darkness.

"Rhys? What –"

"Sshh," he says, ushering me in and closing the door behind us. I quickly make a grab for the small shaving light by the mirror, and the room is bathed in a soft, dull glow. "I just wanted to give you this."

He places a small box in my hand. It is neatly wrapped in purple paper and adorned with a matching ribbon.

I make no move to unwrap it. "Rhys, we can't –"

"Please, Callie, open it. I just want you to have it, that's all."

So I sit on the side of the bath and start unwrapping my gift, careful not to tear the paper because he's gone to so much effort. Inside is a blue Swarovski box. "You shouldn't have done this." I almost don't want to open it. I know whatever is inside I will love, but won't be able to keep.

"Open it," he repeats. He sits next to me.

Inside the box is beautiful crystal horseshoe pendant. "It's lovely. How did you know I would like this?"

He shrugs. "I just did. It's just you, isn't it? It's meant to bring you luck."

I hug him hard, pulling him into me and nestling my head on his shoulder. He will never know how much his gift means. "You know I can't keep it, Rhys," I say, finally pulling away. "Don't you?"

He chews his lip. "Yes, you can."

"I'm sorry I ignored your calls. It was wrong of me, you don't deserve that. But most of all I'm sorry about Saturday night."

Rhys shakes his head. "There's nothing to be sorry for. Nothing happened, did it? But I can't lie, Callie, I wanted it to. I want you." He leans towards me again. "I'm not some stupid kid, okay?"

This time when our bodies touch, the surge is even stronger. And when he cups my face in his hands and presses his lips against mine, I am powerless to stop him.

CHAPTER SEVENTEEN

Now

"Don't look at me like that. Please. I already hate myself enough. It was wrong to kiss Rhys, or let him kiss me, I know that."

DS Connolly turns to his colleague and again they share a secret thought. "Well," he finally says, "legally speaking, Rhys wasn't underage."

My hands are clammy and I clench them, hoping the two officers won't notice the sweat. I see it clearly now, how easily things might have turned out differently, if only I hadn't stepped over that line with Rhys. "But morality is another matter, isn't it?" I say. "I was married and he was too young for me."

"So you knew before the kiss that he had feelings for you. Why didn't you just refuse to be alone with him in the bathroom?"

"I've wondered that many times. It was a reckless action. I was paranoid and scared that everything was crumbling around me. But it's easy to see this now.

Then I only thought of how good he made me feel, how much I needed his comfort."

DS Connolly frowns. Perhaps he finds it hard to understand how an eighteen-year-old can offer any comfort to a woman my age.

"I was so full of self-doubt. I felt that I wasn't good enough, that I couldn't be a mum to the boys or keep my marriage together. But Rhys made me feel different. Like myself. He looked at me and really saw *me*. He gave me a break from everything else. I needed that from him."

DS Connolly opens his mouth to speak but someone raps on the door, throwing it open without waiting for an answer. It is a uniformed male officer and he rushes over, whispering something I am clearly not meant to hear. DS Connolly glances at me and turns off the tape recorder, saying he'll be back in a minute. He stands up and heads out of the door, the uniformed officer following him.

Left alone, neither DC Barnes nor I speak for a few minutes.

"He'll be back soon," she says eventually, her voice stern.

I am relieved when the door opens and DS Connolly reappears, carrying more paperwork. "Sorry for the delay," he says, and I wonder why he is still being kind to me. If we were alone I would ask him this question, but I can already tell DC Barnes would not approve of overfamiliarity.

"Now, where were we?" He sits down, setting his pile of papers to one side. "Oh, yes. The kiss."

I lean forward. "I felt awful, DS Connolly. Words can't describe my guilt. But the problem was, I also felt…great. That doesn't make sense, does it? How could it feel so good when I loved James? I'm not sure. All I know is that my feelings for Rhys had been growing, and I'd tried my best to shove them aside. Until that kiss. That kiss changed everything."

CHAPTER EIGHTEEN

When I wake the next morning, I immediately remember what I have done. I should feel sickened that I kissed Rhys – part of me does – but I also feel good. I can still feel his hands on my face, and I smile to think of it.

I turn over and there is James, still asleep, nearly hanging off the edge of the bed. A stronger wave of guilt floods through me but quickly subsides when I remember our marriage has already been violated. Perhaps the thought of James and Tabitha together shouldn't hurt anymore, but it cuts as deeply as before. I could try to pretend the kiss was about revenge, but it wasn't; it was about my desire for Rhys, my need for him. And that just makes things even more complicated.

It is not yet six o'clock, but I get up and run a bath. As I lie soaking in the bubbles, I wonder if Rhys is awake. If so, what does he think now that morning is here? What if he regrets what happened? What if he tells Dillon? But then I remember the necklace, safely hidden in the pocket of a coat I never wear, and I know he doesn't regret it.

Every part of me knows it is wrong, but I also know I haven't felt at peace like this for a long time. A kiss changes everything.

James is already in the kitchen, gulping down coffee. "Got to get going," he says, grabbing his jacket from the back of a chair. "Harry's mum is picking him and Luke up at about ten and taking them back to their house. Luke's staying there tonight. And I don't know what Dillon and Rhys are planning but they can sort themselves out." As he walks off, I stare at his back and feel a rush of sadness that both of us are lying to each other.

I hang around in the kitchen for a while, hoping to see Rhys. I know it is unlikely I will be able to catch him on his own but I just need to see him.

But by nine o'clock, when there is still no sign of any of the boys, I start to fear the worst. Did I somehow take advantage of Rhys? At this very moment is he reporting our encounter to Dillon? The more I think about it, the more possible it feels.

At nine fifteen it is time to wake Luke and Harry. Harry's mum will be here soon and I need to make sure they're ready to go. And then I can leave too, escape from this mess I have created.

There are no sounds from either of the boys' bedrooms and I take this as a good sign. I tap on Luke's door and wait for him to mumble. Eventually he calls out, "What?" When I tell him they need to get up and get ready for Harry's mum, there is no further reply.

But I'm not worried; Luke might detest me but he won't want to get on the wrong side of Harry's mother.

As I go downstairs to sort out breakfast, I remember I need to speak to Mrs Simmons. In the aftermath of kissing Rhys, it has slipped my mind. Leaving the front door on the latch, I step over the flowerbed separating our front gardens, smiling at my rebelliousness, and ring her doorbell. I can hear it echoing inside her hallway, but there is no sound of feet shuffling along the tiled floor. I am about to turn away when she suddenly appears, staring through the glass.

"Oh," she says, as she opens the door, looking me up and down, the usual judgement she reserves only for me on her drawn face.

"Hi, Mrs Simmons," I begin. I will be polite to her today, despite her attitude towards me. "James sent me. He said you needed to talk to us?"

Her face twists into a grimace. "No, it was James I wanted to speak to."

"Well, I can help you too," I say, trying to keep the desperation out of my voice. "Is something wrong?" I picture Rhys clambering into the cab in the middle of the night, but the image is quickly replaced by another one: his face moving closer to mine. I shake it off and try to focus on Mrs Simmons.

"I'd rather speak to James."

"He'd be happy to talk to you, but he's really busy at the moment. I hardly even see him myself these days. I'm sure you can imagine what it's like running your own business."

She tuts at me, incapable of imagining anything of the sort.

I soften my voice. "You can talk to me, Mrs Simmons, and I'll do my best to help however I can. Whatever the problem is. I am James' wife, after all." The words lodge in my throat like swallowed chewing gum; *James' wife* is the last thing I should be calling myself.

Mrs Simmons takes a moment to consider what I'm saying and then nods. "Okay," she says. And I prepare myself to be asked what the hell Rhys was doing leaving our house at midnight when everyone else was away. "I'm going into hospital on Saturday. For…well, never mind. Anyway, I'll need James to keep an eye on the house for me. Water the plants, feed the fish. That kind of thing."

This is such a relief that I almost hug her. I don't even care that she won't tell me what she's going in for. I have got myself worked up over nothing. *Paranoia.* "I can do that for you. It's no problem."

"I'd prefer it if you could ask James to do it." She won't even entertain the idea of letting me in her house. "It's just that I've known him for so many years. Since he was first with Lauren. So I trust him." I am so relieved that she didn't see Rhys that night, so ignore her unspoken accusation.

I offer a compromise. "Because James is so busy, how about the boys do it? They could take it in turns. Or do it together. It will be good for them."

She seems pleased with this suggestion and agrees to the compromise. "But I'll need to give James a spare set of keys. Today. Just in case I don't see him before I go in."

"I can take them for you."

But she shakes her head and we are back to square one.

After several minutes of persuading her that her keys are safe with me, she finally agrees, shutting the door on me while she goes to find them. "Be sure to give them to James, won't you?" she says, when she comes back, dropping them into my hand. "I don't want them lost."

"Course. Anyway, I hope it's nothing too serious," I say, but she closes the door without another word.

Harry's mother arrives promptly at ten, but she doesn't come to the door. Instead, she beeps her car horn and does a U-turn, waiting for Luke and her son to appear. I accompany them to the car, so she won't think they've been left alone all morning. I have no doubt she knows about the accident and there is no telling what other stories Luke has been passing on about me.

"Thanks for having him," she says, smiling.

"No problem. Thanks for letting Luke stay at yours tonight."

I say goodbye to Luke and Harry. With his head down, Luke forces out a response, while Harry at least looks at me to say his.

Back in the house, there is still no movement or sound from Dillon's room, and it worries me. Rhys must know James goes to work and I have to get up early, so why didn't he try and sneak down to see me?

The house seems claustrophobic now, even though I am the only one awake. I need to get out of here so I decide to visit Dad. Perhaps today will be a good day.

The park opposite Dad's flat looks even more picturesque with the sun shining down on it. It's quiet today, so if I brought Dad out here we would almost have the whole place to ourselves. There aren't enough strangers around to freak him out. But I have only managed to get him out here a handful of times before, so I don't hold out much hope for today.

"Of course!" he says, when I suggest it. "It's summer, we should make the most of it! I'll even buy you an ice cream."

I don't tell him it's not quite summer, but hastily grab his jacket and usher him out. I need fresh air today; I can't bear the thought of being cooped up in his tiny flat.

Dad heads straight for the ice cream van and orders two vanilla cones with chocolate flakes. He fiddles around in his pocket to pay, but only pulls out a handkerchief and piece of scrunched-up paper. I have no idea what it is but it's best not to question him.

"Don't worry, Dad," I say, handing a five-pound note to the man.

There is a huge circular lake in the middle of the park and we sit on one of the benches surrounding it to eat our ice cream. On the opposite side, a young man sails a remote-controlled boat in the lake and we both watch him, although I have no idea if Dad has actually noticed him, or if he is staring straight through him.

"Lovely," Dad says, wiping ice cream from around his mouth with his handkerchief. He stuffs it back in his pocket, oblivious to the melted ice cream that now covers it. I'm not sure whether he is talking about the ice cream or sitting here with me, but I hope it is both.

We talk about my course for a few minutes and Dad seems more aware than usual of what I'm saying. Today must be a good day. I give Jenny credit for this; since I informed her about Dad's medication she has been supervising him even more closely. I decide to take a chance and ask him what's been on my mind since I got here.

"Dad, have you ever done anything you're...I don't know...ashamed of? Anything reckless?"

He turns to me, scrutinising my face for so long that I begin to regret my question. Who knows what it will lead him to say? "It was reckless marrying your mother." He turns back to the man with the boat. "I knew she didn't love me. Not really. Not enough to stand by me when..."

I reach for his hand. He has never told me this before. In fact, he rarely mentions Mum other than to rant about what an evil woman she was, abandoning her husband and child. So to hear him speak her name calmly is a first. I think of James, and wonder – not for the first time – if he would have the stamina to see things through if *I* got bad. But the truth is I have no idea. Even if our marriage was in a good state, would he be able to live with someone like Dad? Or even someone like the old me, the troubled person I was after my baby died? Max didn't stand by me, so why should James? And now James has Tabitha. Unsullied Tabitha. There is nothing hanging over her, threatening to drag her down.

And now I think of Rhys. Of course I couldn't expect him to stand by me if the worst happened, especially given his age, but there is a warmth in his every word and action that James no longer shows for me.

"She may have had other reasons for leaving, Dad. We don't know, do we?"

But he has switched off now, and is pulling at the hairs on his arm. I try to get him to put on his jacket because there is ice cream all over his shirt, but he brushes me away. "Stop fussing, Caroline."

My phone beeps and I pull it out, holding it so that Dad won't be able to see the screen. When I see it is a text message from Rhys, my heart thuds. He says he can't wait to see me again.

Tonight, I text back. I need to see him tonight. I need to tell him this is wrong. And whatever we're doing is over.

I sit on the bed, feeling out of place in Rhys' bedroom. There are posters of rock bands plastered over the walls and more musical instruments than furniture. All that's in here is a desk with a laptop and some school books open on it, a computer chair and, of course, the bed I am sitting on. I feel like a teenager again, as if I am in my first boyfriend's room. Rhys is nothing like Sean, but there is an unmistakably similar scent lingering in the air. It is neither pleasant nor unpleasant, but reminds me I don't belong here.

I could have ended this over the phone or even somewhere public, but I can't risk being seen. Thankfully, Rhys' parents are away and we have the place to ourselves.

Sitting at his desk, Rhys watches me sip my coffee. "How is it?" he asks.

"Getting better," I say with a grin. These days my sense of humour only seems to surface when I'm with him.

"Good. Can I sit next to you?"

"Rhys, I think we should talk."

"Okay, but let me sit with you." He moves towards me and I don't stop him. He looks beautiful today, his dark fringe flopping in his face, and I don't know whether I've always thought this, or if kissing him has changed my perception. But I can't do this. No part of it is right, despite how it feels.

With Rhys sitting on the bed beside me, I yearn for him again, like a drug addict desperate for another fix. I was like this with James in the beginning, before life got in the way. But something is different with Rhys, like nothing I've felt before. Perhaps this is because it is so wrong?

"Callie, I really like you. Last night was…"

I want to agree, to tell him how good it felt to kiss him, but I have to remind myself why I am here.

I take his hand and draw circles on his palm with my finger. "Nothing can happen, Rhys. It just can't."

"Why?" he whispers, leaning in to kiss me.

I pull back. "So many reasons. I'm married. You're *seventeen*. You're Dillon's best friend. Do I need to carry on?"

"I'm *eighteen* in a few weeks." He smiles triumphantly.

"It doesn't matter!" I stand up. "I'm sorry it's gone as far as it has, but we can't do this any more. Whatever it is, stops now."

"But you came here. You came here to see me."

It is now I realise my actions are inconsistent with my words and that he is only observing what my presence proves. That I want him, I need him.

"I'm not giving you up," Rhys says, pulling me down onto the mattress. And then he is kissing me, and once more I am powerless to stop him, my strength to end this before it's begun evaporating. He reaches under my shirt, his hands smooth and cool, and I groan in his ear. "You like me too," he says. "I know you do."

I don't answer, but wrestle his t-shirt over his head and pull him on top of me. His body feels thick and heavy on mine. He is not a boy.

Afterwards he can't stop smiling, and he clutches me as I rest on his chest. As good as I felt seconds ago, I am now swamped with guilt and feel as if I'm being crushed. I have crossed a line and there is no going back. This can't be undone. But when I look at Rhys, I only think of the pleasure he has given me, the way he sees my true self.

Pushing my doubt aside, I listen as he chatters away about his university plans. I take in every word as he tells me he wants to take a gap year and travel to America this summer. "I'd just busk out there," he says. "And drive around from city to city. I've been researching Route 66 on the Internet and I really want to do it. I'll be taking my driving test soon."

I feel a twinge of regret that I never thought of doing something so exciting when I was his age. Travelling, seeing the world, living. All I wanted to do was become a mother. "That sounds like fun," I say, staring at his chest. There are a few scattered hairs on it but nowhere near as many as James has.

"Come with me."

I run my hands over his body, wanting to take in every inch of him, to remember when I get home. "Oh, Rhys, I can't even think about tomorrow, let alone this summer."

"Well, we can talk about it later," he says. I can tell he is disappointed but he doesn't mope or sulk. He holds me tighter and kisses my shoulder.

"So tell me how your gig went on Friday," I say, lying back and listening to the melodic sound of his voice. I can't remember the last time I was so relaxed. It is as if everything negative has slipped away, and even if I wanted to I wouldn't be able to think about home.

Until I notice it is almost ten p.m.

James is sure to be home by now and wondering where I am. "I have to go," I say, jumping up. "Sorry." I start reaching for my clothes, which are scattered on the floor by the bed.

Rhys doesn't move but turns on his side to watch me, still naked. "When will I see you?" he asks.

"Soon. I'll sort something. I promise."

At the front door we kiss, and he watches as I drive away. As soon as he is out of sight, guilt once again threatens to suffocate me. Until I think of James with Tabitha.

I pull onto our road and spot James' car parked a few houses down from us. I check myself in the rear-view mirror, just to make sure there are no visible signs of Rhys on me. I can tell without checking that I smell of him, but I will rush to the shower. I wonder if James does this after he has been with Tabitha. The scent of her perfume can't be easy to erase.

"Where have you been?" he asks when I walk into the front room and find him on the sofa. There is no light on but the television illuminates his face. He squints at his watch and looks as if he has just woken up.

"Out with Debbie." The short drive home has given me time to concoct a cover story.

"Oh," he says. He doesn't ask anything further, but stands and stretches before turning off the television. "I'm knackered, I'm going to bed." When he walks past I back away and even in the darkness of the room, I'm sure I see something flicker across his face.

He knows something is wrong. He must do, because my whole body is screaming out that I've betrayed him in a worse way than he could possibly imagine.

CHAPTER NINETEEN

I haven't seen Rhys for two days and I have mixed feelings about this. Part of me thinks it is a blessing, and as each hour passes without sight of him, I hope my need for him will lessen. But it only grows stronger. As does my guilt.

I have proved I am not fit to be a mother to Dillon and Luke. People would consider me a monster if they knew, and what could I say in my defence? I picture Rhys' parents if they found out, the devastation it would cause to both our families. But still I cannot stop. I cannot give him up when he is the only part of my life that is not in shreds.

We text each other at every opportunity, and I call whenever I am alone in the house and he is not in class or with Dillon. These moments are rare; he and Dillon seem inseparable. Each time we have contact, Rhys asks when he can see me, but all I can tell him is *soon*.

It bothers me that I can't share my awful secret with Bridgette and Debbie but they would never understand. Infidelity is one thing, but indulging in it with a teenage boy is another. They won't be able to fathom that he is so much more than that. Or that I feel free when I think of him.

James arrived home early from work yesterday, but I didn't ask him why, even though it was unusual. Either something has gone wrong with Tabitha or he is suspicious of me. But other than one late night, I have given him no reason to question me. I delete Rhys's texts as soon as I've read them, and keep my phone in sight. I am playing a dangerous game.

"Remember Emma's coming for lunch today," James says. It is Saturday morning – his busiest day – but he still hasn't left for work. He sits at the table with his coffee, smoothing out the pages of his newspaper.

"Okay. What shall I cook?" I only have a vague recollection of him mentioning Emma's visit and cooking is the last thing I feel like doing today.

"The thing is, she's bringing her new partner to meet us all so she wants to cook herself. Make a good impression. She'd do it at her place but there's no space. You don't mind, do you? She'll bring everything."

"Well, she won't want me getting in the way, so maybe I'll pop out for a bit." I am already planning to tell Rhys we can see each other sooner than expected.

But James has other ideas. "What? Why would you do that? She wants us all here."

"What about the shop?" I ask.

"Tabitha will be fine if I pop back for a couple of hours. She knows what she's doing." His eyes light up when he says her name, and my stomach sinks. I know

I am caught up in my own betrayal, but that doesn't make his any easier.

After he leaves, I remember Mrs Simmons is going into hospital today. I deliberately haven't told him or the boys I've got the keys because I have been planning to escape next door to clear my head and focus on my studies without worrying about the boys and their tricks. But now a different plan forms in my mind. It is reckless and crazy but it fills me with excitement.

Taking my phone outside, I head to the bottom of the garden. Then I call Rhys, still keeping my voice low, just in case the boys are awake. I tell him my idea and let his excitement fill me up. "We'll have to be careful, though. Everyone will be home and it's only next door. I'll say that I'm going to see a friend in town, so meet me there at eight-thirty. There's a gate at the side of her house that leads round to the back garden. I'll leave it unlatched so go through it and I'll let you in through the kitchen." I sound as if I'm delivering instructions for a bank robbery and Rhys laughs.

"Got it," he says. "Callie? I miss you."

"Not for long. Just look forward to tonight. But be careful. You really can't be seen. At least it will be dark by then."

"You panic a lot, don't you?" Rhys says, chuckling down the phone.

And now it hits me that I am the only one with everything to lose. I should call him back and tell him to forget the whole thing, but, of course, I don't. I am in too deeply now, heading for a cliff at a hundred miles an hour and unable to brake.

I check on Jazzy before I go back in and he is just waking up in the shed. At the sight of me, he stretches and begins purring. I top up his bowl from the packet of dry food I have stashed in the shed and he saunters over to it, rubbing his head on my hand before tucking in. He looks healthier already. His fur is growing back and he is definitely fatter. I am growing fond of him and wish he could be in the house with us. Perhaps when things are better I will mention him to James. I just don't want Jazzy to be the cause of more conflict. Thinking of this, I'm surprised the boys haven't already told James about him.

But will things get better?

For now I leave Jazzy to eat, making sure the shed door is open so he can come and go as he pleases. As I cross the lawn, I am sure I can see Dillon watching again from his window, but as I draw nearer he vanishes.

Dillon and Luke eventually appear in the kitchen, still in their pyjamas. "Where's Dad?" Luke asks. "He said he'd still be here when we got up."

I watch their faces fall as I tell them he's left. Now they know I will be making their breakfast. Lauren always gave them a cooked breakfast at the weekend and this tradition has lived on.

"How about just eggs on toast this morning? Emma's coming over to cook a big lunch so you probably shouldn't eat too much."

"Yay, Aunty Emma!" Luke says, to Dillon rather than me. "It's always better when she's here."

Dillon, still half-asleep, slumps on the table, but nods his agreement. As I reach for the bread, I smile because they don't know I have armed myself against them. I have Rhys. He may be Dillon's best friend but I am confident that for someone his age, sex will always win.

While they eat, I pop next door to check on Mrs Simmons, desperately hoping her plans haven't changed.

"Oh, it's you," she says, as she opens the door. "Where are the boys? I thought they were coming."

"They are, Mrs Simmons," I lie. "But I just wanted to see you before you left, to wish you..." I search for the right words. "All the best for your...operation?"

She doesn't deny or confirm this, but I let her coldness wash over me. In a few hours I will be in her house, alone with Rhys, and nothing else will matter. "So what time are you off? I'll send the boys over this evening to check on things."

"Hmmm." She peers past me to the road. "The taxi's coming at twelve. I hope it's on time."

I tell her I'll leave her to get ready and she closes the door without a thank you.

Back in the house, the boys have finished eating but their dirty plates remain on the table. There is egg smeared over the wooden surface, soaking in pools of orange juice. I should be used to their vindictiveness by now, but not even the thought of seeing Rhys later can soften the blow.

Emma turns up at eleven and I am forced to endure the boys' fussing over her, acting as if they haven't seen her for years. Eventually she tells them she needs to start preparing lunch, and they leave her in peace, disappearing to the front room to play on the PlayStation.

Left alone with her, I offer to help. She accepts, although I can tell she'd rather I didn't. "So how are things with you?" I ask, peeling carrots while she sets to work on the potatoes. For some reason she has decided we are having a Sunday roast, even though it's Saturday. She must really want to impress this new man of hers.

"Great. I just want to get this meal right." She seems nervous, a trait I've not noticed in her before. I feel sorry for her, and put more effort into preparing the food.

"So, what's his name?" I ask, as if we are best friends, chatting about the latest man on the scene. Perhaps it will diffuse some of her coldness.

"Ha," she says. "*Her* name is Natalie. Don't tell me James hasn't told you?"

I had no idea Emma liked women, and it's none of my business, but it puzzles me that James has never mentioned it. "He…I, um, he probably just wanted to protect your privacy."

Emma turns to me. "I'm not ashamed of who I am," she says. "He can tell the whole world if he wants." She goes back to peeling potatoes and we say no more about it.

Natalie is not at all who I pictured. She is tiny, not just in height but her whole frame, and she looks fragile. Her skin is tanned, perhaps a sign of Mediterranean blood. Next to her, Emma is a plain, dull giant. I immediately like Natalie; she smiles shyly as she shakes my hand. "Nice to meet you," she says, her soft voice matching her appearance. I wonder if Emma talks to her about Lauren, if she compares me with her dead friend.

Emma pulls her away from me and into the kitchen, where the food is waiting. I take a deep breath and follow, counting the hours until I can be next door with Rhys.

The boys seem intrigued by Natalie, once again displaying the amicability they never show to me. Dillon bombards her with questions about where she lives and what she does, and she answers as best she can, letting her food go cold in her attempt to make a good impression. I feel sorry for her; it was not fair of Emma to introduce her to us all at once. I wonder if she feels as much of an outsider as I do, whether she notices that neither Dillon nor Luke have said a word to me since we sat down to eat.

I try to distract myself with thoughts of Rhys, but all I feel is guilt. I should be thinking of James, of saving my marriage, of trying to sort out how we will deal with the boys. I should not be obsessing over a teenage boy I have no business being with. It is bound to end badly. How can it not?

When everyone has finished eating, I clear away the plates and make coffee. I'm relieved when the boys go upstairs; it means I can also make an excuse to slip away.

"I've got some coursework to finish," I say, which is at least half true. I have been so distracted lately that I'm not keeping up with my studies. James and Emma don't seem to mind me rushing off, but I am sure I see a hint of disappointment on Natalie's face.

Upstairs, I close the bedroom door, sit on the bed and text Rhys. When he replies, telling me all the things he wants to do to me later, I feel a mixture of shame and longing. I delete the text, but smile at the memory of his words. Then I think of Dad, and wonder if he was ever so out of control that he betrayed Mum by sleeping with another woman. This idea scares me. Not for the first time, I am frightened of myself.

I stand up, suddenly needing some fresh air, and as I open the door, I almost bump into Natalie. She jumps when I emerge, looking so anxious and lost that I feel another pang of pity.

"The bathroom's just there," I say, pointing across the landing.

"Oh, thanks." She starts to pass me but then turns back. "Are you okay? You were very quiet at lunch. I hope me being here isn't an inconvenience?" She smiles up at me. She can't be more than five feet tall because I tower above her.

"No, not at all. I'm fine. Thanks for asking. Are you okay? This must be nerve-wracking, meeting us all at once."

She nods, apparently relieved that someone has bothered to point this out. "Emma kind of sprang it on me, last-minute. I thought the two of us were going out for lunch or something, but then she told me I'd be meeting her friend, James, and his family." She rolls her eyes. "I think she thought I'd run a mile if she gave me too much notice."

"Well, that probably wasn't fair of her, but…"

She smiles. "Yes. But I'm afraid that's Emma all over, isn't it?"

My silence only stems from not knowing Emma very well, but Natalie must interpret it differently because suddenly she is opening up about their relationship, telling me she's been thinking of breaking it off.

"To be honest," she says, lowering her voice, "I'm just not sure we're right for each other." She drops her eyes to the floor.

My first reaction is to tell Natalie to give it a chance, to speak out for Emma. I open my mouth to form the words but quickly close it again.

"I hope you don't mind me saying this, but I couldn't help notice the boys don't really speak to you. Emma said you and James haven't been married long. It must be hard." Her eyes widen. "Oh, sorry. I shouldn't be saying all this."

I glance at the boys' doors. Thankfully both are closed, and there is music thundering from inside Dillon's room. "No, it's fine. You're right. They're still having trouble accepting me."

"It's not easy bringing up kids, especially when they're not your own. Kids can be conniving. Even good ones. I can't believe they didn't talk to you at lunch."

I almost hug her when she says this. Finally someone – someone other than Rhys – understands. "Thank you. Just for saying that. Thank you."

"Anyway, she'll be wondering what's taking me so long." She turns towards the bathroom door.

"So what are you going to do?" I quickly ask. It is none of my business but I'm curious to know.

"Tell her tonight, I think. I've been putting it off long enough."

Only when she's gone into the bathroom do I notice the gap in Dillon's door, and the set of eyes peering through it.

Rhys smells of aftershave tonight – I can't tell which brand – and I pull him towards me and breathe him in as soon as we're safely in Mrs Simmons' kitchen. We are in darkness, apart from the dull light of a mini key ring torch I found in the shed last time I fed Jazzy.

"I feel like a thief breaking into someone's house," he says.

I jangle the keys at him. "We're not thieves." What I don't say is that I, at least, am far worse than that.

"I've got supplies," he says, holding up a plastic bag I haven't noticed until now. "Everything we'll need for tonight." He hands it to me and I look inside. Crisps, cans of Red Bull, chocolate, biscuits. Everything a teenager dreams of eating for dinner. It's a good thing I had a big lunch.

"Thanks, Rhys. I didn't even think about food."

"That's because all you need is me," he says, chuckling at his own joke, oblivious to the degree of truth in it. He grabs my hand and kisses it. He's not supposed to be thoughtful. Or a good listener. Or able to talk about anything. And I'm not supposed to be sleeping with him. "This place is a bit creepy, don't you reckon?"

I have never been inside Mrs Simmons' house and now that my eyes have adjusted to the dark, I begin to take in the décor and furnishings. The kitchen is exactly the same size as ours but is in desperate need of modernisation. And there is clutter everywhere. Every inch of worktop space and shelving is crammed with everything from utensils to complete junk. Mrs Simmons is definitely a hoarder, and Rhys is right: it's creepy in here.

"Maybe it looks better with the lights on?" I suggest, not convinced. "Let's go upstairs." Hanging around down here, where the neighbours behind the house could spot the torchlight, is starting to make me nervous.

Upstairs, we check the rooms. "Not in there," Rhys says, when we find what is clearly Mrs Simmons' bedroom. It smells musty and, like the kitchen, is cluttered with junk. "That would just be too weird."

We find a spare room that is not too cluttered, although it has no bed or chairs. "It's kind of like camping," Rhys says, making the most of it. I am grateful that I thought to stuff a thin blanket into my handbag, and spread it over the floor.

Rhys lies on his back, and I climb on top of him, feeling an overwhelming surge of desire. Rhys is under my skin now, and this is scary. It is over in seconds, but I feel no disappointment; we have hours left to be together and this isn't just about sex.

"I've never done it like that before," he says. "You're amazing."

He grabs me as I slide off him and pulls me against him, nestling his head on my shoulder. I feel amused that he finds sex with a twenty-nine-year-old woman amazing. Surely my body now cannot compare to those of the girls he has slept with before? I'm not doing too badly, but bodies do change. Especially after a pregnancy.

This thought is like a sharp pain in my gut and I turn away from him.

"What's wrong?" he asks.

"Don't you want to be with someone your age? Or at least close to it? I'm too old for you, Rhys."

He pinches my arm. "I don't give a fuck about your age or mine. Why does it matter if we both like each other? And I know you do, or we wouldn't have just done *that*. I just want to keep seeing you, Callie."

Of course it is that simple for him. He doesn't need to think about the future. Or the fact that our actions will devastate lives.

Sitting in our underwear on the blanket, we eat the junk food Rhys has brought. "Have you had a chance to speak to Dillon yet?" I ask.

Rhys raises his eyebrows. Perhaps he is surprised at my timing. "No. Not yet. Do you still want me to?"

I put down my half-finished bag of crisps. "Of course. The problem won't just go away."

He considers this for a moment. "No, you're right. I will. But I'll have to be careful. We don't want him to suspect anything. He's such a jerk sometimes."

"Don't let me come between you and Dillon," I say. "Nothing's more important than your friendship."

Rhys kisses my forehead. "Don't think about all this now. Just think of you and me tonight."

And in that moment, I allow myself to believe that somehow everything will be okay.

CHAPTER TWENTY

Rhys and I only meet once more at Mrs Simmons' house before she comes home from hospital. It is not easy to make excuses to James because he knows Debbie and Bridgette are usually too busy to go out during the week. I hate myself for lying, so I will go without seeing Rhys instead, until there is an easier way. For now, though, I make do with his text messages, which come hard and fast, full of declarations of how much he misses me.

On Thursday evening, I drop the keys next door and check on Mrs Simmons. I have no doubt she is making a good recovery – she is a battle-axe and will probably outlive us all – but I worry Rhys or I may have left something behind. If we did, she will spot it immediately, but everything seems fine. She even thanks me, although her gratitude is delivered in a brusque manner. "Thank the boys for me," she adds, more warmly. I don't know how I will keep her from speaking to them and thanking them herself, but for now I have enough to worry about.

When I get back in, James is standing at the bottom of the stairs, his arms folded and a frown on his face. This is it. He has found out about Rhys. My deceit is about to unravel. It feels as if my heart has stopped beating and I come to an abrupt stop in the hallway, waiting for him to speak.

"Emma's just been on the phone in tears. She says Natalie ended it with her after the lunch on Saturday and she seems to think the two of you spoke about it. I told her that's rubbish, but she's in a real state, Callie."

I breathe again. Whatever this is about, it has nothing to do with Rhys. We are safe.

"I don't understand. What does she think I've done?"

James repeats himself before I remember. This is about my conversation with Natalie on the landing last week. But somehow things have become warped and twisted. Does she really believe I could have something to do with her break-up?

I explain the conversation to James, leaving out the part about Dillon and Luke. "She did tell me she was planning on ending things with Emma. But I had nothing to do with it. I don't even know the woman. Even if I had told her to leave Emma, why would she listen to me?"

James sighs. "I know. We just don't need this grief on top of everything else."

And that's when I remember Dillon's face peering though the gap in his door. I consider telling James, but restrain myself. As with the other grievances, it's futile to bring it up, especially without proof. No, I will deal with Dillon myself. "I'll talk to Emma," I say. "Clear things up. Don't worry."

He smiles faintly and says he needs to do some work upstairs. A few minutes later, when I'm passing his study to use the bathroom, I hear him on the phone. His voice is low and I can't make out every word but I have no doubt he is speaking to Tabitha.

I go outside to check on Jazzy and he runs towards me, rubbing against my leg, his fur tickling my skin. I scoop him up and cuddle him.

"What am I doing, Jazzy? How did I make such a mess of things?"

The cat looks at me with wide eyes and then tries to wriggle from my arms. I check nobody is watching from any of the windows, then step inside the shed to text Rhys. I need to see him and there is only one place we can go.

He is there waiting for me on the corner of his road, dressed smartly as I asked him to be, in dark trousers and a blue collared shirt. He has even polished his shoes and I am touched by his effort. He smiles when I pull up and rushes to open the door, sliding into the seat and planting a kiss on my lips. He has doused himself in aftershave, but this time has used far too much, and it drifts up my nostrils, making my nose twitch.

"You look good," I say. And he does. Older. More sophisticated. He looks the part and any doubts I have about this evening vanish.

I drive from Rhys' road as quickly as I can, just in case either of his parents decide they need to go somewhere. Rhys must be able to tell I'm nervous because he doesn't say anything; he just gazes out of the window until we are almost out of Wimbledon.

Finally, when I am sure we won't be spotted by anyone we know, I relax, and he does the same. He places his hand on my thigh. "So tell me again. You're taking me to meet your dad, and he's ill so I have to be careful what I say to him?"

I take a deep breath and tell him the whole story of my father. Things I have never told James. He waits until I've finished before asking the first of the many questions he must have.

"So, Dillon's dad doesn't even know about him?" I have noticed Rhys only ever refers to James as *Dillon's dad*, never by his first name or even Mr Harwell.

I nod. "James thinks he lives abroad somewhere and that I barely know him. But the truth is I visit him every week."

"But why can't he know about him? I don't get it."

I try my best to explain but now that I am saying it aloud, voicing my fear of burdening James with my uncertain future, of him changing the way he looks at me, it seems irrational and ludicrous. More evidence that I am not in control, that it is catching up with me.

Rhys strokes my thigh. "It must be hard. You've got such a lot you're dealing with, Callie. I think it's pretty incredible." There he goes again, putting me on a pedestal when praise is the last thing I deserve.

"I'm just doing my duty as a daughter. And I love him. Even though, with his…condition…it's hard sometimes." As I say these words, I wonder – for the millionth time in my life – if people will be saying this about me one day. *She has a condition. It's hard sometimes.*

"So why me? Why do I get to meet him?"

"Because I want you to be the person I have no secrets from. That's why I'm telling you this. There has to be someone, doesn't there? There has to be at least one person I can be myself around."

It should be James.

Rhys nods but I wonder if he truly understands. He is too young to have any baggage, too inexperienced to have built up protective walls. He doesn't know how lucky he is. He is planning a future, without being held back by his past or present. Am I contributing to the heavy weight he will one day cart around with him?

"So I just have to pretend I'm older. Twenty or something?"

Dad will see the difference in our ages immediately, if he's having a good day. If he's lucid enough to even remember how old I am. My birthday last week went by without a mention. It suddenly occurs to me that Rhys might be nervous. Meeting a parent of someone you're seeing is hard enough without the added difficulty of Dad's condition. And Rhys' age. But it is too late to turn back now.

"Don't worry, it will be fine," I assure him. "He won't judge you or try to work out if you're good enough for me. It won't be like that."

Rhys smiles. "So, does this mean we're together then? In a relationship? Because that's what it feels like. I mean, it's not just sex, is it?"

Keeping my eyes on the road, I shake my head. "I don't know what this is, but I know I want to keep doing it. It's complicated, though, isn't it? I'm married."

"Yes, but you don't love him. Soon enough you'll love me, I guarantee it!" Although Rhys chuckles, I sense he is being serious.

The trouble is, he is wrong about James. I do love him. But everything has become blurred.

We stand outside Dad's building, waiting, neither of us sure what to say. We are both nervous now.

"Maybe he's not home?" Rhys says. This is what anyone unused to Dad would assume.

"No, he's home. He's always at home." Just as I speak these words, the door clicks open without Dad answering the intercom. A change to the routine. He does this sometimes. We head inside and Rhys grabs my hand as we climb the stairs.

I should have warned him that the flat will be in a state. That he'll have to take a deep breath before we step inside and the thick stench of old smoke and rotting food assaults us. To his credit, he doesn't react and holds out his hand to Dad as I make introductions.

"Who are you?" Dad asks, eyeing Rhys up and down. "What's going on, Caroline?"

I step forward and explain that Rhys is my friend and we've just stopped by before we go out. I can feel Rhys look at me when I say this because nothing has been discussed about what we will do after our visit. Thankfully, he plays along and keeps quiet, realising it is our get-out clause, to be used if Dad is having a bad day.

"I didn't know about this. Did you tell me you were coming? Well, you'd better come in anyway. Stop those damn people knocking on my door." I try not to look at Rhys, and hope he won't react. Dad needs little encouragement to rant about these non-existent people.

I suggest we sit in the front room because it is the place that will be the least messy, and Dad gestures for Rhys to go in first. "He's all right," he says, turning back to me. "I don't know who the hell he is, but he's not one of them. I can tell."

To prevent Rhys from having to deal with the state of Dad's crockery, I have brought some cans of Red Bull. I pull one from my bag and hand it to him as he sits down next to Dad.

"So my tea's not good enough, eh?" Dad says, staring at Rhys with wide eyes. But then his mouth spreads into a grin. "I'm just messing with you."

Satisfied that Dad will not begin a verbal attack on Rhys in my absence, I slip off to the kitchen to make tea. Dad doesn't drink coffee, and won't even have it in the house. He claims there is something in it that helps *them* control his mind. I never argue with this, or ask who he is talking about. I learnt long ago that it is pointless to do so.

When I carry the two mugs into the front room, Dad and Rhys are engrossed in a conversation about football. Before now, I didn't even know Rhys liked the sport, but then there will be a lot I don't know about him.

I watch them for a while and try to relax. Right now I am relieved to forget my troubles, happy to pretend nothing exists beyond these walls.

"Is he your boyfriend?" Dad asks, when Rhys excuses himself to use the bathroom.

Although I have been expecting this question, I don't know how to answer it. "We're just...good friends." Just like with our affair, I am dealing with things as and when they happen.

Dad takes a sip of tea. "Well, I like him. Bit young, though, isn't he?"

I shake my head. "He's just got good genes. Shall I make you another tea?"

He shakes his head, clearly lost in his thoughts again.

We stay for an hour, Rhys chatting away to Dad, and as we leave I am sure I sense Dad's disappointment. He doesn't seem to be in his usual hurry to get rid of me and even watches us walk down the stairs, something he's never done before.

"I really like your dad, Callie," Rhys says, once we are in the car. "I know he's...ill, but I could really talk to him."

I pull my seatbelt across me and start the engine. "Thanks for coming with me."

"You know, I really think Dillon would like him too. Why don't you –"

"No!" The word shoots from my mouth and Rhys looks taken aback. I have never snapped at him before.

I try to soften my voice. "There's just no way any of them can know about Dad."

"But why? I don't understand. He's really nice. Friendly."

The urge to shut down overwhelms me but I try to resist it. Rhys deserves explanations. After all, I am the one who brought him here tonight.

"Don't you get it? He's got a disease. One that is quite possibly hereditary." I look away from him and stare out of my side window. It has started to drizzle and as droplets collect on the window, tears form on my cheeks.

It seems to take a while for Rhys to get the gist of what I'm saying, and he doesn't realise I am crying. "But it doesn't mean you'll end up the same, does it? Look at you, you're completely fine. Aren't you?"

I have to laugh at this, but it comes out as a sarcastic snort. How can he think I'm fine? I'm sleeping with a teenager, I can't bond with my stepsons, and I've been married less than a year.

Rhys grabs my arm. "What did I say?" And then he sees my tear-stained face and pulls me towards him, smothering my head with soft kisses. "Don't cry, Callie. Whatever it is, you'll be okay. I'm here for you, no matter what."

I cling to him, digging my fingers into his back, and want to believe he is right. That we can deal with everything together. It is wrong to depend on him, yet he is the only person I *can* depend on.

We stay like this for what seems like hours until finally Rhys pulls away. "I don't want to go back to

Wimbledon yet. Let's go for a walk. There's a park over there."

I have never been in Dad's park in darkness. There aren't many people around and it is eerily quiet. It is still drizzling but not enough to spoil our walk. Rhys grabs my hand as we stroll around the lake. It is only then I realise how much freedom the night shadows bring us. I would never hold hands with him in daylight.

"Let's cut through there," Rhys says, "I think I see a bench."

I let him lead me and it is both strange and comforting; just one more example of when Rhys does not seem his age. We sit down and cuddle up close because it's cooled down now the sun is hidden.

We kiss for a while, but restrain ourselves from going further, and I long to be somewhere more private. "I can wait," Rhys says. "I'm just happy being here with you." He leans forward to tie his shoelace so I am the first to notice when a figure appears in front of us.

"Callie? Is that you?"

My heart feels like it's stopped in my chest – I haven't heard anyone approaching us – and I look up to see a face I have not set eyes on for over six years. A face I have not missed. Grinning, Max Hunt looks down at me. "Long time," he says. "How have you been?"

Rhys looks up and Max nods at him, his grin disappearing. Has he seen us kissing? Surely not, otherwise he wouldn't be greeting me so warmly. But how can I explain what I'm doing in a park at this hour, with a teenage boy? Max is shrewd; he will know straight away Rhys is too young for me.

Nobody says anything for a moment, as if we are all in a twisted tableau: me, my teenage lover and my ex-boyfriend. What comes out of my mouth next is not a fully-formed idea; there is no time for that.

"This is…my stepson, Dillon," I say, searching Max's face for any sign of disbelief.

But his expression is hard to read. "Nice to meet you, Dillon. I'm Callie's ex, by the way. I don't suppose she's ever mentioned me."

Rhys stares at him, unsmiling. "No. She hasn't." I can't tell whether he is angry at me for introducing him as Dillon or the fact that my ex-boyfriend is here.

"So you got married then?" Max plonks himself down on the bench and Rhys edges away from me. This is good; until now we have been sitting far too close for my introduction to be believable.

"Yes." Now it is Max who is sitting too close to me. Even without looking at him, I can tell Rhys is silently fuming beside me.

"That's great. I'm glad I bumped into you. Listen, I've been wanting to call you but –"

"What are you doing around here anyway?" I don't want him to finish his sentence. I don't want to remember. I am having enough trouble dealing with the present.

"Remember Simon? He's just moved here and we're meeting for a drink in half an hour. I got here a bit early so thought I'd go for a walk."

I nod, silently cursing my bad luck. Seconds earlier and I daren't think about what conversation we would be having now. "Well, we better be off," I say, standing up. Rhys does the same.

"I'll give you a call and we can catch up properly," Max says, but I am already walking away, Rhys dragging his feet behind me.

Neither of us speaks until we are in the car, the doors shut and the engine running. Rhys is the first to utter a word. "So that was your ex?"

"Look, I'm sorry. I...I didn't know what else to say. It just looked dodgy, us being in the park like that. Imagine if he'd seen us kissing."

"You could have said I was your husband."

"What? He would never have believed that."

Rhys slinks back in his seat and doesn't look at me. "Do you still like him?"

Surprised, I turn to face him but he continues staring straight ahead. "Of course I don't. I got married to someone else, remember? It was over with Max a long time ago."

Rhys snorts. "It doesn't sound like it's over for *him*. You told him you were married and he still wants to *catch up*." He says the last two words with a sneer and I don't like this side of him. Although I've trusted him with knowledge of Dad, there is no way I can tell him what Max and I went through together, how we will always be connected by our silent baby. Even if Max never wanted her.

Forcing the memory aside, I try to understand how Rhys is feeling. "You've been with girls before. That doesn't change anything between us, does it?"

He considers this for a moment then finally turns to face me. "You're right, Callie, sorry. It's just the thought of you being with...you know...it drives me nuts."

I lean in to kiss him then because it is what he needs. He has been here for me every time I've needed him so I need to be here for him too. I let his hands wander and eventually I lose myself, forgetting we are in a car, parked up a side street around the corner from my dad's flat.

Only when someone walks past the misted windows do we stop in our tracks. I hurriedly straighten my clothes. "Shit, Rhys, we need to be more careful."

Checking the rear-view mirror, for a fleeting moment I am sure the figure heading down the road and turning the corner is Max.

No, I tell myself. *It's dark outside; you didn't get a proper look.*

But later, after we've returned to Wimbledon and I've dropped Rhys at the bottom of his road, I am convinced that it was.

CHAPTER TWENTY-ONE

Now

Without looking up I can feel DC Barnes' hard stare on me. Perhaps she could forgive the kiss, but now she knows I have slept with Rhys it is a different matter. But it's okay. I fully deserve her judgement because what I did was wrong.

"But if you'd just been caught in the park by your ex, why would you go on to do anything in the car?" she asks. "Isn't that asking for trouble? Asking to be caught? Maybe that's what you wanted?"

I hang my head, my whole body wracked with shame. "We didn't have sex in the car. We just…we got lost in the moment." I straighten. "Look, I know this doesn't make sense, but I'd grown fond of Rhys very quickly. He made me forget who I was. He made carrying on bearable."

"But why all the risks?" DS Connolly asks, his voice so kind I almost forget who I'm talking to. He could be a friend or a counsellor rather than a detective who has arrested me for murder. "Your neighbours' house, the car, his house. That I don't understand."

"Well, that's clear enough now," I reply. "It's part of the disease, isn't it? Reckless behaviour?" I have learnt this too late. "It was a way to hide from myself, from the person I had become."

Silence fills the room.

"Look, I'm not defending my actions," I continue. "Far from it. I'll take all the punishment I've got coming to me. But the truth is, I was becoming detached from everything. And that's a dangerous position to be in."

CHAPTER TWENTY-TWO

After the close call, it would be logical to slow things down with Rhys, to be more careful and keep ourselves hidden. Bumping into Max last week, in a deserted park in north London, of all places, means nowhere is safe.

But instead of learning from the incident, I start to take more risks. It's not the excitement of getting caught, I am not interested in that. It is only that I am blindly walking through my life without thought to consequences. To anyone else it would seem I'm acting only out of selfishness, but this isn't true. My head is a fuzzy blur and I am living moment to moment.

Rhys comes to the house in the afternoons, skipping lessons when we are sure James is on a shoot somewhere out of London. He sneaks around the back of the house, avoiding Mrs Simmons' gaze.

"I've spoken to Dillon," he says on one of these afternoons. It is a rare early summer's day and the heat is sweltering so we sit in the kitchen with the door wide open, hidden from the neighbours' view. Even in my vest top and shorts, the sweat is pouring from my body and Rhys tugs at the neck of his school shirt, unable to get comfortable. Outside, Jazzy lazes on the grass, rolling around and swiping at butterflies. I have never seen him so confident in the garden; it's as if he knows the boys aren't here so it is safe to come out.

"Okay. Tell me." He has been here for over an hour without bringing up Dillon, so I know the news can't be positive.

"Callie, I don't think I can change his mind. He said…oh, it doesn't matter, he just wouldn't listen to me. And I couldn't push too much or he'd get suspicious." He says this too casually, as if Dillon finding out about us wouldn't be such a big deal.

"What exactly did he say?"

Rhys looks away from me, towards the garden. "Are you sure you want to know? It's kind of hurtful." He lifts his can of Red Bull to his lips, tilting his head back and taking a long sip.

"More hurtful than anything else he's said or done? Not sure that's possible. Just tell me. I can handle it." I am putting on a show of bravado but my insides feel loose like jelly. No matter what I am doing with Rhys, the boys' hatred still hurts.

Rhys scrunches his empty can and clears his throat. "He reckons you're not good enough for his dad. But it's bullshit, Callie. I never met his mum but there's no way she was even half as amazing as you are." He reaches for my hand. "Anyway, isn't it pointless to worry about all this now?" He picks up his can before he remembers it's empty. I would offer him another but only bought three and that was the last one. It's not as if I can keep a stash of Red Bull in the cupboards;

everyone knows Rhys is the only one who drinks the stuff. "When we tell everyone, Dillon's not exactly going to be your biggest fan anyway, is he?"

It takes me a moment to digest Rhys' statement. *Tell everyone.* This is the last thing I have planned to do. The past couple of weeks I have been ignoring what I am doing, living every moment with Rhys as if the next day won't exist. But the bubble in which I've been encapsulated has just burst.

Lifting my feet from the chair they're resting on, I turn to face Rhys. "Listen, we can't tell anyone, Rhys. Ever. Can you imagine what would happen?"

He frowns. "But I'm eighteen soon. I thought we could wait until then and it wouldn't be too bad. I know you want to be with me, Callie, but we can't keep this a secret forever. And why should we? I'm proud to be with you and I want to show you off to the world."

His idealism, although touching, frightens me. I have never stopped to consider that I might be Rhys' first love. That first love that grips you so tightly, never truly lets go and leaves an indelible trace, even years later. Even if that person is out of sight. Even if, like Lauren, they are no longer here.

I have to be careful what I say.

"Rhys, I really like you, but my life is such a mess at the moment. I just can't do anything to make things…even worse."

"But…so…" He trails off. Clearly he hasn't expected me to say this. "But you don't love Dillon's dad, do you? You can't, otherwise you wouldn't be with me." He seems pleased to have reached this conclusion, as if there is no other explanation.

Seeing the serious expression on his face, it occurs to me that Rhys wants me to address things I don't want to think about, like what we are doing, or at least what *I* am doing. But I can't. My involvement with him is heinous enough, but if it is all for nothing, if my intention is not to leave James to be with him instead, then what does that make me?

But there is no way I can explain all this to Rhys. How can I expect him to understand that I do love my husband, but have somehow managed to keep our affair separate from that? I have stuffed Rhys into a neat compartment, not letting any edges hang over, so he can't overlap or spill out onto my marriage. I wonder if this is also what James has done with Tabitha. Why else has he not left me when he has had every opportunity?

So I lie. I take Rhys' hand and assure him that I just need more time to sort things out. He visibly relaxes when I say this but now I am the one who is on edge. Something has changed this afternoon. This is getting out of control.

In the late afternoon I have a tutorial in central London. It lasts two hours and gives me breathing space, albeit temporarily. Somehow I manage to focus on what our course tutor says, but seeing how focused the other students are is a stark reminder that I have let my studies slip.

Going home on the packed District line, I grab one of the only empty seats and for the first time force myself to consider the future. I love James, but I can't see how things can ever change, even if he stopped seeing Tabitha. It is too late for me to confront him; I would just be a hypocrite because I am doing far worse. My relationship with the boys is beyond hope, and how could I ever have a life with Rhys? We would be outcasts, our relationship frowned upon by everyone. No, I need to have the conversation I've been putting off with James. It is time we sorted out our problems.

But when I get home, all my intentions fizzle out when I realise Tabitha is here, in our house. I hear her before I see her: that deep, throaty laugh echoing from the kitchen, followed by a chuckle from James. My first thought is that I have caught them together, and James has forgotten the time of my tutorial. But the boys will be home and I know he wouldn't stoop so low. She must be here about work.

I smooth down my hair, still surprised by how short it is, and open the kitchen door, unprepared for the scene that greets me. Tabitha and James sit at the table with the boys, the four plates in front of them piled high with fish and chips. They all look up as I enter but James is the only one who speaks.

"Callie, hi. I thought you'd be later than this. Tabby just popped round to go over some work stuff. Have you eaten?" Tabby. When did he start calling her that?

No food has passed my lips since lunchtime, but I nod. Even if I told the truth, it doesn't look as if there is enough food for all of us.

"Nice to see you again," Tabitha says, her voice warmer towards me than it's ever been. She is mocking me, letting me know she has won.

"I'll just make a cup of tea," I say, rushing past them to the kettle. I can feel Tabitha's eyes on me and wonder why she still hasn't told James I confronted her at the shop that day.

While I wait for the kettle to boil, I grow increasingly anxious. Tabitha is here in this house, flaunting their affair as if she has nothing to be ashamed of. Even when I think of what I have done here with Rhys, as recently as this afternoon, it does little to stop me hating her. If it weren't for her I would never have looked at Rhys. I would never have needed him to help me escape.

There is always an excuse, isn't there?

And then things get worse. Behind me, Dillon turns to Tabitha and tells her how nice it is to see her again, fawning over her as if she is a celebrity. Even though I know this is for my benefit, it is too much to bear.

"I'll have this outside," I announce, holding up my mug. I don't wait for an answer, but hurry outside to the shed. And someone I can depend on.

For over an hour I sit on the dirty shed floor with Jazzy curled up on my lap. I stroke his fur, much softer now, and let the rumble of his purr comfort me. When someone appears in the doorway, Jazzy springs up and cowers in a corner at the back.

James stands there, shaking his head. "Callie? What are you doing here?" He notices Jazzy. "So this is the cat the boys were talking about. He's cute." Of course the boys have told him about Jazzy; why would they miss an opportunity to stick a potential nail in my coffin?

"I don't let him in the house," I say. "He sleeps out here."

"Callie, it's fine. I'm surprised they didn't want him. They always used to hound Lauren to get them a pet." To my surprise, he joins me on the floor, brushing away some of the dirt before he sits down. "Tabitha's gone," he says. "We need to talk, don't we?"

So the moment is here. James is going to tell me he's leaving me for Tabitha, that he never meant for it to happen, but somewhere along the way they have fallen in love. He will probably spare my feelings by omitting that she will make a much better stepmother than I have. A better wife.

He takes my hand and it startles me; we've hardly touched in weeks. His skin feels so different from Rhys'. Not better or worse, just different. And being this close to him feels odd now. It is funny how you can get used to someone new in such a short space of time.

"Callie, there's something I need to tell you. I should have said it a while ago but things have been so...strained for us."

I nod, tears forming in my eyes. I don't try to wipe them away; I will not hide from the truth anymore. James squeezes my hand. "Tabitha just told me you went to see her. That you found a text from her?"

"Yeah." It is all I can manage to say.

"Why didn't you talk to me?"

This is a good question, and now that it's out there I feel foolish for not doing it. "I don't know. Things were just bad, with the boys and…everything. I suppose I didn't want to deal with that as well." I can no longer look at him because he's about to say something that can never be undone, so I turn to watch Jazzy instead. He seems more relaxed now and has nestled into his bed.

James keeps hold of my hand. "I know I should have told you this before, but Tabitha and I…we, well, we…" He pauses. "Before I met you we kind of had a thing."

I look at him again now. Why doesn't he just spit it all out? "Okay." This doesn't feel the way I thought it would. I don't feel as if I'm being crushed by his words. I am numb to it all; perhaps blocking it all out until it explodes from me like a river bursting its banks.

"But it was over way before I met you," James continues. "And the only reason I didn't tell you is because she still works with me. I just didn't want any problems. In my head it was completely over. I have no feelings at all in that way for her. I just thought you might doubt me or worry about it if you knew. But I swear to you, nothing has happened since I met you."

It takes a moment for my brain to decipher what he has just told me. This is not what I have been expecting him to say. It is all wrong. "So…you mean you're not sleeping with her? Now, I mean?"

James snorts. "Ha, not a chance. I mean, I'm fond of her but it was over before it even started. For me, at least. I think I was just trying to get over Lauren. It was a mistake. You have nothing to worry about."

"But…the text? How can you explain that?"

"She was apologising because she was a bit drunk and made some suggestive comments, but I put an immediate stop to that. Trust me, there is no way I'd do that to you."

"But what about the last part of that text?" I quote it back to him, the words still fresh in my memory. "'But it was good, wasn't it?'"

"She must have been referring to when we were together years ago. Callie, I swear to you, our relationship is strictly professional now. I promise there is nothing going on. No way in hell."

I feel like I have been struck across the face. This changes everything. It makes what I have done with Rhys even more despicable. James has been innocent all along. He's done nothing wrong, nothing to tarnish our marriage. His worst flaws are only his optimism and blindness where his sons are concerned. My whole body starts to shake and I can't stop myself from crying. James wraps his arms around me and pulls me into him. "We're okay. Everything's okay." He thinks I am crying tears of relief. He doesn't know they are borne of guilt.

We stay like this for a while until eventually I calm down. "We still need to sort out the boys," James says. "But I've been thinking a lot about that. I know how hard it's been for you so maybe we can all sit down together and, you know, thrash things out. Air any grievances. Obviously me talking to them on my own hasn't helped, and I'm sorry. But *we'll* make them listen this time, we'll do it together. Do you think that might help?"

"I don't know," I say, but quickly add, "I hope so." James is really trying so being positive is the least I can do. He really believes there is a way forward for our family.

But with a sinking feeling, I know it is too late. Just like words, actions cannot be undone, and I can't pretend Rhys doesn't exist.

James kisses me then, and it is both unfamiliar and recognisable at the same time. It is right. I cling to him, burying my face in his neck, hoping he won't notice his t-shirt is becoming soaked in more of my tears. "Let's go to bed," he says, rising and pulling me up with him. I take a quick look at Jazzy, sleeping contentedly now, and walk with my husband back to the house.

It's quite dark now but as we approach the door, I glance up and see Dillon at his window, watching us. He moves away when our eyes meet.

We lie in bed for a while, even though it is not very late. He apologises again and each time I hear the words it's like a knife piercing my skin. He has nothing to be sorry for. I am the one who has betrayed us all. And now, ironically, I am betraying Rhys by sleeping with James.

My phone, buried in the pocket of my jeans, vibrates for the third time since we came upstairs. I know without checking that it will be Rhys, wondering why I haven't replied to his last text.

I tell James I need the bathroom and, sliding out of bed, pull on my jeans. I am right. All three messages are from Rhys. The first one says he misses me and the other two are asking if I'm okay. I sit on the floor by the side of the bath and start typing a response. Short and simple. *I'm fine. Just busy. Speak soon.* He will know something is wrong but at least it will stop him texting any more tonight.

I'm about to put the phone back in my pocket when it pings with a new voicemail message. I nearly ignore it – it will only be Rhys again and the thought of hearing his voice right now is too much – but curiosity gets the better of me.

The voicemail isn't from Rhys. Instead, it is Max's voice I'm listening to, saying something about the park last week, about the boy I was with.

Max telling me he knows that boy is not my stepson.

CHAPTER TWENTY-THREE

"I'm taking the day off work today."

I open my eyes and see James lying on his side, staring at me. He looks alert and I wonder how long he's been watching me sleep. I ask him to repeat what he's said, just in case I have misunderstood in my sleep-fuddled state. He rarely allows himself time off work.

"It's fine. I've already texted Tabby…Tabitha, and she's getting a freelancer in to cover my shoots for the day. We need to spend some time together. Do something nice."

I rub sleep from my eyes and try to ignore the wave of anxiety I feel at the sound of her name. Surely now that James has explained himself, I shouldn't feel threatened?

But it's your paranoia. You can't forget that she's slept with him, even if it was before you met. She knows what your husband feels like.

"Thank you." I sit up and lean against my pillow, trying to shrug off the doubts. I have no right to dwell on James' past. "That sounds great."

And just for a second I believe everything will work out. Until I remember Max's voicemail. He is the real threat from the past because if he wants to, Max could destroy everything. And now I know that James still loves me, I will fight even harder to keep my marriage together. I won't let Max, or anyone else, destroy us.

I have Max's number in my phone now so I will call him back today to find out what he's playing at. Despite what happened, he has no right after all these years to worm his way back into my life, especially not this way. I try to tell myself it is some kind of joke, that he is winding me up just to get me to speak to him. He has not been successful the other times he's tried. But I know this is a fantasy. He is calling only because of what he knows.

Then there is Rhys. I will need to speak to him, try to end things amicably; this is the least he deserves. But one thing at a time. I need to fix things at home first.

"So," James says, lifting up the duvet and swinging his legs over the side of the bed. "I'll wake the boys and tell them we're going bowling. The four of us."

My heart sinks again. This is not what I thought he meant when he said we need to spend some time together. It's too soon. But then I remember our agreement in the shed yesterday, and how I tried to believe confronting the boys together would help. I want to be optimistic, but there is no way the boys will suddenly accept me just because James wants it, just because he is embedding his latest lecture in a fun day out. In fact, if anything, they will resent me more when he confronts them right in front of me. Perhaps they will even escalate their hate campaign. But I will give them a chance and try to make this work. For James. For our family.

I watch James pull on jeans and a polo shirt. I don't deserve him. If he had any idea what I have done, he would throw me out and never look back. I have no doubt that his love for me is based on my loyalty, the picture of the person he thinks I am. When we said our vows, he would have had no idea I could be capable of such deceit. I had no idea myself. But still I can't give him up. I will have to learn to bury my guilt. It will have to be yet another secret I am forced to keep from my husband.

"Maybe it's best if you talk to the boys first, without me?" As soon as my words are out I regret them.

James sits on the bed to pull on his socks. "But I've done that plenty of times." He pauses. "Actually, you're right. I'll give it another go. Make them listen." He smiles, as if he has solved a difficult puzzle, then jumps up and tells me he's going down to make breakfast. There is lightness in his voice, as if a weight has been lifted from him. I only wish I could share his optimism.

I take my time in the shower, putting off the things I have to deal with today. Rhys. Max. Bowling with Dillon and Luke. When I sit on the side of the bath to dry myself, I think of how reckless I have been. It doesn't matter what I thought James was up to; nothing can excuse my behaviour. And now, when I remember the feel of Rhys' mouth pressing against mine, it is not excitement I feel, but nausea.

In the kitchen, James and the boys are finishing their breakfast when I walk in. Luke's eyes flick to his father when he sees me, but then he murmurs a *good morning*. Dillon eventually does the same, while James beams at all of us as he sips his coffee.

"Good morning," I say, joining them at the table. It feels odd. Despite James' pleasure, there is still something wrong. They will not give in this easily.

"We've saved you some eggs and bacon. Your plate's warming in the oven," James says.

The boys' plates are empty but they make no move to get up when I sit down, as they usually do the minute I appear. Instead they sit like Stepford children, obedient and robotic, until I have finished eating. Nobody talks, but I notice the looks James gives them.

"Can we go now?" Luke asks, finally losing his patience.

James scowls. "Yes, but don't forget we're leaving at one. Okay?"

Luke scrapes back his chair and springs up, eager to get back to his room. Dillon, taking out his phone, stands up too and I remind myself I need to give this a chance, that it's only the first day of a fresh start and it will just take time. And I almost feel better, until I feel the hard impact of a shoe crashing against my shin. I stifle a yelp and turn to see Dillon hurrying out of the kitchen.

James' head is buried in his newspaper so he saw nothing. I was right to be sceptical. Nothing has changed.

Later, when James heads to his study to work on his new website, I go outside to check on Jazzy. The shed has become my private space, the only one where I don't feel claustrophobic, despite its size.

I call Max, but get his voicemail. Within seconds of hanging up, I receive a text from him. *Can't talk now. Meet me this evening. 8pm in Kingston. We should talk. Will text address later.* I sigh heavily as I read; this is not going away. I will have to meet him and hear what he's got to say. Whatever it is, I will tell him he is wrong. He can't possibly know that Rhys isn't Dillon. And even if he has managed to work it out, he can't know I have been sleeping with him. But then I remember the shadowy figure walking past the car that evening, how I was so convinced it was Max. I need to come up with something plausible, just in case he saw us together.

I take a deep breath and prepare to make my second call. Rhys has been texting all morning and I haven't responded so he must know something is wrong. But I can't end it over the phone, I need to speak to him face-to-face. I owe him that much.

He picks up immediately, as if he has been staring at his phone, willing me to call. "Callie, finally! I've been texting you loads. Are you okay? I've been worried. Has Dillon done something?" He is talking too quickly and breathing heavily, as if he is pacing.

"No, no, it's nothing...I've just been really busy. Sorry."

"Good. When can I see you? I need to see you, Callie." His voice sounds strange; his words are desperate but he delivers them as a command. Perhaps

216

he has become so used to looking out for me, taking control, that now he feels he is in control of things. Of us.

"Soon, I promise. We need to talk. I, um, got a message from Max, my ex. Do you remember him from last week?"

There is a long silence and I wonder if we've been cut off until Rhys finally speaks. "What does he want?"

I tell him about Max's voicemail and text, and his breathing slows. He must have stopped walking. "He knows," I say. "We need to –"

"I don't care if he knows, Callie. It was bound to come out sooner or later. We'll get through this together. He just wants to meet up with you. He wants you back. You don't have to go. Please."

Stunned by his response, I lose track of what I was about to say. "No, Rhys, listen. It can't come out. Not like this. Do you understand what it will mean? I have to go and find out what he knows."

He falls silent again, but I can't tell if he is contemplating how serious this is or whether he is just sulking. "Rhys, are you there?"

"Yep. So you're seeing him tonight? Your ex." It sounds as if he is talking to himself rather than me, getting it clear in his head. He is insecure, threatened by Max. Yet he has no problem with James, which is why I am only now seeing this side of him. Have I been so blind this whole time? How could I have thought he was mature?

"I don't have a choice. Look, I'll text you later to let you know how it goes. And we'll meet up soon. Talk things through."

Jazzy strolls into the shed and I kneel down to stroke him. Somehow, the vibration of his purring calms me down. I make him a silent promise to let him sleep in the house.

"Okay," Rhys says. But when I disconnect the call, I know that things are far from okay.

Bowling would be fine if it hadn't been for Dillon's kick to my shin earlier. It didn't hurt for long, but the memory will not fade so easily. So now we all take turns knocking over skittles, cheering whenever anyone gets a strike. Dillon puts on an Oscar-winning performance and while Luke is taking his go, asks me how my studying is going. Although I am not looking at him, I can sense James nodding his approval. I don't know what he said to the boys at breakfast, but he's only made things worse. Now they are putting on their phoniest act yet. I can forgive James for being laidback, for wanting to believe the best, but I know that's unrealistic. My stepsons won't give up until I am gone from their lives.

Finally the game is over and we can leave. Dillon has won but when I congratulate him, while James collects his shoes, he ignores me and strides ahead, pulling Luke along with him.

During the drive home, James delivers his lecture about us all sticking together, being the family we should be, and how he won't tolerate any more coldness. "We've had a good day out today," he says. "And this is how it should be all the time. I know nothing's ever perfect but we need to accept and support each other, okay?"

A few moments of silence follow, and then Luke speaks up. "Sorry, Dad," he says. "I'll try harder. Sorry, Callie."

"Dillon?' James says.

"Yeah, sorry."

Beside me, James smiles, apparently still feeling victorious. It doesn't affect my love for him but does he really have no idea that he hasn't helped at all? That he never has? And his idea for the four of us to air our grievances has come to nothing. But this is a relief, because like everything else, it would only be futile.

We pull up to the house and immediately I see Rhys sitting on the front step, in exactly the same position I found him in weeks ago. My whole body heats up. There is only one reason he is here. He could tell on the phone I want things to end and he wants everyone to know what we have been doing. I almost scream at James to keep driving, the excuse of having left my phone in the bowling alley on my lips, but then Dillon says, "There's Rhys. He's a bit early."

So Dillon has invited him over. I have almost forgotten that they are best friends, and perhaps in my mind I have written him off now that I have come to my senses. But here he is, waiting for Dillon, a painful reminder that he will never be gone from my life, his presence a constant threat.

As we get out of the car, Rhys stands up to greet us, fixing his eyes on me. I daren't look at the others to see if they notice. Dillon rushes over to him and slaps his arm, pulling his phone out to show him something, but the whole time I am the focus of Rhys' attention.

"Nice to see you," I say, when it is no longer possible to avoid him.

He doesn't answer for a moment but then says, "Hi, Mrs Harwell," before turning to Dillon.

For a moment I stay where I am, rooted to the spot by fear. I haven't even broken if off yet but Rhys will always have power over me because he will still be my stepson's friend. Even if he takes the breakup well, avoiding him will be impossible. And I will always wonder if the moment has come for me to face what I've done.

We traipse inside and I watch the boys head upstairs. Before Rhys reaches the top he turns back to look at me, offering a quick smile before James appears beside me.

"I was thinking," James says, "I've just got a bit of work to do and then do you want to watch a DVD or something tonight? I might even stretch to some popcorn from the corner shop!"

I'm about to agree but then remember I have to meet Max tonight. The only excuse I can give is that I am seeing Debbie or Bridgette. At least it is the weekend so it is more believable that they will be available. I open my mouth and the lie floods out; I have got far too good at deception. The lies need to stop, and I vow to myself that they will, as soon as I've sorted out this mess.

James looks disappointed but he pats my arm. "Don't worry, you go out and have fun. You probably need a break anyway."

When I hear loud voices upstairs, I almost change my mind and tell him I will stay home after all. What if, in my absence, Rhys decides to tell Dillon? Or goes directly to James? Both scenarios are unthinkable and will have only one consequence. There is nothing to stop him exposing us while I'm still here, but at least I might be able to control the situation. I can keep an eye on him.

But if I don't meet Max then what will he do? Will he turn up here? He somehow found my mobile number, which I've only changed recently, so there is every chance he knows our address. I am trapped like a hunted animal. I have no choice but to meet him.

"Callie?"

James nudges me, snapping my thoughts away. "You look like you're in a trance! Did you hear anything I just said?"

"Sorry, what were you saying?"

"I was telling you that when you get home tonight I'll run you a bath. You know, pamper you a bit. I know I'm not romantic, but I've seen it in loads of films!"

I turn away from him because I can't bear him being so nice to me. My deceit was far easier to deal with when we were barely speaking.

CHAPTER TWENTY-FOUR

Max lives in Kingston now, in a three-bedroom flat overlooking the Thames. I don't want to be here but the only other option was meeting somewhere public and I can't risk being seen. It would just be one more thing I can't explain.

This place is a far cry from the minuscule studio flat he rented years ago and let me move into. I still remember the rickety old furniture that the landlord refused to replace, even though most of it was falling to bits. But Max didn't care then. He was a free spirit, refusing to be tied down by possessions, especially those that didn't belong to him.

And now, being in his new flat – one that he owns – I can immediately tell he has changed. The furnishings are still sparse, but what he does have is tasteful and expensive-looking. He has done all right for himself.

I sit on his brown leather sofa and lean forwards, clutching my bag to my stomach because I can't get comfortable here. And don't want to try. I don't know what Max wants from me but he hasn't asked me here to make small talk.

He sits in a chair opposite me, studying and scrutinising me. "I'm glad you came," he says, lighting a cigarette. I'd forgotten that he smokes. He holds the box out to me but I shake my head. "You used to have the occasional one," he says, reminding me that we share a past.

"Not often," I say, determined not to let him win whatever this is.

He shrugs. "Well, it's been a long time since I've seen you. It's possible you could have got addicted."

I ignore him and watch as he pours us each a glass of red wine. He has already laid everything out on the coffee table so clearly there was no doubt in his mind that I would show up. He hands me a glass, which I don't want but accept anyway, and I stare at his plasma television screen, taking in the muted flickering images of a music video.

I watch him inhale on his cigarette. It doesn't feel as if we were ever together, as if he ever witnessed my pain. The six-year absence has made us strangers; we were barely more than kids when we broke up, so I know nothing about Max as a thirty-year-old man. It took me a long time, but eventually I learnt to leave him, and everything else, in my past. But now he is intruding into my future and I just need this evening to be over.

He finishes his cigarette and squashes it out on a silver ashtray that sits on his coffee table. When he stands up, I pray he won't sit next to me on the sofa.

But he does. Not so close that I can justify shifting over, but too close for my liking.

"So it's been a long time, huh?" he says. "What are you doing these days?" He takes a sip of wine and swills it around his mouth before swallowing. "Aside from being *married*, that is." He draws the word out but smiles innocently. I wonder what he thinks of the fact that I'm married. He was never one for settling down, despite how long we were together, despite the fact we were nearly parents. The idea goes against his nature. It was the cause of much conflict between us because I knew one day – far in the future, of course – that I would want marriage.

I have no patience for his question. "Look, what's this all about? You've obviously got something to say so just spit it out." My words fly from my mouth with more anger than I intend, but it is too late to take them back. And I won't apologise.

He pulls another cigarette from the packet and sticks it in his mouth, but doesn't light it. I wonder if he is nervous; he never used to chain-smoke. "Callie, I'm offended. I haven't seen you for six years and within five minutes you're jumping down my throat." He places the cigarette back in the box, lifting his glass instead and staring at the dark wine inside. "I just wanted to catch up. Explain things. You know. What happened. With us."

I have no wish to revisit the past. Whoever Max thinks I am, I am no longer that person. The one who made him feel trapped. Who he thought needed looking after. But perhaps he was right to believe those things. I was young. In some ways, I did inadvertently trap him.

He waits for me to say something and anything is preferable to talking about what I was doing with Rhys, so I give him what he wants. "What happened is you packed up my stuff, threw me out of your flat and disappeared."

Max looks taken aback that I have said this so blatantly. "I know, I'm –"

"You didn't even have the decency to talk to me or leave a note. Anything. So what's the point of explaining now?"

He stares into his glass. "I was a jerk."

I almost tell him that he still is, or he wouldn't have forced me to come here tonight. He puts down his glass and rubs his chin. "I couldn't handle it, Callie. Your grief. My grief. I tried to help you, but you wouldn't let me. It was like we had nothing to say to each other anymore. But I never stopped caring about you. I didn't want children – I never lied about that – but I accepted your decision to have her…" He trails off because there is no right choice of words.

"But you left years after we lost her, Max. No, what was too much was the thought that I'd end up like my dad. That's why you did it." Over the years I have accepted the truth: any tiny argument Max and I had, anything I did that he considered not normal, would have him picturing me like Dad. And he couldn't deal with that.

"Callie, you're wrong. I tried my best to help you, don't you remember? But I just couldn't, could I? I'm sorry for that."

At least now he has the decency to look ashamed. Taking out the cigarette he has only just replaced, he wastes no time lighting it. "But it did freak me out. I was twenty-three, for Christ's sake. Practically a kid. We both were. If I could change things, I would."

I think of Rhys. Of how different he was with Dad, even as a boy of seventeen. He didn't fear him, and he didn't care what might or might not happen to me down the line. I feel a momentary stab of regret, but it passes quickly.

"I don't care about all that now. I got over you, Max. I don't want to talk or think about the past."

Still holding his cigarette, he uses his other hand to lift his glass again, this time taking a long, slow sip. I haven't yet touched mine.

We both watch each other, consumed with our own thoughts. Max is probably planning to make his demand, finding a way to phrase it, while I search for a way to get out of this mess.

"So how's your husband? I hope he's a good guy." A smile appears on his face, which is not warm, or smug. Just blank.

I place my drink on the table. "Why did you ask me here? It wasn't just to apologise, was it? Because you're six years too late."

He finishes the last of his wine and looks at me with the huge eyes I used to love. They are so dark his pupils are difficult to make out. "Who was that boy you were with in the park?"

I have been expecting this question, but my face starts to burn. I grab my glass and finally take a sip. A long one. Anything to draw out this moment because once I speak, nothing will be the same. "I told you. He's my stepson. Dillon." I put my glass back on the table with too much force, causing some of the wine to slosh over the rim. A red pool forms on the coffee table but Max doesn't seem to notice.

He leans back in his chair, speaking slowly. He is in control and we both know it. "Cut it out, Callie. I know he's not your stepson. Well, I know that now, and to be honest, I'm relieved."

When I frown at him, he quickly explains. "I saw you both. In your car. That Golf. I was on my way to meet Simon and I saw you. I saw everything, Callie. Do you still want to claim he's your stepson?"

So my instincts that night were correct. I feel as if I will suffocate if I don't get out of here soon. There is a balcony outside and I eye it with longing before turning back to Max. "You're sick. Watching like that." Attacking him is the only defence I have.

He thinks about this for a moment, putting out his cigarette. "It wasn't like that, Callie. You'd just told me he was your stepson so of course I wondered what the hell was going on. I can't help being curious. Hazard of my job, I'm afraid."

"What job? What are you talking about?" My hand is trembling and I want more wine but don't dare to reach for my glass.

Max refills his glass. "I'm an investigator with a law firm in the city. So there's no point lying about anything because I already know that boy is Rhys Marshall and he's seventeen. *Seventeen*, Callie. What the hell are you playing at?"

"How did you find out?" I cannot begin to imagine the lengths Max has gone to.

"It doesn't matter. Just talk to me, Callie. What have you got yourself into?"

It is almost a relief not to have to lie anymore. I am trapped in a corner once more and the lies just make this worse. So I tell Max everything, hoping that by the time I have finished he will have just the tiniest bit of empathy. He listens without interrupting and there is no hint of judgement on his face.

But what he says next is not what I expect to hear. "So are you taking any meds? What are you doing to help yourself?"

"What? I'm not...I don't –"

"That was always your excuse, Callie, wasn't it? You don't want to deal with the truth. You just brush it under the carpet and hope the pile won't trip you up." He chuckles. "Well, I guess it finally has. And now you're ruining your marriage."

There is nothing I can say because he is right. I reach for my wine and repeat that it's over with Rhys. "I made a mistake. I'm putting it right now."

He shakes his head. "So you think it's as simple as that, eh? We can do whatever we want in life as long as we're sorry afterwards?"

I shake my head. "No, that's not –"

228

"He's practically a kid, for fuck's sake. You took advantage of him."

"It wasn't like that. Rhys was the one who came after *me*. He knew exactly what he wanted."

"It doesn't matter. You should have known better. Of course he was going to be ruled by his dick. He's a teenage boy."

"He's eighteen in a couple of weeks." I don't know why I'm trying to make excuses for my behaviour when there is no justification for what I have done.

"You know, Callie, it sickened me when I saw you in your car. I couldn't sleep that night. Not just because of the boy, but because of you. Because I hadn't seen you for years, and when I spotted you in the park I wanted to believe you had sorted your life out. But this was worse than I could have imagined."

My glass is nearly empty and Max grabs the bottle from the table and tops it up. I don't know why he is doing this. Lecturing me when he should just get to the point. I know he wants something in return for keeping my secret, and I am just waiting for him to spell it out so I can release the anger that's built up inside me.

"Stop this," I say. "Just tell me what the hell you want! I know there's something. In return for your silence. So what the fuck do you want?" I can't stop my body trembling.

Max's eyes widen. He shakes his head before getting up and walking to the window. It almost reaches to the floor and even from my seat I can see what a beautiful view he has. "Please tell me you're not saying what I think you are."

I don't answer him. I want to hear how he worms his way out of this.

He turns round to face me and there is a visible change to his face. "You think I was going to force you to sleep with me to keep my mouth shut about this boy? Is that it?"

I turn away from him.

"Jesus…fuck…Callie, what the hell? You're so…deluded. You seriously think I would do that? After everything we went through together? Forget how it ended, it was still five years of our lives. Fuck!"

He walks back to his chair and sits on the arm, squashing his leather jacket as he does so. I have made another mistake. I am out of control and everything he has said is right. "The reason I wanted to see you is because I was worried about you. Because part of me will always care about you. You're being reckless and it's a downward spiral, Callie, if you don't get help. Surely you can see that? I want to help you. You can't go on like this. You say you're ending it with this boy, but what's next? Because there *will* be something, won't there? Unless you get help."

I am scarcely aware of what happens next. I am not present in my own body. The only thing I know is that I have to hurt Max. I pick up my glass and hurl it across the room, watching as it smacks against his face, falls and shatters on the wooden floor.

I scream as I leave. "I am *not* my Dad!"

CHAPTER TWENTY-FIVE

Somehow I manage to sleep the whole night, and when I wake up, for a few seconds I have freedom from my thoughts. But then I remember what I did to Max and my throat constricts. How did I get things so wrong? And how many other times have I done this without realising? Things have spiralled out of control just when I am meant to be getting a grip. My hands slip from whatever they touch. And I haven't even dealt with Rhys yet.

James' side of the bed is still warm and I roll over and breathe in his scent, letting it comfort me. I can't lose him; I won't let anyone destroy what we've got. We have been through too much for it to fall apart now.

It is eight o'clock, so he must have left for his photo shoot. He told me where it was when I got home last night but I was too shaken to take in what he was saying. Birmingham? Manchester? Either is just as likely or unlikely as the other. But his absence will give me a chance to speak to Rhys.

I shower quickly and run a comb through my hair. It doesn't need drying now that it is so short and today

I am grateful for the time it saves me. I text Rhys to ask if he can meet me this morning. His reply is immediate. *My house. Parents away. Come now if you can.* He has added two kisses to the end and I wonder how he can be so oblivious.

I drop Luke at Harry's on my way to Rhys' house and he barely says a word. I try to ask him about school but he tells me to mind my own business. I am almost tempted to record him on my phone to show James that his latest talk hasn't worked, but I won't burden him with that now. And Dillon and Luke need to believe I am not fighting anymore, then when they least expect it, I will catch them unawares.

I feel anxious walking up the path to Rhys' front door. What if his parents have come home unexpectedly and he hasn't had a chance to text me a warning? What if he has chosen not to? An excuse forms in my mind: I will tell them I am looking for Dillon and thought he'd be here. That will work. It is perfectly plausible. Feeling more confident now, I ring the bell and look around, grateful Rhys doesn't have a neighbour like Mrs Simmons.

Rhys answers the door and the first thing I notice is the familiar scent of his aftershave. It is overpowering as usual and I wonder if I should mention it to him. But I've got to get the more difficult matter out of the way, and after that it will no longer be my business how much he douses himself in aftershave. *He* will no longer be my business.

As soon as he closes the door behind us, he leans forward and tries to kiss me. Instinctively I move my

232

head aside and his lips only brush against my cheek. "Let's talk," I say. "We need to."

He ignores my snub. "I know. I can't believe your ex. I've made you some coffee and it's still hot. It's in my room."

I should tell him I'd rather stay down here, but there will be enough bad news in a moment. I can at least allow him this much. So I follow him upstairs, all the time wondering how I've come to feel so differently about him in the space of just a couple of days.

It's because of James. He is the only one you can love. And you can't even get that right.

"Where are your parents?" I ask, watching his t-shirt crinkle as he walks up the stairs two at a time.

"They've gone to see my nan and grandpa. I was supposed to go with them but I got your text so told them I wasn't feeling well." More lies. I just want this to stop.

"You should have gone. Where do they live?"

"Not too far. Kent."

I make a quick calculation. If anything happens and his parents decide to come back early, they will need at least an hour. Even so, I need to make this quick, I can't take the chance of being found here, especially when I am putting an end to this today.

Once we're in Rhys' bedroom, he hands me a mug of coffee. It is lukewarm and tastes bitter but I don't want to offend him so force myself to drink it.

"So what did he say? Tell me," Rhys says, sitting on the bed and patting the space next to him. "Come and sit." He thinks I am here to talk about Max. How is this possible? A few days ago I couldn't keep away from him so how has he not noticed my recent avoidance?

The images of shattered glass and Max's shocked expression form in my head but I push them aside. I consider telling Rhys that Max knows, that he saw us, but has promised not to say anything, but then I realise what a mistake this would be. Rhys will be pleased that someone has found out; it is what he wants. He wants us to be forced out into the open, so that James will leave me and I can be with him. This is what he believes will happen.

"It was fine," I say. "Max doesn't know anything. You were right. He was just messing around to get me to meet up with him." I avoid Rhys' stare by taking another sip of tepid coffee.

He frowns, even though this was his theory to begin with. "What? I don't get it."

"He just wanted to apologise for how things ended with us. That's all." It doesn't feel good lying to Rhys. Until now, he has been the one person I can be honest with.

The frown remains on his face and I wonder if he sees through my lie. "Okay," he says. "So we don't have to worry about him then?" He still doesn't understand.

I place my mug on the floor by the bed and turn to him. "Look, Rhys, we can't do this anymore. Me and you. It's not right. Sorry." I turn away from him again; I don't want to see the look on his face when my words sink in.

But he grabs my arm, forcing me to meet his stare. "No...you don't mean it. You're just worried. This whole Max thing has shaken you up. We'll be okay. I promise."

And then I have no choice but to tell him everything. How it's not about Max, it's about James, how I want my marriage to work. I *need* my marriage to work.

"But you don't love him. You can't do. Or you wouldn't have slept with me. And not just once, Callie…"

"It's all my fault, Rhys, I'm so sorry. I shouldn't have led you on. I'm completely in the wrong here, I know that. I really am s –"

"Don't say it!" He lifts his finger to my mouth. "I don't want you to be sorry. Not for what we've had. I'll never be sorry about it." His eyes are glassy as he speaks, and it is only now I realise that what I have done goes far beyond sleeping with someone too young. Our relationship has changed him, left a scar on his skin that won't easily be removed, and I am responsible.

When he reaches forward to hug me, I let him, although my arms only touch him lightly. I pat his back, not to patronise him but to show him it really is over, but he doesn't take the hint. Instead he tries to kiss me, more forcefully than he did at the front door a few minutes ago, his mouth frantically pushing against mine until I shove him away. "Stop. We can't do this anymore. I have to go."

Standing up, I knock over my half-empty mug of coffee in my haste to leave his bedroom, his house, his life. Fumbling in my bag for some tissues, I bend down to wipe up the liquid, which has already soaked into the beige carpet. "Let me clean it properly. Do you have anything up here I can use?"

"No, don't worry. Just leave it. I'll do it."

I'm about to protest but then I realise he needs me to go. He has to deal with this on his own, without me in sight. I take one last look around his room before I leave – the posters and mess that shriek of teenager – and shudder to think what I was playing at. Like Dad, I have become my own worst enemy.

Reaching the car, I pause and suck in deep, desperate gasps of air. I look up and in the sky are two huge clouds drifting towards each other, their ragged edges slotting together like pieces of a jigsaw. James and I are like these clouds. Pieces of a puzzle that only fit with each other. Nobody else matters; not Rhys, Lauren, Tabitha, Dillon, Luke or anyone else. I make a silent promise to James that I will fight for him and put right the disaster I have caused.

As I get in the car, a black Land Rover pulls into Rhys' drive and two people step out. Mr and Mrs Marshall. I have avoided them by only a few seconds, and only because I rushed out of the house when I did. When they walk round to the boot and start lifting out Sainsbury's bags loaded with groceries, I know without a doubt that this is not over.

The drive home is a blur and I am weighed down by not just my guilt, but the pressure of keeping things hidden. I don't feel good about any of my lies, but all I seem to do is add more. I thought Rhys reacted too calmly to my news. He knew his parents wouldn't be gone long. He wanted us to get caught. And that was before he even knew it was over.

I'm distracted from my thoughts when I pull up to the house and see Mrs Simmons sitting in her front garden. She's in a deck chair piled high with cushions and there is a book on her lap, but I'm sure she hasn't been reading it because her glasses are nowhere on her body.

"Just the person," she grunts, as I open the car door. She attempts to stand up. Her legs are shaky but she manages to pull herself up by leaning on the arms of the chair. "A word, please."

"I'm a bit busy, Mrs Simmons," I say, grabbing my bag from the passenger seat. "Can it wait?"

She tuts. "No, it cannot."

I walk across to her and attempt a smile. I know it won't win her over but it's harder for people to be angry when confronted with a smile. "Everything okay?"

"Why did you lie? What are you playing at?"

I swallow a lump in my throat, praying this is not about Rhys. I have no idea precisely what she is talking about but it is clear she has caught me out with something. "I'm sorry?"

"I've just been chatting to James' boy. Dillon. I thanked him for keeping an eye on the house for me but he had no idea what I was talking about. You better tell me what's going on, right now."

Even though she has caught me off-guard, I have become so used to lying that I instantly have an excuse ready. "Oh, I'm sorry, Mrs Simmons. Dillon was actually grounded that week. He's been playing up at school so his dad and I thought it best we didn't give him any extra responsibility. So I checked on the house for you myself. Sorry I didn't let you know." I offer her another smile, but she continues to frown at me, her lips a tight, thin line.

"That doesn't sound like Dillon. He's a good boy," she says. "Or at least he was."

I lose my composure. I have put up with Mrs Simmons' snide remarks for too long and I won't let her get away with this one. "How dare you judge me? You don't know the first thing about me."

For a second she seems taken aback that I am shouting, but her shock quickly fades. "I know what I saw when you hit poor Luke with your car. What those poor boys tell me. Dillon's told me how awful you are to them. How you just want them out of the way." She folds her arms, happy with her attack, ready for me to try and challenge her.

But it is pointless to argue. She will never take my word over the boys' and I don't need it getting back to James that we've argued. "Believe what you want," I say, forcing my voice to stay measured.

"I know what I saw," she repeats, turning away from me and picking up her book.

I am shaking when I get inside and I shut the door and lean against it, closing my eyes, unable to move. When I look up, Dillon is sitting on the stairs, watching me. My head tells me to greet him, to ignore whatever he has done, to keep making an effort for James. But this is not what I do. "What the hell do you think

238

you're doing? Telling Mrs Simmons all kinds of lies about me? You need to stop this now, Dillon." I try to keep my voice steady but I can't stop myself from shouting.

His eyes widen. "I haven't lied. Everything I said is true. And this just proves it. You're the liar. Why did you tell her we were looking after her house for her?"

"That was a misunderstanding and it's not what I'm talking about. You've been treating me like dirt since I married your dad and I've had enough, Dillon. All the nasty comments, the ignoring, the kicking. All of it has to stop. Now."

"Whatever. I think Dad should know about this." He stares straight at me and raises his eyebrows, standing up so he no longer has to look up at me. Now it is I looking up at him.

"Your dad told you to give me a chance, didn't he? He's spoken to you and Luke so many times. Why do you insist on hurting him like this?"

Dillon shakes his head. "I can't believe he married you. But he'll realise he's made a mistake. You'll never be our mum and I wish you'd fuck off."

He storms off and seconds later his bedroom door slams shut. Then his stereo blasts out some rock music. The song is familiar; I'm sure I've heard Rhys listening to it as well. But rather than being angry, I am grateful for the noise; it drowns out my heavy sobs as I collapse on the stairs and bury my head in my knees.

When I have calmed down, I shut myself in James' study with a cup of coffee and try to focus on studying, but it is difficult with Dillon's music blaring from the next room. I am surprised his eardrums haven't burst because even with the wall separating me from his speakers, the noise is making my ears ache. But he won't care; he is doing this only for my benefit.

Soon I have had enough and pound on his door, shouting at him to turn his music down. Instead the volume increases. Lifting my hand to bang again, I suddenly have second thoughts. There is no point making this worse. It won't matter to Dillon that he is in the wrong here. So I give up and take my books outside to the shed. My safe place.

Jazzy appears and pounces on my lap as soon as I sit on the floor. I still haven't had a chance to clean in here, and dust is already coating my skirt. I lift the cat and nuzzle his neck, letting his purr once again calm me down. Even out here I can hear the thump of Dillon's music, but at least it is less invasive.

I study for a couple of hours until it is time to collect Luke from Harry's. James' last text said he'd be home before five so at least I won't have long to be alone with the boys. It shouldn't be like this. I should be enjoying their company.

It is a relief not to hear from Rhys, and briefly I wonder how he is. Perhaps I have got him wrong after all and he didn't mean for his parents to find us. He seems to be handling this well, better than I expected he would, and I admire him for being dignified about it. But selfishly, I am pleased that perhaps he is one less thing I need to worry about. I think of the horseshoe pendant he got me and wonder if I should give it back. I have only worn it when we've been together, and it's still hidden in my old coat pocket. There is no way I can wear it now so it's pointless to hang onto it. But I won't initiate any contact with him; that would be a huge mistake.

When I leave the shed, Jazzy follows me, trying to rub against my leg as I walk. I look up at Dillon's window, somehow sensing he is there. And I am right. He sneers at me from behind the glass, behind the fog of his music, but I don't look away; I meet his stare all the way to the kitchen door.

I don't want to hate Dillon – he is James' son, and a part of the man I love – but right now I don't think I'd care if he disappeared forever. Trying to get through to him is like smashing my head against concrete.

I can take no more of it.

CHAPTER TWENTY-SIX

Now

"So you'd reached the end of your rope with Dillon." DS Connolly fixes his stare on me and it feels as if he can read every part of me, every flaw beneath the surface.

"Yes, I had. I felt like I was standing on a cliff and Dillon was pushing me closer to the edge every day."

It is hard to read the police officer's expression. I have dared to hope he will understand even a tiny bit of my story, but now I am convinced he can't. Or won't allow himself to.

"But you were desperate to be a mum to both the boys, weren't you, Callie?"

I nod, filing away thoughts of my silent baby for later. "That's all I wanted from the beginning. I think it would have been okay if it weren't for Dillon."

DC Barnes chimes in. "Exactly what do you mean by that?"

"Just that Luke was different when his brother wasn't around. Nicer. I think I could have connected with him, but Dillon was always there, influencing him. And Luke idolised his brother." My throat begins to dry up and I glance at the water dispenser in the corner of the room.

"Would you like some water?" DS Connolly is already standing up, grabbing my used polystyrene tea cup because there aren't any new ones in the room.

I down the whole cupful too quickly and it hurts my throat, but I ignore the pain and carry on. "Luke was always more easy-going than Dillon. He's happy just to play his computer games and see his friend, Harry. But Dillon was uptight, consumed by his vendetta against me. Not willing to give me a chance, not willing to trust his dad's judgement."

The officers turn to each other and I know what they're thinking. *James got it so wrong. Dillon was right all along.*

DC Barnes leans forward. "So Dillon was a threat to you? You held him responsible for the trouble with both boys? The trouble with your marriage? I think that's what you're saying, isn't it?" Her voice is louder than I've heard it, any pity she may have felt for me earlier has completely gone.

"No...Yes...I mean, not how you mean it. What I'm trying to say is *everyone* was a threat to the life I was trying to hold together."

"Including your neighbour, Mrs Simmons?"

"Yes. Especially her."

CHAPTER TWENTY-SEVEN

When James got home last night, Dillon didn't mention Mrs Simmons or our argument and James had already left by the time he emerged from his bedroom this morning, but that doesn't mean he'll keep it to himself forever. In fact, I think he enjoys flaunting the uncertainty, making me wonder when he will speak up. He knows this will get to me more. And it works. I am unable to relax, now more than ever, because there is always something or someone I need to watch out for. I know I will burn out if I keep this up – I am not sleeping and barely eating – but I have little choice.

I am more fearful than ever of losing James. This is why I cling on so hard, why I continue to fight when everything is slipping away. I cannot lose him. Is this how Dad felt about Mum? Did he even try to fight for her? In the end he lost her anyway. To his sickness. That's what it is. To say "illness" is to sugar-coat it. His sickness began as an infection, lurking just beneath the surface, unknown until it decided to show its face. And by that time it was too late because no one had seen it coming. Will this be my fate too?

After breakfast I visit Dad but he is not having a good day. He sits in his armchair, festering in the same clothes he was wearing when I last visited, and asks where my friend is. He forgets my birthday. He forgets what day of the week it is. But he remembers Rhys. When I tell him Rhys is busy today, that he has studying to do, Dad accuses me of lying and starts yelling that they've taken him away from us. Then he smashes up all the crockery in his kitchen, throwing open cupboard doors to see what else he can find to hurl at the walls.

Almost an hour passes before I can calm him down, and even then he is still on edge, his eyes wide and alert. "I can smell burning," he says. "In the bedroom. Check it, quick!"

I go through the motions of walking to the bedroom, opening the door, inhaling deeply and reporting back to him that it's a false alarm. But this doesn't stop him demanding it three more times.

Making the excuse that I need to use the bathroom, I check the cabinet to make sure Dad's taking his pills. The packet is half-empty and I remind myself of Jenny's promise to make sure he takes them in front of her.

When he finally falls asleep in his chair, I clean up the mess in the kitchen and drive to Argos to replace his crockery. I choose a navy blue set of mugs, plates and bowls, because somehow the colour feels right for him: dark and calming. As I key in my credit card pin on the self-serve till, I wonder how long this set will last.

Back at the flat, I make tea, and Dad doesn't notice that he's holding a new mug. It is too late for me to do any cleaning today; I have spent too much time pacifying him and replacing what he has broken. I will have to come back as soon as I can.

"Find that boy, Callie," he says, as I'm leaving. "Don't let them keep him."

Once I've closed the door, I stand outside his flat for a moment, listening for sounds from inside. I don't have the energy to deal with another episode but thankfully all is silent. It is hard to pull myself away and leave Dad like this and I almost turn around and go back, before I remember that sometimes it is better to leave him in peace.

Too shaken up by the outburst to drive home straightaway, I walk around the park, following the footsteps of where Rhys and I walked that night I brought him here. I love Dad, but I know now, more than ever, that I can't end up like him. He is a prisoner of his own mind. He has no more freedom than a criminal in a cell. In fact, he has less. Does he even realise it? If so, he never complains, never moans about his life.

There have been other times – although not quite as severe – when Dad has been out of control, but none since James and I have been married. On those occasions I could stay the night and watch over him, just to make sure. But I can't do that now. More pain caused by my lies. Calling Jenny, I fill her in on what's happened and ask if she can visit Dad later. Thankfully, she agrees.

I have only been home for ten minutes when someone raps on the door. I immediately assume it's a deliveryman, as they are the only people who don't seem to bother pressing the doorbell.

So when I open the door a fraction and see Rhys standing on the step, my stomach sinks. He is dressed in his school clothes and swings his rucksack in his hand.

Instinctively I start to close the door but he thrusts his arm out to stop me. "Please, Callie, can we talk? Just for a minute."

I release my hold on the door but don't open it any wider. "You shouldn't be here. Please, just go."

He shakes his head. "No. I'll sit out here until Dillon gets home if you don't let me in."

I think of Mrs Simmons, how she is probably watching us at this very second. If I let Rhys in at least I could say he needed to pick up something that he left here, but how could I explain him sitting outside on the doorstep for hours while I am inside? "Five minutes, Rhys. That's it, okay?"

He traipses in, his usual bounce conspicuously absent. I have done this to him. I lead him into the lounge rather than the kitchen, so I won't need to offer him a drink. I want him to leave as quickly as possible.

He plonks himself onto the sofa and rests his head in his hands. "I thought you might text me."

"Rhys, it's better this way. Better if we don't contact each other."

"I'm eighteen in two weeks."

"I know."

"Doesn't that make a difference? Any kind of difference?"

I move towards him but still don't sit down. "Look, Rhys, I've said all this before, it's not about your age. I love James. He's my husband."

He looks up finally. "But if you love him how could you sleep with me?" He has used this argument before and it highlights his naivety. But I don't have the time or energy to explain it to him. In time, after a few more girlfriends, he might come to realise how things can be this way.

It is tempting to tell him it was a mistake. Perhaps I have been too nice about the whole thing. It is true that sometimes cruelty is necessary in order to be kind. "Things aren't always black and white, Rhys. James and I were…having issues."

He looks up at me and his eyes are red but dry. Perhaps he is more angry than upset. "So you used me? Is that it?"

I wonder if this is true. "No. I really liked you. Like you. It just can't work. It's not right."

He doesn't say anything for a moment but shakes his head. "I love you, Callie. I can't just walk away and forget about us. How can you?"

I sit then, making sure there is space between us. "Because sometimes we have to do things that hurt. There's no future for us, Rhys, surely you can see that. I'm a married woman and the stepmother of your best friend. It's too complicated."

"Why do you even care about all that? Dillon hates you anyway. His feelings shouldn't matter."

I think about this for a moment and wonder why I do care. "*Your* feelings matter. Your friendship with him. Women…girls…should never come between you."

My words seem to make Rhys even more agitated. "Don't do this," he says. "Give us a chance. Please, Callie."

"I think you should go now. Just go." I stand up and head towards the living room door. Within seconds he is behind me, grabbing my arm and forcing me to face him.

"Callie, will you just meet up with me one more time? If I ever meant anything to you. Just once, that's all I'm asking. Kind of like a goodbye. Nothing has to happen, we can just talk." He is desperate now, trying everything he can to delay the end.

"I don't –"

"Please just think about it? That's all I'm asking."

And then I find myself nodding, even though I have no intention of meeting up with him. I only want him to leave.

"Thank you." He pulls me towards him and kisses the top of my head, stroking my hair and my cheek. "You're so beautiful," he says, leaning into my neck. I pull away before he has a chance to try anything else

And then I look up and my stomach sinks for the second time. Behind him, at the window, Mrs Simmons stares at us, her mouth hanging open.

"Fuck!" I run out to the hall, leaving Rhys with no explanation, and fling open the front door. Mrs Simmons has already gone. I rush down the path but there is no sign of her. For a second I wonder if I imagined seeing her – isn't this what happens to Dad? – because it seems impossible she could have got back inside her house so quickly. But then I hear her front door click. This is real. And now I have an even bigger problem.

Rhys joins me on the path but I push him back inside. "Callie? What's going on? What's wrong?"

I can barely speak and my whole body is shaking. "My neighbour…Mrs Simmons…she saw us through the window. She was looking right at us!"

He frowns. "What? But I didn't see anyone."

"Rhys, I'm not making this up for the hell of it! She was right there at the window. She saw us! You had your back to her."

"That's so weird, why would she do that? But we weren't doing anything."

"You were hugging me! And from that angle it could have looked like more. Just you being here is bad enough! Don't you get it? She already hates me."

"Well, shouldn't you find out if she did see anything before you panic?" Rhys says. Only a few seconds ago he was the one in a state, but now it is me who needs calming down. Like Dad. And as I look at him, at the way he manages to remain so relaxed, I know I am on my own with this.

"I have to go and talk to her. Now. You need to go." Back in the hall, I fling open the front door again.

Rhys follows me, lifting his rucksack onto his back. "Callie, you'll still meet up with me, won't you? Like you promised?"

"Just go," I say, forcing him outside. "Quick." I haven't got the space in my head to deal with this right now.

"Let me know what she says," he calls as he heads off. Now I am left to clear up this mess, and I have no idea how I will do it.

I check my watch. It's nearly half past three so I don't have long before Dillon and Luke are due home. I grab my keys from the phone table and head next door. Rather than stepping over the flowerbed separating our two gardens, I use the path, just in case she is watching. There is already enough for her to accuse me of so I won't let ruining her roses be one more thing.

Rapping on the door, I take a deep breath and wait to see the shape of her head through the glass. Seconds pass. I knock again. Minutes. But still no sign of her. Knocking yet again, I turn to look at the street. All is quiet; not many people on our road are home at this time of day.

"What do you want? Go away!" I spin around and there she is, concealed behind her half-closed door, shouting.

"Please, Mrs Simmons, can we talk for a minute?" My words echo Rhys' earlier; now it is my turn to beg.

"I've got nothing to say to you. I'll be talking to James as soon as he gets home." She closes the door but I pound on it. I am desperate now.

"Please. Just for one minute. Let me explain. Please, Mrs Simmons. The boys will be home soon." I don't know why I say this. Perhaps I am trying to appeal to her humane side; surely she won't want Dillon and Luke to come home to find me banging on her door.

It works. She slowly opens the door, her head peering around the narrow crack. "You are a worse person than I imagined. I just don't know what to say to you." There is disgust in her eyes.

"Can I come inside for a minute? Or you come next door? I can explain everything."

She doesn't move and for a moment I think she will slam the door in my face, just like I tried to do to Rhys earlier. Like I should have done. But then she opens it wider. "I know what I saw."

Anger wells inside me; she shouldn't have been standing in my garden, staring through my window, invading my privacy. *You nosy, senile bitch. Always interfering.* The words nearly escape before I remind myself it's better to try and put this right peacefully.

I edge forward. "No, you've got it all wrong," I say.

She turns around and I waste no time stepping into the hall and closing her door behind me. It would not be good for anyone else to hear this conversation. Mrs Simmons shuffles into the kitchen and I follow her, grateful she isn't screaming at me to leave.

Without inviting me to sit down, she eases herself into a chair and rests an elbow on the table, shaking her head. She can barely look at me. Being here reminds me

252

of Rhys but I try to shake off the memory of what we did in this house.

I am about to deliver my latest lie but Mrs Simmons speaks first. "You're disgusting. That was a *boy*. I'm calling the police."

I try to stay calm. "Mrs Simmons, that was Dillon's friend, Rhys. You must have seen him around?" She doesn't say anything so I continue. "He's eighteen, by the way. He just came over to wait for Dillon, but then he got upset – something about his parents – and had to leave."

"Stop!" Her voice is a shriek and takes me by surprise. "Just don't say another word." Her mouth begins to tremble and despite how much I detest her, I actually feel sorry for her. She won't be able to express half the anger she feels because it will take too much of her energy. "I saw you. You were kissing. I saw clearly. Don't try and lie. Like you lied about hitting Luke with the car. You're..." She gasps for breath and I can see she is trembling.

"Mrs Simmons, please calm down. Don't get worked up, it's not good for –"

"Don't you dare pretend you care about my wellbeing. You only care about yourself. I don't want you in my house!" She tries to push herself up but her arms, weak from shaking, can't support her weight and she drops back onto the chair.

I watch her for a moment, a jumble of thoughts whirring through my head. This was inevitable, wasn't it? I had to get caught eventually. The irony is that things with Rhys are over and nothing was going on when she found us. And looking at her now, how much frailer she seems to have become in the last few minutes, I feel as if I will suffocate. And then I am crying. Not out of sympathy, or to manipulate her, but because it is all too much. My chest heaves and I can't control the flood, but neither can I look at her. She will only tell me my tears aren't real.

She stays silent, her breathing slower now, as if her anxiety has transferred directly to me, and lets me cry for what seems like ages. And finally, when I am drained, she opens her mouth to speak.

"What have you done?" she says. Her voice is not angry, but wary.

I give no thought to what I say next. I have no control. The words want to come out, to release themselves, and so I let them. I am numb again, living in the second, much as I was during every moment with Rhys.

"You've been right about me all along. I'm a terrible mother. I don't deserve James or the boys."

When I look up I expect to see satisfaction on her face. Pleasure that she has won. But there is only disappointment. And then something else. Hatred.

"I have no words for what you are," she says, her voice stronger now. "All I know is this. Out of respect for James, I'm giving you until tomorrow evening to tell him everything or I'll do it myself. And either way, I think we both know what that means for your marriage. Now get out of my house or I will call the police."

CHAPTER TWENTY-EIGHT

It is three a.m. and once again I haven't slept. Beside me, James mumbles something indecipherable in his sleep. My mind replays everything that happened yesterday, repeating the events over and over. How I was walking down Mrs Simmons' front path when the boys suddenly appeared. How Dillon eyed me suspiciously but didn't say a word. And how I sat down to a late dinner with James and kept my mouth shut. There was no way I could utter those words of betrayal. The act was bad enough, but speaking it out loud is unthinkable.

There is always another way.

I receive a text from Rhys – he too is clearly suffering from insomnia – and I have no choice but to reply. I need him on my side to back up my story that Mrs Simmons has got it wrong. If it comes to that.

He asks me what she said and I reply briefly. *It's fine. I convinced her there was nothing going on.* He questions me more after this but I ignore his pleas for answers, hoping he'll assume I have fallen asleep.

It is muggy in our bedroom tonight, despite the open window, and I pull the duvet lower so that it only covers my knees, but it makes no difference. I will not sleep tonight. Three a.m. is a strange hour. A dead hour. It is neither last night nor this morning, just a no-man's land of loneliness.

This time is also a devil's playground for the mind and as I lie here on my side, facing away from my husband, I am forced to think of Max. What would I be doing now if we had stayed together? If we hadn't lost the baby? If he hadn't left me? Would I be better off? Or would I still have made mistakes?

It was inevitable that somewhere along the line I would fall. Mum didn't change Dad and neither did having a daughter. He is who he was meant to be. And so am I.

At six o'clock, I go downstairs and make a cup of coffee. I can't remember a time when I have been up before James and I hope he doesn't dwell on what it means. I will just say I needed to study.

Jazzy's face appears at the kitchen door, peering in at me, just like Mrs Simmons did yesterday. I unlock the door and go to the shed to feed him. It is already warm out here, too warm for June. It is making headlines on the news, this unexpected heat wave, but I wonder why the weather matters to anyone. Don't people realise what's truly important?

Instinctively I look up at Dillon's window as I walk back to the house, but his curtains remain closed. He is having no trouble sleeping.

I'm on my third cup of coffee by the time James comes down for breakfast, already dressed for work. "You're up early. Are you okay?"

I try to reassure him and offer a smile. "Just anxious about my next assignment. It's due in a week and I haven't even started it yet."

James smiles. "You'll do it. You always do."

We sit together at the breakfast bar and look out into the garden. Jazzy is prancing around on the grass, swiping at insects, but James doesn't say a word about him. His top lip turns up slightly, though, so I am sure he is finding the cat amusing. He would let him in the house if I asked him, but right now I can't bring myself to ask for anything.

"Callie?" he says, turning to me.

"Yeah?"

He pauses for a moment. "You'll do well on your assignment. I'm sure you will."

I'm grateful for his encouragement but am sure this is not what he wanted to say.

"Right, I'll get going."

My whole body feels heavy as I walk James to the door and kiss him goodbye. I don't deserve him.

I have half an hour before it's time to wake the boys, too much time to sit and stew about Mrs Simmons. Nothing is the same now. I can play along as if it is, but my gut knows the truth. How long do I have before everything falls apart?

When James' key turns in the lock and he rushes back inside, I immediately fear the worst. "It's Mrs Simmons!" he says. "There's an ambulance outside her house. They said she collapsed yesterday and she's been lying there all night. She's had a nasty knock to her head. They think it happened as she fell."

"Is…is she okay?"

"They're not sure. That's all they told me. I feel awful. I should have looked in on her more often, even if she's a bit difficult. I better wake the boys and tell them what's happened – I don't want them to see the ambulance and panic. You know how fond of her they are."

He rushes upstairs and I am left to ponder his words. I should feel something at this moment. Sadness? Guilt? But then I picture Mrs Simmons' face as she threatened me, the pure hatred in her eyes, and I am only relieved. This has bought me some more time. It is a godsend.

Footsteps pound on the floor upstairs as the boys wake up and no doubt rush to the window to see what's going on. I go into the kitchen; I don't want to hear their displays of sorrow. I should feel guilty for feeling this way, but I don't. Mrs Simmons will not die. She will be back home, causing me more trouble soon enough.

I open the back door and step out onto the patio so that their voices are mumbles. Then James pops his head into the kitchen and says he's off, leaving me alone with the boys.

There is some bread in the cupboard so I toast a few slices and lay out butter, marmite and jam. As usual, I get no thanks, and the boys ignore me as they discuss Mrs Simmons.

"She won't die, will she?" Luke says.

Dillon pats his brother's arm and butters a slice of toast for him. "No, I'm sure she'll be fine. They'll look after her in hospital."

Luke seems appeased by this and I feel both sad and angry that I am not the one delivering words of comfort.

"What were you doing there yesterday?" Dillon says. At first I don't think he is speaking to me – he hasn't so far this morning – and it is only when the room falls silent that I turn and see them both staring at me.

My heart pounds so heavily I am sure they can hear it. "I just popped over to check she was okay." I turn away, not wanting to scrutinise their faces to see if they believe me or not.

"But she hates you!" Luke blurts out.

I open my mouth to respond but quickly close it again. There is nothing I can say to this, and I am already buried under an avalanche of my own lies. "Your lunches are in the fridge," I say, before walking out of the kitchen.

As soon as the boys leave for school, I hunt around in James' study for Mrs Simmons' son's number. I know he has it, but the chances are it's in his phone rather than scrawled on a piece of paper somewhere. I have to try, though. I have to find out how she is and if she has said anything. I can't even remember his name: Darren? Dominic? I will know it when I see it. But there is nothing. James is too organised to have scraps of paper lying around.

I pop next door to see if anyone happens to be at her house, my hand trembling as I ring the doorbell. But there is nobody home. The house is silent. Ominous.

My only other option is to call the hospital, but how would that look? I could say I'm a relative, but I'm sure James has mentioned before that her son is her only family. There aren't even any grandchildren. No, I will have to sit tight and wait for news from James. Whatever it will be. I go back inside and upstairs to the study again to try and make a start on my assignment.

At lunchtime Rhys texts again, asking how I am and when we can meet. I don't reply. And when he texts three more times, before school has even finished for the day, I delete them without reading a word.

My eyes open and I'm not sure what's woken me. I have fallen asleep on James' chair, my text book slumped on my lap. The sound of voices drifts up from downstairs and I grab my phone to check the time. Ten past four. That means the boys are home from school.

With the heaviness in my legs that seems to be a constant companion, I head downstairs to make my presence known, before they call James to tell him I'm not here. The last thing I expect to see when I walk in the kitchen is Rhys digging around in the fridge while Dillon leans against the counter.

"Oh, hi, Mrs Harwell," he says, beaming a smile only I can read. Dillon doesn't even glance at me. "Dillon invited me for dinner. That's okay, isn't it?"

I hesitate. "I, um...I'll need to check with James."

"Dad said it's fine," Dillon snarls, still not looking at me.

"I don't want to be any trouble," Rhys says.

"You're not." Dillon pours out a glass of apple juice and hands it to his friend.

"I'm afraid it won't be anything special," I say, avoiding Rhys' gaze.

"It never is," Dillon mumbles.

I ignore his comment and go outside to check on Jazzy. But as I walk off I can still hear their conversation. Dillon telling Rhys what's happened to Mrs Simmons, and adding, with a raised voice, that I was the last person to see her yesterday. He can't know this, of course. It's possible she had a visitor after I was there, but he won't care about this. He is too excited to suggest I am somehow guilty.

Once I'm outside, out of earshot, I call James to find out if he has heard anything. Tabitha answers but falls silent when she realises it's me, handing the phone to James without another word. I won't let her get to me. She is bitter and twisted because I have something she wants. For how much longer, though?

"Do you know how Mrs Simmons is?" I ask James as soon as he says hello.

"No. I spoke to her son this morning when I got to work but he didn't know much at that point."

"What's his name again?"

"Duncan. He's in Exeter and can't get down until late tonight. I said I'd go and see her for him this evening."

"I'll go. You've got enough to do. I can go after dinner." There is no way I can let James visit Mrs Simmons.

"Are you sure? That would really help. I've got so much work to do on this website. We need it to go live tomorrow."

I tell him it's no problem, that I'm happy to help, and can hardly bear to picture him nodding and smiling, thinking what a good wife I am.

"How are the boys?"

"They're…fine. Rhys is here. Did you say he could stay for dinner?"

"I don't remember Dillon asking, but I don't mind if it's okay with you?"

"It's fine," I say, glancing towards the house. Through the glass door, I see Dillon and Rhys guzzling their drinks, huddled together over the breakfast bar, conspiring. I say goodbye and feed Jazzy before I go back inside, sickened by the thought of sitting round the table with Rhys. And the visit I have to make to the hospital. It is hard to say which is worse.

Somehow at dinner I end up sitting next to him. He has nudged his chair as close as possible to mine and I am surprised nobody else seems to have noticed. James sits opposite me and devours his chicken, talking about Mrs Simmons in between mouthfuls. I can feel Rhys' eyes on me but I daren't look at him. I can tell he is bursting to talk to me alone. There are questions he will want to ask me, so I have to ensure he doesn't get the opportunity tonight. When his leg nudges mine under the table I still don't turn to him, but focus on forcing down my food quickly so I can get to the hospital.

When he's finished eating, James excuses himself and goes upstairs to work. Eager to spend some time on his computer, Luke follows him up, and I am left alone with Dillon and Rhys.

"I'll help you clear up, Mrs Harwell," Rhys says, and my chest tenses.

"Don't bother," Dillon says, before I can answer.

But Rhys insists, staying behind while Dillon slouches off, scowling.

I wait for a few moments before turning to him, my voice a whisper. "What are you doing? Just go upstairs with Dillon."

He shakes his head. "No, we need to talk. You've been ignoring my texts all day. You promised we could talk." His voice becomes louder. "And what happened to your neighbour?"

"How would I know? She's elderly, Rhys. She was fine when I left her."

"I'm not saying —"

"Shhhh! Keep your voice down."

"When are we meeting up? You promised." He reaches for my arm but I shake him off.

"Rhys, let this go. Forget about me. Move on." It is hard to keep whispering when I am telling him something so important. So final.

For a moment I think I may have got through to him. But then he speaks, not bothering to keep his voice down. "No, I won't do that. Not until you talk to me like you promised. You can't treat people like shit, Callie."

I pick up the casserole dish, needing both hands to lift it, and for a flicker of a second I picture smashing it across Rhys' face, wiping the smugness from it, destroying all the power he holds over me. But the thought is gone as quickly as it appeared and I load the dish in the dishwasher and close the door.

"Leave me alone, Rhys. Get over this and just stay away from me." I turn from him and walk away.

He remains silent until my hand reaches for the door handle but then he says, calmly and quietly, "You can't stop me coming here. Dillon's my best friend. I'll be here all the time, Callie. There's nothing you can do about that."

By the time I get to the hospital, visiting hours are over and the nurses won't let me see Mrs Simmons. They huddle around the desk and tell me that because I'm not family they can't make any allowances. "She wouldn't be able to talk to you anyway," one of them says, and I take comfort from this thought. It means she won't be able to carry out her threat.

I drive around for a while, hoping that by the time I get home Rhys will be gone. The problem with Mrs Simmons might be dealt with for now but I still have Rhys to worry about. And the boys. And Tabitha will always be lurking in the background, ready to take my place. I feel as if I am in a maze, with no idea where the exit is.

My phone beeps with a text message so I pull over to check it. Not Rhys this time, but James asking when I will be back.

The house is dark and silent when I get home and I have no idea if Rhys is inside. Upstairs, I see light coming from under James' study door, but it is closed so I leave him to his work.

When I climb into bed, my phone beeps again and this time it is Rhys. *Meet me at the end of your road at 1.a.m. Please.* I delete it and roll over, hoping I will sleep right through until morning.

CHAPTER TWENTY-NINE

Over the next week, Rhys' visits to the house become almost a daily occurrence. He doesn't speak to me in a way that might raise flags for anyone listening, but I feel the heavy weight of his stare whenever we are in the same room. His presence is like a noose around my neck, which can be pulled tight at any moment.

I have come to realise that Rhys is a far greater threat than Mrs Simmons, lying in her hospital bed. At least her claims, if she ever makes them, can be dismissed as the delusional ramblings of an elderly woman in a bad state of health. But when Rhys chooses to expose what we have done, everyone will listen. There will be little doubt as to the truth of his words. I am sure he will even be able to produce proof if necessary, describing things about my body only James would know.

It is hard to make the most of time spent alone with James when the foundations of our marriage are about to crumble around me, and although I blame myself for starting something with Rhys, he is now responsible for not walking away and accepting it for what it was.

On Tuesday I arrive home from a tutorial session in the West End, fully prepared to find Rhys in the kitchen. Or living room. Or wherever he has decided to make himself at home today. But I am greeted by silence. I know Luke has gone to Harry's after school but James hasn't said anything about Dillon not coming home.

There are no shoes or bags sprawled under the coat rack so, deciding nobody is home, I slip off my shoes. I will have a soak in the bath before anyone gets home, anything to try and scrub away the stress of the last few weeks. It hasn't helped that my tutor is worried I am falling behind. Ian is a tolerant man but his frustration at my lack of progress was palpable today. He smiled and nodded when I assured him I would catch up, but like everyone else, I am sure he has written me off. For a moment, as we stood outside the lecture room, everyone brushing past us in their rush to get home, I thought he was going to ask me if everything was okay. But he didn't, and this is probably for the best.

When I pass Dillon's room I hear a thud, followed by silence. I freeze. He can't be home because he never takes his shoes or bag upstairs; there is always some evidence of the boys downstairs. Then I hear giggling. A female voice. And then another thud. I throw open his door, having no idea what I will face on the other side.

I stare at Dillon and Esme, sprawled on the bed, both of them naked. Esme's legs are wrapped around

Dillon but the second they notice me, Dillon scrambles to pull the duvet over them. Their limbs are splayed everywhere and I should turn away and give them a moment, but I am too stunned to move. Disentangling herself from Dillon, Esme lets out a scream, as if I am an intruder in their home. I do turn away then, rushing from the room without a word.

In the kitchen, I sit at the table, listening to the whispers in the hallway. The front door opens and there is more talk, louder this time but not loud enough for me to hear, until finally the door clicks closed again. All of this gives me time to think about what I will say to Dillon. I am furious with him, of course, but without realising it, he has given me the upper hand. I now have something to hold over him, something that might put a stop to his behaviour towards me. I can't help but smile.

I already know, without asking, what James would say if he had been the one to find them. Easy-going as he usually is, he would not take an offence like this lightly. Dillon and Esme are both underage. This is his house and they have disrespected it and him. Dillon would get a lengthy lecture and probably be grounded for weeks, but that would be nothing compared to the shame and embarrassment of knowing the image of him and Esme would be permanently etched on his father's brain. Their relationship would be irrevocably altered.

Staring out into the garden, I realise I haven't seen Jazzy all day. He wasn't there when I fed him this morning and there is no sign of him now. But I am not

268

too worried; I have heard that male cats often wander off.

The kitchen door opens and Dillon peers in. He stands there for a moment but doesn't come in. Perhaps he is waiting to hear what I will say before he decides what to do. I stay silent and watch him. Not knowing what to expect will freak him out.

Soon enough he tentatively steps forward, sheepishly staring at the floor as he plods in with no shoes or socks. His t-shirt is inside out and I almost laugh. This is the first time he has willingly come to speak to me. He stands in the middle of the room, still keeping his usual distance between us, but looks up slightly. "Please don't tell Dad."

That is it. Four words. That is all he can be bothered to offer. "So now you want a favour? You want me to help you out? Is that right?"

His eyes widen. His nod is slow and cautious.

"After the way you've treated me?"

"He'll hate me. He'll be disappointed and say I've let him down." He turns his stare from me and once more gazes at the floor.

"Yeah, he will, won't he? Maybe he'll finally see the real Dillon." I know I shouldn't be talking to him like this; he is only fifteen, after all, but the more submissive he is, the greater my urge to continue. This is my chance to end this feud, or whatever it is.

But then something changes, I can see it on his face before he speaks. His body straightens. "D'you know what? Fuck you! Tell him if you want, I'll just say it's lies like everything else that comes out of your mouth.

Esme will back me up. She wasn't even here today." His mouth twists into a gloating smile, and I am right back to square one.

I can't let him see he is regaining control. "Okay, you do that. Tell him. He'll be home at six."

"You're such a bitch, I hate you! I wish you were dead!" Dillon screams his words at me then turns to leave. When he reaches the kitchen door he turns back, suddenly calm again. "By the way, good luck finding that manky cat."

As soon as the door closes I rush outside to the shed, feeling the heavy weight of horror and emptiness, praying he was just trying to hurt me. I search the garden but there is no sign of Jazzy. His food and water bowls remain untouched.

I rush to the front of the house and walk up and down the street, looking in gardens as I call Jazzy's name. He is nowhere to be seen. I try to convince myself that Dillon wouldn't hurt him, but if his hatred towards me is this strong then how can I be sure? Either way, Jazzy has gone and Dillon is responsible. I picture the helpless creature letting Dillon pick him up, purring at the attention, an innocent party in all this, and my sadness turns to rage. He has crossed a line.

I storm back inside and run upstairs, screaming Dillon's name. Without waiting for an invitation, I throw open his door.

Hours later, I am sitting at the computer, immersed in my assignment, when James gets home. All around me the house is quiet and I have managed to make a good start on it.

James comes into the study and kisses my cheek. "You look busy," he says. "How's it going?"

"Not bad," I lie, trying not to think about Jazzy. "How was work?"

He takes out his laptop and puts it on the desk. "Good. Tabby…" he trails off, remembering that I know. "Never mind. Where's Dillon?"

I look up. "He went out a couple of hours ago. Sorry, he didn't tell me where."

James rolls his eyes. "So things aren't any better? I'm getting sick of telling them."

"No, no, it's fine. I was just stuck up here. Maybe he didn't want to disturb me?"

"He's probably with Rhys. When he gets home I'll have to lecture him about making sure one of us knows where he's going."

It is strange to hear James say Rhys' name and I force down the lump in my throat to ask what he wants for dinner.

In the kitchen, I make spaghetti bolognese while James sits at the table with his laptop. "I'll make enough for Dillon," I say, "in case he hasn't eaten. And Luke too, he might still be hungry when he gets home later. Harry's mum is still dropping him back, isn't she?"

James nods, but he is distracted, engrossed in his project. "The website's doing well," he says. "We're getting a lot more online bookings." As I watch him I know that whatever I have to go through for him, whatever I have to do, is all worth it.

We talk over dinner as if we are catching up after an absence, filling each other in on all the small things that time – or life – has prevented us from discussing recently. But behind it all are the huge things I cannot say to my husband. The stack of lies that is as fragile as a house of cards. I push this to the side and focus on James. It is rare to get him alone so I am determined to make the most of this time. It is a venomous thought, but it occurs to me how different our lives would be if he didn't have children.

Even as we are enjoying each other's company, I notice James glancing at his watch and I know he is wondering where Dillon is and why he hasn't called. I can understand this. It is out of character for him not to let James know his whereabouts. I picture the shock on Dillon's face as I stormed into his room, but quickly force away the image.

"I'm going upstairs to do a bit more work," James announces, placing his knife and fork together. He has only eaten half the food on his plate. "If he's not back in an hour I'm making some calls."

I can't let James call Dillon's friends. Who knows what Rhys will say? And then there is Esme. If James speaks to her she will tell him I found them together, or at least that she was here. And then how will I explain why I didn't mention something so important? I will offer to make the calls myself.

Just after seven o'clock, Harry's mother drops Luke back. I wave to her from the door and beckon her over to see if she wants a cup of tea, but she gives a quick wave back and speeds off. Luke rushes upstairs and I hear him knock on Dillon's door. I will leave it for James to tell him what's going on.

I offer to call Dillon's friends and James hands me Rhys' number on a slip of paper. "It's his home number. I don't have his mobile. I don't know any of his other friends' numbers but Rhys should know them, shouldn't he?"

"I'll make the calls outside, I need some fresh air."

He thanks me and I am weighed down by his gratitude.

I take the phone into the back garden and dial Rhys' number, fully prepared for him to answer. But thankfully it is Mrs Marshall who picks up. I ask her if she's seen Dillon, my self-hatred increasing, and she immediately becomes alert, shouting out to Rhys, who she tells me is in his bedroom. As I expect, Rhys has not seen him. Mrs Marshall says she will get the numbers from some of their other friends and text them to me as soon as she can. Thanking her, I hang up quickly, knowing that the hole I have dug is too deep to clamber out of now.

Once I receive her text, I make some more calls, secretly grateful Esme doesn't pick up her phone, and report back to James that nobody has seen Dillon. He thanks me again for trying and checks his watch once more. "I'll just do a bit more work, and then...I don't know."

I hug him then, I can't bear to look at him, but I pull him close to my chest and offer him silent comfort.

I stare out at the garden, part of me expecting Jazzy to come creeping across the lawn at any moment. But I know he won't. So I stay down here to keep myself from telling James that Dillon is probably doing this on purpose. It is best if I don't say anything. Not about Jazzy, or my terrible fight with Dillon this afternoon. I don't want to think about any of that, so I bury my head in my textbook, scribbling down notes to add to my assignment.

I am still perched on a kitchen stool when James comes in. I offer to make coffee but he shakes his head. "I just called Emma," he says, "in case he decided to turn up there, but she hasn't heard from him either. And Tabby's still at the shop and said he hasn't been by there."

Glancing at the kitchen clock, I see it is nearly eight thirty. I can't help but think James is only worrying so early because he doesn't know his son. It would never cross his mind that Dillon could be punishing me. "Okay," I say. "Shall we go out and look for him? Drive around or something?"

But he isn't listening. "Callie, you saw him after school, didn't you? Did he say anything? Anything…unusual?"

I shake my head, nausea sweeping through me because I am lying again. And now I am getting worried.

Something registers on James' face and I'm sure it is mistrust. Is he thinking about the accident, about the time Luke was sick? Piecing things together that won't quite make sense? "Right. I'm calling the police." He goes out to the hall to grab the phone, leaving me feeling as if my legs will collapse beneath me.

I wait until he has finished talking then join him in the hall. "They're sending someone over," he says. "As soon as they can."

"I'll go out in the car," I offer, and James smiles and squeezes my arm. Once again, his gesture of gratitude is almost more than I can bear.

Driving around for over an hour, I am too numb and dazed to notice my surroundings. My lies and deceit are suffocating me and being out here is just another one of them. There is no way I can be at home when the police get there. I was the last person to see Dillon so they are bound to have questions for me, and how long before I trip myself up?

When I get back, it is nearly ten p.m. and James and Luke are huddled on the stairs. James looks up but I shake my head. Both of us know what this means. Luke's eyes are red and his face is flushed. I have never seen him look so helpless and I want to hug him and tell him I'm sorry for everything. But then he looks at me and his eyes narrow. "This is all your fault. He's gone because of you. Because you hate us!"

"Luke, enough," James says. "Just calm down. This has nothing to do with Callie and you know it. The police are looking for Dillon now, everything will be all right." He looks at me and I can tell from his glassy eyes that he doesn't believe his own words. "They've got all his details, Callie. We just have to wait now."

Without a word I escape to the kitchen and put the kettle on. I know cups of tea won't solve anything but I have to do something while the minutes tick away.

James joins me and paces around the room. "The police said he's low-risk. They'll talk to his friends and keep an eye out, but that's about all they can do at the moment. Can you believe that? He's a kid, for fuck's sake!"

I go to him and hold him against me, trying to keep his twitching body still. He wants to keep moving. "He'll turn up, James." It is a hopeless offering but what else can I say?

When the doorbell rings I freeze. It must be the police again. But then I hear Emma's voice, followed by Luke's, both quiet and deflated. James pulls free and goes to greet her. At first I don't follow, but fill another mug and take them out on a tray, with a Ribena for Luke.

"Hello, Emma. Thanks for coming," I say. I wonder if I sound like a robot or whether only I can tell my words are forced.

She gives a nod, but doesn't speak. I still haven't cleared things up with her about Natalie and put her straight about Dillon's lies, so I understand her wariness. Turning away from me, she pulls Luke into her huge body for a hug. He grips her tightly and even after everything I feel a pang of envy.

We all head into the living room. It is almost Luke's bedtime, and he has school tomorrow, but none of us mention this as we sit down.

"So who saw him last?" Emma asks, looking straight at me.

"Well, I didn't exactly see him. He came home from school and I was upstairs in the study. And then he left without a word."

She turns back to James. "Shall we go out and look? It just feels wrong, sitting here doing nothing."

James mulls this over. "Callie's already been but we could go again. As long as someone's here. Callie, would you stay here with Luke in case he comes home or the police come back?"

"No!" Luke says. "I'm coming with you."

James glances at his watch. "Well, okay."

Within minutes they are gone and I am wrapped in silence once again. But this time it is not peaceful.

I walk around the house aimlessly, wondering how I can fill this void. Somehow it is worse to be left alone with my thoughts than to put up with Emma's chilliness. I need to hear a friendly voice so I decide to call Bridgette. I don't want to use the home phone in case anyone tries to call, but when I look for my mobile it isn't in my bag, or in the kitchen, and I can't recall having it with me when I drove around earlier.

When I check upstairs, it is there in James' study, underneath my textbook. I scoop it up and notice I have four missed calls and five text messages. All from Rhys. Without checking them, I delete every one. What if James had found my phone up here? How would I explain these messages? But I can't think about Rhys right now. James and Emma will be back soon and I need to prove I am just as concerned as they are.

CHAPTER THIRTY

Dillon has been missing for five days. There is a strange atmosphere in the house now, as if it knows something isn't right, as if Luke and James' anguish has seeped into the walls. Everything I do feels wrong: eating, making a cup of tea, even having a shower each morning. James looks at me through narrowed eyes and I know what he is thinking. How can I do normal things when we don't know where Dillon is? When we may never see him again?

James does none of these things. When he is not out searching, he is holed up in his study, printing posters with Dillon's smiling face plastered all over them, or making desperate calls to the police for updates. Each time he speaks to them, they assure him that teenagers go missing all the time, and more often than not, turn up after a few days with humble apologies for their frantic parents. But no matter how many times he is told this, James remains fraught. He barely sleeps and all he eats is an occasional packet of crisps or the odd burger when he's out on one of his searches.

He calls Dillon's phone several times a day, even though it has been switched off since he went missing, but all he ever gets is his son's pre-recorded voice, the energy with which he speaks incongruous now.

Emma is here every day, offering her futile support. And so is Tabitha. I don't mind; James is in no state to concentrate on work or even call into the shop, so she has no choice but to come over to give him an update each evening. Of course she barely speaks to me, but this is not important.

I can no longer keep track of the flurry of visitors passing through the house: friends, neighbours, even strangers, all offering their support. It is hard to say whether James is grateful for, or annoyed by, their warm wishes as each time someone shakes his hand, his face is impassive. He won't speak about how he feels, but as long as he is doing something to help the search, he seems able to cope.

It is Sunday morning and already the phone is ringing constantly. As soon as one of us puts it down, the bleeping starts again. Always another well-wisher or, just now, the police. They still assure us he will turn up and that they are keeping up their questions and search. I tell James it is a good sign that they are not more concerned. It means they have found nothing to suggest harm has come to Dillon, so we should cling to this thought. When he shakes his head, it doesn't surprise me that he is not jumping to agree.

Esme turning up or calling is a worry, but I learn through Rhys' texts – most of which I ignore – that she is too worried to tell her father she was here that afternoon, for obvious reasons.

What does surprise me this morning is Luke. I have just come in from the garden – another pointless attempt to see if Dillon was lying about Jazzy – and he is standing in his pyjamas, clutching his Nintendo DS to his chest as if it is a security blanket. He is twelve but at this moment he could easily be eight years old.

He inches towards me, staring at the floor. "Callie? He'll come back, won't he? I've tried to talk to Dad but he's always busy. It's not the same without Dillon here. It's weird."

I fight back the urge to tell him it's much better without Dillon. I am a terrible person for thinking this, however fleeting the thought.

Luke plonks himself on a chair and looks up at me. He needs me; something I have been desperate for since I met the boys. For the first time, he is displaying trust in me. I'm shocked and pleased at the same time.

"It will all work out. He'll come back and things will be better, I promise." This is only half a lie, so I am able to smile at Luke as if I mean every word.

Mrs Simmons arrives home from hospital at midday. I watch from the downstairs window as Duncan pulls up in his BMW. I almost laugh at how strange it looks: an elderly woman hobbling out of such a flashy car, but then I remember her face when she threatened to tell James what she had seen. What I said to her. With all the worry over Dillon, I have almost forgotten about her, but now she is back, I need to speak to her.

While I am still standing at the window, Bridgette texts, asking if she can call me, and hearing the beep reminds me I haven't had a text from Rhys today. But I don't dare hope I have heard the last from him. He will not give up so easily. Perhaps he is just being considerate because Dillon is missing.

I type back *Yes, of course* and watch as it tells me my message has been delivered. Within seconds Bridgette is on the phone, apologising for not having called before now, for not having had time to meet up. "I've been so busy with work," she explains, "and I hate myself for neglecting you. Especially when you're dealing with all this."

I know the truth is that Aaron is consuming her time, not just work, but I don't say anything. She deserves happiness. I tell her it's fine and she asks if I can meet this evening for food. When I explain I need to be at home for James, she insists we can make it quick, and that we can plan a strategy for searching for Dillon. "That's doing something to help, at least, isn't it?" she says.

By the time we have made the arrangements and hung up, Duncan is already leaving, hurrying to his car and whizzing back to Exeter without a backward glance. Seeing this, I feel sorry for Mrs Simmons. He could at least have stayed for a bit longer and made sure she has settled in, but his quick exit leaves me the opportunity to go to her now and get this conversation over with.

There is no answer when I slip next door and press her doorbell. I wonder if she is asleep, resting after her ordeal in hospital. I leave it a few seconds and then head round to the back, every step I take reminding me of Rhys, making me shudder.

She is in her kitchen, sitting at the table with her back to the door. It is strange to see her in this position; she usually prefers to observe everything that is going on outside. I stop for a moment and take a deep breath. I have to be careful this time.

"Oh, it's you," she says, turning around when I rap on the door. I can hear her clearly because the window is open. "I'm not up to visitors."

"I just wanted to check you're okay. I saw Duncan leaving."

She shakes her head and I prepare myself for an attack, or maybe for her to shuffle off and leave me standing here. What I'm not prepared for is to watch her lift herself up, a grimace on her face as she does so, and hobble over to open the door. Without a word, she goes back to her chair and pulls the cup and saucer she has left on the table towards her.

I'm not sure whether she wants me to come in so I hover by the door. "Are you okay?"

She ignores my question. "Have they found him yet?" So she has already heard, probably from Duncan because I know James hasn't seen her yet.

"No. But we haven't given up hope." Why isn't she talking about seeing Rhys and me together? Perhaps her head trauma has caused her to forget what she saw; why else would she not mention it? But can I really be getting off so lightly?

"Poor boy. Poor James and Luke. When I think what they must be going through. I wouldn't be surprised if he's run away because of...trouble at home." She tries to slot her trembling fingers through the handle of her cup but it takes her a while and she emits a heavy sigh. So nothing has changed. She still hates me as much as she ever did.

"Can I get you anything or do anything? Anything at all?"

She snorts, lifting the cup to her thin, cracked lips. "No. Just tell James and Luke I'm thinking of them."

I tell her I will – ignoring her dig – and turn to leave.

"Oh, just one other thing." She shakes her head and breathes heavily. "I had a lot of time to think while I was in hospital. I don't like you. I never have. But I'm not going to be the one to rip James' life to shreds. You are responsible for that. We all get what we deserve in the end so I know you will. I don't want any part of your life. Don't come here again. If James sends you over, make an excuse."

Hearing this, I feel as if I have shrunk to the size of an ant. Without a word, I walk out, closing the door on Mrs Simmons, her words ringing loudly in my ears.

Tabitha is at the house again when I get back. I have only been out for a matter of minutes, yet here she is in the hall, her arms wrapped around James, his head nestled on her shoulder. They pull apart when I open the door, James rubbing at his eyes, Tabitha watching me with a smirk. Even with all James is going through, she misses no opportunity to try and rile me, but I don't take the bait.

"Hello, Tabitha," I say, in my sweetest voice. "It's nice to see you again." James' eyes widen for a second but then the familiar sadness wipes away his surprise.

"Where did you go?" he asks. He looks at me with hope in his eyes, as if I am about to tell him I have found Dillon.

"Just to check on Mrs Simmons." For once I am not lying, yet it feels as though I am.

"I was just making coffee. Do you want one?"

"No thanks. I'll just be upstairs." I daren't tell him I need to finish my assignment. It is one of the ordinary tasks he considers indulgent while his son is missing.

"Oh, do you mind if I pop out later to meet Bridgette quickly? She said she'd help me think of things we can do…you know…to find Dillon. But if you need me here then I won't go."

James smiles and squeezes my hand. "Tell her I said thanks."

Bridgette is already inside Café Rouge when I get here. She waves me over to her table and when I get to her, jumps up, almost suffocating me with her hug. "Your hair!" she says. "It looks great!" It must be two months since I've seen her, if it was before the haircut, and my hair, though still short, has grown a bit. She quickly tones down her excitement. "Any news?"

I sink into my seat, a foamy bench stretching across the whole back wall, and pull off my cardigan. "Nothing. It's been five days now."

"Fuck! Are you okay? I mean, I know you didn't get on, but still, this is horrible, isn't it?"

The waiter appears before I can answer and asks me what I'd like to drink, his accent revealing that he is Italian. I notice Bridgette already has a glass of wine so I ask for the same, grateful for a distraction from her question.

"So do you have any idea what's happened to him? Has he run away?"

"Bridgette, I just don't know." With my nail I scratch tiny circles into the table and avoid her gaze. "Do you mind if we talk about something else? How are things with Aaron?"

Her eyes light up when I ask this and her bright pink smile expands across her face. "Great. Really good. I like him a lot."

I smile and nod while she provides details of their relationship and I am pleased she has finally found someone she can stand still with. Yet at the same time it saddens me that Bridgette was once the person to whom I told everything. But there is no way I can tell her about Rhys and what a mess I am in. There are limits to what people will accept and I don't want to find out hers.

The waiter brings over my wine and asks if we are ready to order. As usual, I haven't even looked at the menu yet, so when Bridgette orders chicken, I once again ask for the same. I don't know what it comes with but I have no appetite so it makes little difference.

By the time our food arrives, she is eager to talk about Dillon again. I can feel myself shutting down, but

285

it would be unfair to ask her to change the subject again because it is such a big deal. She only wants to know if I'm okay. So I push food around my plate and endure her questions.

"So you were the last person to see him? That must be weird."

"Yeah. Well, I don't know. It depends where he went afterwards, I suppose." Do I sound guilty as I say this? Too defensive? As if I am trying too hard? "He could have gone anywhere. To a friend's house. Who knows?"

She digs her fork into a chunk of chicken. "But won't the police have spoken to them all? I would have thought that's the first thing they'd do."

"But we don't know everyone he was friendly with. At this point they'll only be able to talk to people his friends from school can name." I think of Rhys but push the thought away.

Still chewing, Bridgette shakes her head. "But do you think they're doing all they can? It's just it's been, what, five days? Shouldn't they be out there with search parties or whatever?"

"Bridgette, he's almost sixteen. They're not going to prioritise him like they would a small child. They probably think he's run away."

She mulls this over for a moment. "Do *you* think that?" There is something in her expression then. Mistrust?

"I don't know what to think."

"And he didn't say anything strange the last time you saw him?"

I roll my eyes. "Everything he said to me was strange, wasn't it?"

"I'm sorry. Enough of the questions. This must be hard for you and James, you know, with your...strained relationship."

We both focus once more on eating. My lies have created a wall between us, our friendship just another casualty of what I have done.

After our main course is finished, Bridgette orders dessert, but I opt only for a cappuccino. It is a bit easier now that she is talking about other things, but then she brings it up again. "Remember your ex, Max? He connected with me on LinkedIn and apparently he's an investigator now for a law firm. I wonder if he could help in any way? Or if he has any contacts?"

I am so shocked she is bringing up Max, when neither of us has mentioned him for years, that I almost can't swallow the cappuccino that's sitting in my mouth. There is no way I want Max to know about this. No way. "I doubt he can help. Or would want to." I leave it at that, hoping to prevent a detailed conversation about him.

"Perhaps you're right. Anyway, did Debbie tell you her news?"

I try to recall whether Debbie has said anything significant in her recent calls or texts but my mind is blank. "Um, what news?"

Bridgette's expression suddenly changes and she doesn't answer. "Oh...it's nothing."

"Come on, tell me."

"She and Mark are trying for a baby. They've decided it's the right time now that they're living together." She pauses. "Oh, Callie, I'm sorry, I shouldn't have brought it up. Especially not now with everything else you've got going on. Sorry if I've upset you."

"It's okay. Please don't worry," I say, my eyes filling with tears. "I don't want anyone walking on eggshells around me."

"I know, but it's still hard, isn't it?"

I nod, keeping to myself that not a single day goes by when I don't think of my baby. How I was nearly a mother to her, but couldn't protect her inside me, couldn't keep her alive. And how I've also failed Dillon and Luke. But Bridgette reaches for my hand and gives it a squeeze, as if she knows my thoughts.

"Shall we get the bill?" I say, before any more tears escape. "My treat." We have barely even discussed strategies for finding Dillon.

Outside we hug goodbye and Bridgette decides to get a taxi home. "I've got a headache all of a sudden," she says. "But listen, one of Aaron's friend's works for the police so I'll get him to have a word. See if there's anything else you could all be doing. Okay? But let me know what else I can do to help. Posters, you know. Anything you need me for."

I thank her, wondering if she is actually going to Aaron's place; I have never known her to get a taxi such a short distance before. But I don't question her. We each have our secrets.

Even though it is dark, I decide to walk home. It will help to clear my head, and delay the moment when I have to confront James' sadness again. Sadness that I am responsible for.

When I reach the corner of our road, I see someone walking towards me. I pay no attention until the figure gets closer and I realise who it is. Rhys. His hands are stuffed in his pockets and his hood is up but it is unmistakeably him.

"Callie," he says. "I've been waiting ages to see you. We need to talk."

At first I think this must be about Dillon. They have found him. But Rhys grabs my arm and pulls me from the middle of the pavement towards a bush, where we are only slightly hidden from passing cars.

"What are you doing here?" I don't know which will be worse: news of Dillon or Rhys being here just to see me.

"Why aren't you answering my calls, Callie? I've been going out of my mind. Worrying about you, worrying about Dillon."

"You shouldn't be thinking about me, Rhys. It's over. You know that."

He shakes his head. "You promised me we could talk. When? I need to talk to you." Part of me wants to scream at him that he should be thinking about Dillon at this moment and whatever has happened between us shouldn't matter anymore. But I stifle this thought. I don't want to talk about Dillon.

I look at my watch. It's nearly ten o'clock and James will be expecting me back. "Well, I'm here now. We can talk for a minute but then I have to get home."

Rhys shakes his head, drawing closer towards me. "No, not here. Not in the middle of the street. You owe me more than that, Callie."

I cringe when he says my name. He has no right now. "There's nothing to talk about. I won't change my mind. I wish you would get that through your head." I almost spit my words and Rhys looks taken aback. I have had all I can deal with from him; I just want him to leave me alone. He doesn't say anything so I carry on. "I'm going now. Don't come to the house again. James will let you know if we hear from Dillon. Okay?"

I turn my back to him and begin to walk off but he grabs my shoulder and forces me around. "I won't let this go. James should know the truth. You've lied to us all. I'm telling him everything."

CHAPTER THIRTY-ONE

Luke and I sit together in the living room. The television is on but neither of us is watching. My textbook is on my lap, open at the page I should be reading, and Luke plays half-heartedly on his Nintendo DS. Since Dillon went missing it has become his constant companion. And he even seeks out my company, just to fill the void his brother's absence has left. He is supposed to be at school today but claims to have a stomach ache so James has allowed him to stay at home. But both of us know the more likely truth: he is too distraught to drag himself there.

James is out searching again today while I look after Luke. He has urged me not to leave the house in case Dillon returns or there is news, making me promise that if I need anything I will call him so he can get it while he is out. If he does come home, I have strict orders to alert James the second he appears. Even after six days, his hope has not diminished.

I am relieved that James is out of the house. Since Rhys' threat last night I have been on edge, wondering when he will show his face here. At least he can't get to

James for now; he won't know his mobile number, and bumping into him is unlikely. Rhys should be at school today but he has the excuse of his best friend being missing to blag a day off.

"Can I have a drink, please?" Luke asks, clutching his stomach but not letting go of his DS. It is a pleasure to be asked so nicely; it's all I've wanted for nearly a year. To have a role in the boys' lives. I never expected to take Lauren's place, just to be given a chance to be there for them. Perhaps it is true that trauma brings people closer together. But it's a shame it's had to come at such a cost.

While I'm pouring a glass of apple juice, the home phone rings. I have brought it into the kitchen with me; since last night I have kept it by my side, telling James I am filtering calls for him, so he doesn't have to deal with all the questions and updates people are desperate for.

Even though I know there is every chance Rhys will be on the other end, I am still shocked when he begins speaking. He is obviously serious about carrying out his threat because he had no way to know I would answer.

"What are you doing?" I hiss, cutting him off midsentence. I haven't even heard what he's said. I glance at the kitchen door to make sure it's closed.

"You have to meet me, Callie. Tonight. We need to talk."

"We've been over this. There's nothing to –"

"This won't go away, Callie. *I* won't go away. In fact, I thought Dillon's dad would answer just now. I thought he'd be by the phone, waiting for news."

I have never heard Rhys speak like this before, calm and measured, as if he has clearly thought out what he is doing. Even last night his words were thrown at me in anger. This is worse. Anger can be calmed down, pacified. But this is final. I should meet him, put a stop to his obsessive behaviour for good. I can't live like this anymore. I can't live in fear of when he will appear and ruin everything I've worked so hard to keep hold of.

"Okay," I say.

The silence that follows is a measure of his shock. I have given in and perhaps he thinks if he can persuade me this far, I can be talked into more. But this is fine. I will let him believe it for now.

"I'll pick you up on the corner of your road at eight o'clock. Don't be late because I won't be able to hang around."

"It's okay, my parents are away. You can come to the house."

I remember them arriving home the last time I was there, how I missed them by seconds. There is no way I can risk Rhys arranging something else like that. And how can I trust him now that he knows it's over? In fact, meeting up tonight is starting to feel like a terrible idea, at least until I've had more time to figure it all out, make sure I've considered every scenario. This feels too rushed.

When I remind him what happened last time, insisting it's not a good idea to meet tonight, he gets defensive. "I didn't lie to you, Callie. They *were* meant to be going to my grandparents' but on the way there, Grandpa called to say Nana wasn't feeling too well. So they had to turn around. I didn't know!"

"Rhys, they'd been shopping. Stop lying."

"I'm not! They went on the way back, I swear."

I no longer know what to believe. For months my judgement has been unreliable and I can't afford to make another mistake. Perhaps Rhys has learnt to become dependent on lies, just as I am, from his time with me.

"Look, Callie," he says, when I don't reply. "I can prove it. Just call my mum and say you couldn't get hold of me and wanted to check if I've heard from Dillon. She'll understand. Then she'll tell you she's in Dubai with my dad. For his work. Go on, do it now."

It is a juvenile game to play but I agree to call Mrs Marshall. I do need to see him tonight and it will be safer if we are shut away in Rhys' house. In my car it's possible someone could see us together. "If you're telling the truth, I'll see you at eight," I say.

"Thanks," he says, the relief in his voice palpable. He must really believe he will win me over and things will resume between us. It is then I know for sure that meeting him tonight will not be the last time he demands something, or threatens me with exposure.

I make the call to Eva Marshall and I know before she picks up that Rhys was telling the truth; at least about her. The ringtone is different, each elongated beep single instead of double. And when she picks up I quickly learn that her husband is with her and they are in Dubai, not due back until tomorrow morning. I thank her and hang up. The brief call will cost a fortune, but at least now I can prepare myself for tonight without worrying about being caught.

Back in the living room, I give Luke his juice, relishing the thank you he gives me in a squeaky voice.

"Sorry I took so long, just had to answer the phone."

"It's okay," he says.

This is how it is supposed to be. This is what I have longed for since I married James. I know Luke has only just begun to warm towards me, but I won't let Rhys or anyone else ruin things.

I think of Dad, how, if he was having a good day, he would be proud of me sitting here with my stepson in comfortable silence. I wonder if I will ever be able to introduce everyone to him, to let him see that he is a grandfather. But then I remember Dad's recent outburst and know without doubt this is impossible. It would be too traumatic for him to suddenly learn I have a family. And not only that, he has met Rhys now, so how can I know he won't bring it up? Trying to convince Dad to keep a secret would be impossible.

It has been over a week since I have been to visit him – James has needed me here – and I can't see how I will be able to go any time soon. Thankfully, Jenny has agreed to visit him on extra days; I just hope Dad is okay with this. It's not just because Luke is home from school, but thinking of excuses to present to James is becoming difficult. I am his wife. Why would I leave his side when his son is missing? I can't even call Dad; having a phone only incites his paranoia.

When James gets home, Luke and I are eating lunch together in the kitchen. He is so distracted he doesn't notice the significance of what he is witnessing. I ask him if he wants a sandwich and he shakes his head. "No, got to get on with stuff." And as he walks out, Luke and I turn to each other, not saying a word but probably thinking the same thoughts.

I find him upstairs in his study, trawling the Internet, researching statistics on missing teenagers. When he looks up at me, his eyes are swollen and red. I sit down on the armchair by the window and lean forward so I can stroke his arm.

"Do you think we'll find him?" he asks.

There is only one answer I can give. "I think he'll turn up. I just don't know when."

James tries to smile. "I keep wondering what he's doing. I look at the clock and I think: what's Dillon doing at this very second? And then I wonder if he's even breathing."

I am surprised James says this. So far he hasn't allowed himself to believe something has happened to Dillon. "Don't think like that," I say, and I wonder if my words are more for my benefit than his.

"Thank you, Callie," he says, grabbing my hand. "For being here for me. Always."

My chest begins to feel heavy, a physical manifestation of the burden I am carrying. Of the lies I have been forced to deliver to my husband. "Don't thank me. I'm your wife. I love you." I can't look at him as I say this but at least the words are true.

"We'll get through this together, won't we?" he says, and I sink to the floor and crawl closer towards him, leaning my head against his knee.

"No matter what," I say.

The words stick in my throat.

Rhys answers the door within seconds, as if he has been hovering in his hallway, waiting to see me though the glass, or watching from a window like Mrs Simmons.

"I told you I wasn't lying about my parents being away," he says. He is dressed in jeans and a hooded sweatshirt with a designer logo emblazoned across it, and I wonder how I ever thought he looked older than his age. At this moment he looks every bit the teenager he is.

He tries to hug me but I pull away. He smells strongly of alcohol and the familiar overpowering scent of his aftershave, and it almost makes me retch. I have no inclination to warn him now how off-putting it is.

"But it's my birthday! You remembered, didn't you?"

"Yes. Where did you get alcohol?" I say, backing further away.

He smiles proudly. "It's my dad's. I took it from the cabinet. Well, I am eighteen now. I'm allowed to drink. Do you want some?"

I shake my head. "Rhys, I haven't come here to drink with you."

"How about coffee?"

"No, I'm fine."

He shrugs and flicks his hair out of his eyes. "Let's go in there." He points towards the living room and I am relieved he is not trying to get me upstairs today. I follow him in, watching his unsteady steps as he negotiates his way to the sofa. Clearly he isn't used to drinking. Flopping down, he tugs at the neck of his top and I see a bead of sweat trickle down his forehead. He looks me up and down. "Why are you wearing trainers? You never do."

I stare at my feet but don't say anything. He is right; I don't think I've ever worn these trainers before. I'm also wearing jogging bottoms that I've only ever worn around the house, and the oldest top I could find. "Look, you wanted to meet me tonight," I say, ignoring his question. "What's so urgent?"

He squeezes his eyes shut, then opens them again. "Why do you have to be such a bitch? I haven't done anything to you."

"Just forced me into coming here. It's practically blackmail. Can't you see that?"

Rhys shakes his head then leans back against the headrest. "Just sit down, will you?"

I sit at the far end of the couch. I never thought I would be here again and it's making me nervous. My head is pounding and my heart thuds in my chest. I am desperate for water but to ask Rhys to get me some will waste time I don't have.

"Do you remember our first time? In my bedroom? Don't tell me you don't think about it." He inches closer to me. His words sound false, as if he has memorised them from a film. This is not Rhys. At least not the Rhys I spent time with. I would never have labelled him desperate.

"It was a mistake. We were a mistake. Look, I've said all this before and nothing has changed. I love James." Saying his name gives me strength. I know that I can do whatever is necessary to end this now.

He looks away from me. "I just –"

"What, Rhys? Did you think I would come here to sleep with you? One last fuck, for old times' sake?"

He doesn't say anything.

"Or is it that you want me to keep sleeping with you to keep your mouth shut? Is that it?" I am echoing the incorrect suspicion I had about Max. But this time I'm sure I am right. Rage is boiling in me; I can no longer see any good in Rhys. Everything he did to help me in the past has been wiped out by the stranger before me.

"I'm not giving you up. I love you, Callie. Doesn't that mean anything to you? I don't care about uni or my music, or anything. I'd give it all up for you. To keep us together."

He is scaring me now, the words he is speaking still at odds with the Rhys I have known. What if he tells James? I can't let that happen. For a second I picture taking him for a drive. Perhaps he is too drunk or upset to think about putting on his seat belt. I imagine finding a long stretch of road, pressing my foot to the accelerator then slamming on the breaks until he smashes through the windscreen.

"Callie, I'm not a toy you can play with then throw away when you're bored." He stands up and walks over to a cabinet in the corner of the room, pulling out a bottle of gin and taking a long swig. The room has fallen so silent I can hear the glug of the liquid slipping down his throat. I should stop him, but I don't say a word. It will be easier this way.

"I need to use the bathroom," he says.

While he is gone I notice he has left his phone on the sofa. I don't know if he knows it is there or whether it fell out of his pocket, but either way it is good for me. I grab it and study the screen. It is a Blackberry, so I am not used to the menu and it takes me a while to find his text messages. All the time I listen for his footsteps on the stairs. When I find his inbox I notice he has hundreds of messages, going back weeks. I start at the beginning and delete every message I have sent him, removing any evidence of our communication. I do the same with his call log. Then I delete my name from his contacts.

When he comes back down he sits in the same place and notices his phone. Picking it up, he waves it at me, taunting me with his silent threat. "Is this really what you want?" he asks. "I just think you should be sure, because, you know, once I've done it there's no going back, is there?"

I edge closer towards him. "Please, Rhys, just think about this. What good would it do, telling James? It won't change anything with us. I still can't be with you."

He stares at me, his eyes narrowing. "You're such a fucking bitch, aren't you? You didn't need to say that." And then a smirk spreads across his face and he begins tapping something into his phone.

"What are you doing? I ask. "Stop it, Rhys, just give me the phone."

"You're really not going to change your mind, are you?" he asks, looking up at me.

I don't answer.

"Then I've got nothing to lose. I'm calling Dillon's dad. Telling him everything."

And that's when I lose it.

CHAPTER THIRTY-TWO

Now

DS Connolly stares at me, open-mouthed. I don't think he wanted to believe I am a monster. Up until now, I'm sure he has been hoping this has all been a mistake. Not even my disease can excuse this; after all, Dad is far worse than me and he has never come close to doing what I have done.

"I think we need to take a break," he says, finally averting his eyes. "Someone will take you to a cell until we're ready to resume."

I sit on the hard bed and, now that I'm alone, my thoughts crash around my head until I feel as if it will explode. I need to be calm, to accept my punishment, because nobody is to blame but me.

How ironic that in trying so hard to protect my marriage, I have now lost James for good. I long to see him, to touch his face and feel his hair between my fingers, but from now on I will have to make do with memories. It is for the best that he isn't here. There is no more left to say.

Hours pass like this until finally a uniformed officer comes to collect me. DS Connolly and DC Barnes are already in the room, fresh coffee in front of them. They don't offer me anything this time, but that's okay, I don't want kindness. That will only make this harder.

"So...what did you do when you left Rhys Marshall's home?" DS Connolly asks, all the warmth gone from his voice.

CHAPTER THIRTY-THREE

I rush out of Rhys' house, no longer caring if anyone sees me. The car seems too far away, as if I will never reach it. Everything is distorted, out of shape and unreal. What have I done? It is over. Now there will never be a future for James and me. I thought I was making things better but now they couldn't be worse. I need to get away from here, away from that house, so that I can think clearly.

In the car I lock the doors and turn the radio up as loud as I can stand it, just to drown out my thoughts. But of course it doesn't help. How can it?

Once more I end up at Wimbledon Common, only this time everything has changed. I turn off the engine and the lights and sit in silence, my fingers tapping the steering wheel, my whole body shaking. I have no choice but to think now. I need a plan.

I could go to Dad's. It's past nine o'clock and I doubt he's asleep, but what will his reaction be if I turn up so late? The chances are it won't be good, for either of us. I am alone. I have lost everyone and everything, and now it is only a matter of time.

There is no way I can turn up at Bridgette's. If she is at home it's likely Aaron will be with her and I haven't even met him. What would he think of her crazy friend turning up in such a state? They are still in the early stages of their relationship and I wouldn't want him to judge Bridgette by the company she keeps. Debbie and Mark are not an option either. James will think to look for me there and he will want answers. But how can I give him any when there is no chance he will ever understand what I have done?

That leaves only one other person.

He answers the door in his dressing gown, squinting into the darkness as if he cannot believe it is me standing here. At first he smiles but it quickly fades and I can only assume he is remembering what happened last time I was here. "Callie? What are you –"

I take a step forward. "Please, Max, can I come in?" I know without having a mirror what a state I must look: my eyes bloodshot, black mascara stains on my cheeks and my hair greasy and dishevelled.

He stands aside and lets me pass, checking outside before he closes the door. "Are you okay? What's going on, Callie? What's happened?"

I think of the last time I was here and a flood of shame rushes through me, adding to everything else I am weighed down by. He shouldn't let me in. He doesn't know what I'm capable of. Or maybe he does. He has seen glimpses of me, after all. All those years ago. A couple of weeks ago. I recall his words during our last conversation: *You don't want to deal with the truth.*

You brush it under the carpet and hope the pile won't trip you up. It is only now I realise Max knows me better than anyone else. And he was right.

"I…" Shaking my head, I burst into tears.

Max squeezes my arm. "It's okay. Whatever it is, we'll sort it out. I'll make us some tea and then you can talk to me, okay? Just take your time. You're safe here."

I wonder if that's true. What if Max calls someone? But no, just as he knows me, I know he wouldn't do that.

A nod is all I can manage in reply, but I hope he can see how grateful I am.

I sit on the sofa while he is in the kitchen, in exactly the same place I sat last time. It is surreal that I'm about to have a cup of tea when my world has shattered around me. I have shattered it. Now I know why James has been giving me looks of disbelief every time I do something normal. But this is worse.

By the time Max brings in our drinks, I have become numb and am no longer shaking. Perhaps it is a defence mechanism, to stop my mind twisting in on itself. I have become Dad. It was inevitable, wasn't it?

Max lights a cigarette and waits for me to speak, but now that I am here, I know I won't be able to say a word. I shake my head and he seems to realise what I mean. Perhaps that comes from spending so many years with someone.

He exhales and a cloud of smoke floats above him. "I know you don't want to talk but I'm guessing that pile under the carpet finally tripped you up?"

How does he make it sound so harmless? So innocent? This is more than just being tripped up. I take a sip of tea, knowing with certainty this is what it is like for Dad. Hearing people but not having the ability to answer them.

When I don't respond, he continues. "You know what upset me most about the other night? Not that you threw the glass. It's just a glass, after all, I don't care about that. It bothered me that you got me so wrong. But even more than that, I was powerless to help you. And you need help, Callie. Before…" He doesn't finish his sentence but stares at me. "Is this about that boy? Has someone else found out?"

I shouldn't have come here. Max can't help me. I believe he wants to, but what can he do? My phone rings in my pocket, piercing the silence, and Max's eyes drop to my jogging bottoms. "Don't you need to answer that?"

I pull it out and see James' name flash on the screen. Ignoring it, I place it on the arm of the sofa and wait for the noise to stop. After a moment it becomes easy to pretend I can't hear a thing.

Max watches me and bites his lip. The ash on his cigarette is building up and will surely topple to the carpet any moment, but he doesn't flick it. "Look, Callie, it might help to tell me what's going on."

My phone rings again and I don't even glance at it this time. My eyes are fixed on my tea. Max springs up and picks it up. "It's James. Your husband." He waves it in front of my face. Why aren't you answering? Has he…Does he know?"

I look at my watch. It is after ten p.m. "Probably by now," I say, still not looking at Max. This is the first sentence I have managed to string together since I arrived.

"Well, he obviously wants to talk to you. That's a good sign, isn't it?"

Of course Max will think that. I ignore his question again. It won't be long before he gets fed up and demands I leave. "Can I use your bathroom?"

He nods and I stand up. "Second door on the right."

As soon as I'm inside, I lock the door and bolt to the toilet, throwing up more violently than I would have thought possible. Afterwards I feel drained and my stomach aches with emptiness. But it is also a good feeling.

"Are you all right in there?" Max knocks on the door. "Your husband's called twice more. And texted."

I quickly rinse my mouth and go back to the living room. My phone is still on the arm of the sofa and Max is on his chair, lighting another cigarette.

Snatching it up, I open James' text message. I will have to face it sooner or later. The words are a blur at first but quickly come into focus.

Where are you? Dillon is back!

CHAPTER THIRTY-FOUR

He sits on the sofa, huddled in the corner. He looks smaller, thinner, like a helpless child in need of looking after, not a boy on the verge of manhood. His clothes are filthy and his hair is limp with grease. None of us can take our eyes off him.

Emma is here too and she fusses around, trying to force him to eat a sandwich I am guessing she has made. But it remains untouched on his plate.

He looks up at me, as if he is about to say something, but then bites his lip and remains silent.

James nods towards the door so I walk out and wait for him in the kitchen. "He's been sleeping rough. All this time." He tugs at his hair. "I can't believe what he's been through."

"Did he say where? Or why?"

He shakes his head. "No. Just that he needed to get away. From all of us. And that he's done a lot of thinking since he's been gone. He even said he threw his phone away so no one could find him."

I almost ask James to repeat these words. How is it possible that Dillon hasn't told him I was the one who drove him away? Why hasn't he repeated the horrific things I said to him, the truths that had been bubbling under my skin for too long?

James bangs his fist on the worktop. "I saw this programme once. A documentary. About runaways. It said they're never the same when they come back."

I rub his arm, trying to offer comfort, but I am expecting the house phone to ring any second. I can hear it in my head already, taunting me. Dillon appearing like this is a surprise, but I have bigger concerns. I rushed back here without thinking of the consequences. I should have stayed with Max. Nobody would have found me there. "It's okay now, isn't it? He's back. That's all that matters." This couldn't be further from the truth. James thinks we have got through the worst, but he has no idea our world is about to change.

"What do we do now?" he asks.

"We go back in there and we treat Dillon normally. Don't push him. He'll talk when he's ready."

We move towards the door but James stops and turns to me. "What if something happened to him? While he was out there?"

"Then he'll tell us when he can. Don't let that eat you up."

He nods. "You're right. Where were you, anyway? I've been trying to call you for ages."

"Just driving around. Looking for Dillon."

"What would I do without you?" he says, kissing my forehead.

Back in the living room, Luke is recounting something funny that happened to a teacher at their school last week, in an attempt to make his brother laugh. Dillon forces a smile, but I can tell he is only half-listening.

"You can sit next to me if you want," Luke says to me. Beside him Dillon frowns but stays silent. Luke shrugs at him, as if sending him a private message. Dillon will think it strange that in such a short time – although it would have felt like an eternity to him – things have changed so much. But he has nothing to worry about. This is only temporary.

"I'm glad you're home, Dillon," I say, sitting next to Luke.

He looks at me and forces out a thank you, his words barely audible.

Then Emma starts talking again, still encouraging him to eat the sandwich he doesn't want.

It's torture to sit here in fear, waiting and wondering when it will happen. But until Dillon decides he wants to go to bed, it is not possible for me to leave. After the developments with Luke, I have to be here for Dillon, showing him that I care, just in case the impossible happens and the phone doesn't ring.

But I don't have long to wait before Dillon says he's tired and stands up. Luke jumps up too and we all say goodnight, as if nothing has happened, as if he hasn't been missing for days and is now refusing to talk about it.

When the boys have gone, an idea occurs to me. "Has anyone called the police? To tell them Dillon's back?"

"I didn't think of that," James says. "I was just so happy to see him. I'll do it now."

I jump up before anyone can object. "No, I'll do it. You stay here with Emma."

In the hallway, I grab the phone and take it to the kitchen. I'm put through to an officer called PC Emnett who says he's glad Dillon has turned up and he'll update their system. It is a strange name, I think. Emnett. But then, it is even stranger that I notice this, in the midst of everything that's happened. When I finish the call, I put the phone back in its charger and bend down to reach behind the phone table. Pulling out the cord, I shove it under the table so no one will notice it's not plugged in. At least for now I won't have to worry about the phone ringing. I can't stop anyone knocking on the door, but I can try to get to it first.

Somehow I manage to sleep for a few hours, but I wake to the sound of footsteps. It's not difficult to work out that it is Dillon, pacing up and down in his room, the floorboards creaking with every step he takes. Beside me, James doesn't wake; he is able to sleep deeply now that Dillon is back. How long will this last?

I think about going to check he is okay, but I can't be sure of the response I'll get. Just because Luke has warmed to me it doesn't mean his brother will do the same, especially as I am the reason he ran away. But he didn't seem angry with me tonight. Something, yes, but not angry. I almost wish he *had* shouted at me or told

James about our argument. Maybe he will. It will make things so much easier if he still hates me.

Eventually silence fills the house again and I drift back to sleep. But my dreams give me no relief.

The second time I wake, it is to the sound of James' mobile blaring out. It is barely six a.m. Within seconds he is awake and upright, speaking softly into the phone, and for a moment it feels as if my heart has stopped, until I realise the caller must be Tabitha.

"I don't know what to do," he says, gently nudging me.

I roll over to face him and ask him what he means.

"There's a photo shoot in Putney today. The freelancer had an emergency and can't make it and it's too short notice for Tabby to find someone else. I don't want to let these people down, but how can I leave Dillon?"

I squeeze his hand. "James, he'll understand. And he'll be okay now. He came back, didn't he?"

"I know." James lets out a heavy sigh. "But I don't think he should go to school. Would you –"

"I'll be here all day," I say. We both know what he means. Although if Dillon wants to leave again, I will hardly be able to stop him.

"Thanks. I could be out most of the day."

This is good. It buys me more time.

James gets up and pulls on a checked shirt. He showered before bed last night, for the first time since Dillon went missing. "I think Luke should go to school, though. He'll probably make a fuss but if he does, just call me and I'll speak to him."

Once he's gone, I head downstairs and plug in the phone. I could leave it unplugged, but isn't it better to know? And as long as James isn't here, there is still a chance I can control the situation. I am numb, unable to feel anything but the desperate need to protect my marriage. If there is any hope left at all.

When it's time to get him up, Luke groans himself awake but doesn't hurl insults or abuse at me. Even when I tell him Dillon will be staying at home today, he nods and doesn't grumble.

You don't deserve this, not now, after what you have done.

Dillon sleeps until after ten and I am sitting at the kitchen table when he comes downstairs, my course books spread out and my laptop in front of me. The new Word document I opened two hours ago is still blank and the cursor flashes at me, reminding me what a mess I have made of things.

It is obvious he hasn't showered yet; his hair is still greasy, his arms grubby, and I can smell him from across the room. "Can I have some toast?"

His eyes narrow, as if he is unsure how I will answer his question, and I remember the last time we were alone. How cruel my words were, cutting into him like knives. Perhaps he thinks I am still angry with him. "Course. Sit down. I'll make you some sweet tea, as well. It will be good for you."

He screws up his face but then shrugs and pulls out a chair. All the while I am getting his breakfast, he watches me through cautious eyes.

When I place a plate of buttered toast in front of him, he picks up a slice but doesn't eat it. And in that moment my heart aches for this boy I have spent so much time fighting and hating, and regret surges through me again, for what I have done to him and Luke, as well as James.

"I'm sorry...about your cat," he says, his eyes flicking to the table. "He's not...you know...I gave him to someone to look after. Esme's friend. He's okay." Dillon's words float around me and I breathe them in. Again, this is more than I deserve.

"Thank you for telling me. Look, Dillon, I'm sorry about our fight. About everything."

He doesn't say anything and doesn't look at me, making me wonder if I have pushed too hard. Perhaps to make amends is not what he wants at all, and I have misread everything. "Can I ask you something?"

Dillon shrugs again but remains silent.

"Did something...anything happen to you...you know, while you weren't here? I won't ask you for details. I just need to know you're okay."

The silence feels heavy and I am sure I can hear my heart thumping in my chest. Eventually he nods and stares straight at me. And then he begins to speak, the words pouring freely from his mouth. It is so strange to hear him talking so much that I almost don't recognise his voice. But I listen. I listen while he tells me how cold the nights got while he was sleeping under bridges and in doorways. How half the time he couldn't sleep for fear of other people, because there was always someone hovering around. People like him who didn't want to go home or who had no home. Or others, who he didn't want to wonder about. And how he cried himself to sleep each night but couldn't drag himself home.

"But why didn't you go to a friend's? Esme's? Anyone's?"

He bites his lip and stares at the table once more. "Because Dad would have found me straightaway. I wanted to punish you, make Dad blame you for driving me away. For making me suffer. So I figured it was worth it."

"It's okay," I say, grabbing his hand. It must have been exhausting for him to carry around so much hate. Hatred borne from nothing except grief: the unforgivable fact that I'm not Lauren.

Dillon flinches slightly but doesn't pull away. This is an unfamiliar feeling for both of us. He begins to recount more details and there are tears in my eyes as he speaks, but not in Dillon's. He remains impassive, putting in place the defence mechanism I am all too familiar with. And then he tells me what happened to him on his last night, and there are no words to describe how I feel hearing it. His voice becomes muffled through his sudden flood of tears, and my hand stiffens around his as I sit here, stunned, sicker than I have ever felt.

"Please don't tell Dad," he says. "Please don't."

An hour later, Dillon is asleep on the sofa. I sit by him on the floor, watching over him, even though it is too late to protect him. I have failed him as a mother. He, and everyone else, was right about me. He looks even younger with his eyes closed, and I wonder how I ever hated him so much. The phone rings but I don't rush to answer it. I have to think about Dillon. He is what matters now. Whoever is calling doesn't leave a message, and I let out a breath of relief. The time has not yet come.

Sometime later my mobile rings and that familiar feeling of dread cuts off my breath. But it is only Max, calling to see if I'm okay. I am touched by his concern, even if it is years too late. But I cannot blame him for any of this. It was never his job to save me from myself. I tell him I'm fine and I'll call him later, hanging up on his protests. There will be no later.

When Luke gets home from school he hurries to see his brother. Dillon is still in the living room, lying on the sofa, but is awake now, watching television. At least on the surface it appears he is watching; I doubt he is taking in anything he sees. I tell Luke to stay there while I prepare dinner.

Dillon sighs. "I'm not ill."

"Can we have pizza and chips, Callie?" Luke asks, his wide eyes pleading.

But this would mean a trip to the shop and I can't leave the house in case the phone rings. Unplugging it again is too risky. And what if the police pay a visit? There is no way I can let Dillon and Luke deal with that. No, I will have to stay here.

"How about a Chinese takeaway instead?" I suggest, and both the boys smile their agreement.

It is nearly seven o'clock when James gets home, and the boys are starving. "It will be quicker if I go and collect it," he says, and we all nod our agreement. I call in the order, glad to see Dillon's appetite has recovered. At least for now.

While we eat, Luke chatters away about Harry getting into trouble at school today, but even this cannot distract me. I glance at the clock above the door, at the second hand ticking away, the sound amplified in warning. The food sticks in my throat.

Beside me, Dillon is shovelling down his food. I'm relieved to see his appetite has recovered; perhaps he is making up for those days when he barely ate. I know he is not okay, though. He can't be after what's happened.

James is in the middle of telling us about his photo shoot today when the doorbell rings. I have been expecting this moment to come but still I am unprepared for it, my hand so damp with sweat that I can barely grip my fork. I can't look at anyone. In a second I have to decide who should answer the door. It should be me but I can't face it. But neither can I let James do it. "I'll get it," I say, jumping up. Behind me I hear forks once again clinking against plates.

I can't make out who is behind the glass but there are two people, one taller than the other. Perhaps one male and one female officer. They always come in pairs, don't they?

This is it.

On autopilot, I turn the latch and pull open the door, but a few seconds pass before I recognise who is standing in front of me.

Not the police.
Rhys' parents.

CHAPTER THIRTY-FIVE

I stare at Mr and Mrs Marshall, my chest tight, waiting for them to speak. But neither says a word, and they cling to each other as if they will topple over if they let go. Perhaps they will. I know why they are here, but my mouth won't open to speak either. We are all trapped in this silent scene.

James appears behind me. "Hey, how are you both? You must have heard the good news? We're so…" And then he realises something is wrong. That they are not here to check on Dillon. That Rhys is not standing on the doorstep with them.

Confirming this, Mrs Marshall sinks to the ground, like a sack emptied of its contents. Her husband kneels to help her but can't manage it on his own. James steps forward to assist him and they help her into the living room. After they've settled her on the sofa, James pokes his head into the kitchen, telling the boys to go upstairs.

They sit opposite us, Mr Marshall speaking while his wife sobs beside him. She is wearing casual, loose trousers and a long cardigan – comfortable clothes –

and I assume they're what she wore on the plane. There will have been no time, or inclination, for her to change once they arrived home. She looks a different woman than the one I saw unloading Sainsbury's bags from her car that day.

Mr Marshall, through stuttered sentences, explains how they came home from Dubai this morning and found Rhys' body in the living room, his head concave from where it had been smashed against the marble coffee table.

I let out a gasp, even though I know this already, and beside me James' mouth hangs open. "I...I...shit...fuck. I'm so sorry, I can't believe it." He looks at me and I try to meet his eye, try to match his surprise, even though I have replayed the scene in my head a million times. I should do something. Go over and hug them? There is no right thing to do. Instead, I stay where I am and tell them I'm so sorry. Futile words.

"We'd planned a surprise birthday party for him," Mrs Marshall manages to say. "And now he'll never know..." The heavy sobs drown out the rest of her words and she stares at her shoes.

"We wanted to tell Dillon before he heard it from someone else," Mr Marshall continues. I have forgotten his name, or perhaps never knew it. "We heard he was back and..." His voice trails off. "It needs to come from us. They were so close." I want to scream out that it should be me who talks to Dillon, not them. I am the one whose fault this is.

James speaks now. "I'll go and get him. What have the police said? What do they think happened?"

Now Mrs Marshall looks up, rubbing her eyes so hard they make a squelching sound. "They don't know yet, but the back door was smashed and some things have been taken so they think he surprised a burglar. Everything in the living room was smashed up, as if there'd been a fight. He must have tried to stop them…" She bursts into loud, gut-wrenching sobs again and I can no longer watch her.

"I'll go and get Dillon," I say, standing up before James offers to do it. But when I step into the hallway, he is already coming down the stairs.

James tells Dillon to sit down and he does, a frown on his face. He glances at Rhys' parents, then back to James. "What's going on?" he asks, his voice faint.

James places his hand on Dillon's arm. He breaks the news, sparing him the extra details Mr Marshall gave us only moments ago. Dillon stares at him for a moment, as if he hasn't heard what's been said. He pulls his arm away. "What? Why are you saying this?" Sinking to the floor, he grabs his hair, yanking it on both sides of his head until I think he will pull clumps out. "No…No!" He is shrieking now and sounds like a dying animal.

I drop to my knees and put my arm around him, trying to coax him up so I can get him upstairs. I half expect him to shrug me off and back away, but he falls limp and lets me guide him. "I'll take him up," I say.

For a while I stay with him in his bedroom, trying to ignore how similar it is to Rhys'. He slumps on his

322

bed, resting his head in his hands. Several times he looks across at me, opening his mouth slightly as if he wants to say something, but nothing comes out. I sit at his desk until eventually he lies down and drifts off. At least sleep will bring him some respite.

Closing his door behind me, I step onto the landing, feeling as if my legs will collapse beneath me. I manage to make it to the bathroom and splash cold water on my face, watching the droplets trickle down my cheeks like tears.

Sitting on the side of the bath, I allow myself to think about Rhys. How different things would be if I had pushed him away when he first tried to kiss me. He wouldn't be dead.

I try to work out how I feel about him but there is nothing solid I can grasp. One minute I hate him still, then I miss him, then I pity him. But I have to think about my family now. Something good has to come out of this. It is not callousness that makes me feel this way; it is the need to protect James and the boys, and put right what I have done.

By the time I have summoned the energy to go back downstairs, the living room is empty, the lights turned off. I find James in the kitchen, sitting in semi-darkness, with only the cooker light switched on. The plates from our interrupted dinner are still on the table and the smell of old food lingers in the air.

I head to the table but don't sit down. There is too much to think of and I don't want to be still.

"I just keep thinking…what if it was Dillon who'd been found dead?" James says. "I mean, it could have been, couldn't it? He was out there on the streets. For almost a week. Anything could have happened to him."

James has offered me the perfect opening; I could tell him everything now and unload the burden, but I need more time. I want to relish every second we have left together. "Don't think that way. It's not healthy. Dillon's fine. We're all fine."

And Rhys' body is lying stiff and cold in a mortuary.

"Has Dillon said anything to you?" he says. "About what he did all those days he was missing?"

"No. I mean, why would he talk to me?" I bite my lip. There are some things a boy can never tell his father.

"I don't know. It just seems like things have been better between you and the boys."

Things *are* better, and it does appear that we have reached a silent truce, but it doesn't matter now because it is too late. But until the final moment comes, I will make the most of any family time we can share.

"They have, I think. But it's early days. And who knows how Dillon will be now. After…this."

"You're right. Rhys dying has got to be the worst thing that could have happened to him, other than losing me. Us."

But there are worse things, far worse.

"He's already lost Lauren. What's next?"

I don't know if James expects an answer, but I have none to give. I am out of comforting words.

"I'll go and check on them," he says, leaving me alone in the dark kitchen.

324

Once he's gone I have space to think. For the first time it occurs to me that things might not be hopeless, after all. The Marshalls have said the police aren't sure what happened, so that must mean nobody saw or heard anything. And if they have found any evidence they would be banging the door down by now. Of course, it might take a few days, but I know I didn't leave anything behind; I was there such a short time.

It is now a waiting game and only when enough time has passed will I know it is safe. Is it possible that we can be a normal family? Rhys' death would always hang over us, but with a fresh start, in time it might fade. I get so carried away with this idea that I think about asking James if he would consider moving away now. I could make him see that it would be good for Dillon, good for all of us. He has been against it before, but if he thinks it will help Dillon then surely he will give it some thought? We don't have to go far, just away from this house, these memories that stain every wall.

Do you know what this is? This excitement you are feeling in the midst of everything? This invincibility? It's not real. And soon enough you will crash back down.

I mention my idea to James later, when we are in bed, cocooned in the duvet that is far too warm for this weather. He takes my hand under the sheet and squeezes it. "I don't know, Callie. Do you think that's a good idea? Taking the boys out of school? Dillon's got his GCSEs."

"I know, but by the time the house is sold he'll be finished, won't he? It's not going to happen overnight, it could take months to get a sale. Anyway, we don't have to move far. They could still go to the same school."

"Is this about Lauren?"

His question is a surprise and I'm about to deny it when I realise I can't lie anymore. Of course there are lies I cannot expose, but I won't add any more to the pile. I will be honest with James whenever I can. "Partly," I say, and his hand tightens its grip. "It's been hard for me. Living here. In the house that belonged to you and her. And I think it might be part of the reason the boys didn't want to accept me. How could they, when everything is a reminder that I don't belong here?" As I say these words, it occurs to me how strange it is to be talking about Lauren after everything that has happened tonight.

"You're right. I'm sorry, Callie. The truth is, I don't think I wanted to move because I was scared it would mean there's nothing left of Lauren." I am grateful for his honesty; I know this is not easy for him to say. "But I've realised that the boys are all I need of her, so what else matters? And it's not about her now, it's about you."

Relief floods through me. "Thanks for saying that." Now there is a chance for us all to escape the mess I have made.

James kisses me. "As soon as Dillon feels better, let's get an estate agent round to value the house."

I lean across and wrap myself around him, burying my head in his chest. My tears fall onto his skin but he doesn't seem to notice. At first they are tears of relief.

But quickly I realise I am not sure who I am crying for the most: me or Rhys.

CHAPTER THIRTY-SIX

Sometimes I wonder what I would think of myself if I were someone else. If I could analyse myself from some exterior perspective: my thoughts, my actions, nothing out of bounds or hidden from view, what opinion would I have of Callie Harwell?

It's easy to sum up.

I would wonder how she gets out of bed every day, eats breakfast, showers, talks to her family. How she lives with what she has done. How she puts it aside like a handbag when she needs to get on with something else.

But the body and mind have a way of carrying on, despite what we put them through. It is a protective mechanism, a way of warding off insanity. Only when that breaks down are we in trouble.

Days pass and after Rhys' funeral I start to breathe again. The truth is always there, of course, tainting everything I do and every word I speak, but I cover it with acts of normality and hope it will stay buried. But still, I hold my breath every time the phone rings or someone comes to the door.

James is in regular contact with the Marshalls and they say the police are stumped. There have been no developments, and Rhys' computer and mobile phone show nothing unusual. I don't even want to consider what would be happening if I hadn't thought to delete my texts from his phone that night. The fact that there are so many others, going back months, will hopefully mean the police are satisfied, at least for now. It is a certainty they will look into his phone records, but Mrs Marshall makes no mention of this, so for now, at least, I am safe.

All of Rhys' friends have been questioned, and when it was Dillon's turn, a few days ago, I stifled my nausea and watched as he told them everything he could, in between fits of crying. He asked James and me to stay in the room with him, and although I was surprised he wanted me there, I was grateful to hear what the police asked him. From their questions, I was able to put my mind at ease that they have not linked me to Rhys.

James keeps to his word and, after discussing it with the boys, arranges for an estate agent to value the house. Initially there is some moaning from Luke, until he's told he won't have to change schools. Dillon, on the other hand, doesn't object at all.

Even though we are months away from a house sale, yesterday we took the boys into Kingston to pick out new furniture. "There's no point buying anything yet, but just looking might get them excited about it," James said. "And the important thing is we're doing something as a family." And he was right. Both Dillon and Luke seemed pleased that they could help us choose how to kit out the house we will eventually buy, and I cherished every second in that shop, knowing people in there saw me as the boys' mother.

Dillon remains subdued, but James and I have discussed counselling with him and, after some initial reservations, he's starting to come around to the idea. It is a shame I cannot help him. Although I am making good progress with my studies, this is all too close to home.

I know Jenny is looking after Dad, but I haven't seen him for a few weeks and I can't leave it any longer. At first I couldn't risk leaving the house, but today, once the boys have left for school, I will drive to Palmers Green and spend the morning with him. Dillon has an exam today and will be home early, but he mentioned that Esme might come over so they can study together. He seems to have cut himself off from all his other friends since Rhys' death, so neither James nor I have the heart to uphold the rule barring him from having girls over while we're out. I'm glad he still has someone. I don't know if they are still in a relationship, or if they are just friends now, but at least she is company for him.

Despite what's happened, Dillon has been catching up on all the studying he missed while he was away from home, and he is taking his exams seriously. I hope he will do well. I have already messed up his life, as well as my own, but if there is any chance to salvage it then I want him to grab it.

Thinking of this reminds me of Rhys. I try not to think of him too much, blocking his image out whenever it attempts to appear, but sometimes I let myself. It is only right. He would be sitting his final A-level exams now, and planning his gap year and the trip to America, if it weren't for me. If he were still alive, his band would be playing more gigs; how can they hope to be even remotely successful without Rhys at the helm? I have snatched all this from him.

Dillon and Luke both appear in the kitchen, snapping me out of my melancholy. "I want to get to school early to do some more revision," Dillon says. "I'll grab some breakfast on the way."

Luke looks disappointed but won't want Dillon to head off without him. I reach for my purse and grab a handful of coins, dividing them between the boys. "Get something with this," I say.

Once they have gone, I trudge around Sainsbury's, picking up Dad's regular groceries as well as some things for us. Dad's list is always the same; he never asks to try anything new, just as nothing will ever change in his life. He can never get well. And suddenly, right there in the middle of the aisle, I am powerless to stop my flood of tears. People pass by but nobody says a word, they just avoid me as if I am a crazy person, best avoided. I wonder if they are right, because the truth is I don't know the real reason for my tears. Maybe it is about Dad, but it's just as likely to be anything else. Or everything mashed into one. If I were here only to shop for James and the boys, I would run out of here right now. But I have to get Dad's food. I have already let everyone else down; I can't do that to him too.

By the time I have pulled myself together and made it to Palmers Green, it is nearly one o'clock. I wanted to be home by now, to be there when Dillon gets back, not only just arriving at Dad's.

As I park up and grab the shopping from the boot, I glance across the road at the park. It will always make me think of Rhys now, even though we only went there once together, and I have been many times without him. I know that I will never set foot in there again. I will have to find somewhere else to take Dad when he is having a good day.

Things start off the usual way after I've pressed Dad's buzzer, but it doesn't take long before I realise something is wrong. I have been out here too long. Dad has never taken this much time to answer. But it's not just that. I can feel something is wrong. I just don't know what it is.

I press the other buzzers – all of them – and wait for someone to answer. I know the woman next door to Dad doesn't work, and pray that she is home. After a few seconds a female voice answers. Quickly I explain who I am and she lets me in.

When I reach the top of the stairs she is waiting for me, poking her head out of her door. I can't see much more than her curtain of grey hair but she looks a bit younger than Dad. "You come every week, don't you? His daughter?" she says. Her eyes drop to the shopping bags I'm holding. "Is Mike okay?"

I tell her I don't know, that this is the first time he hasn't answered his door.

"Maybe he's fallen asleep? I do that sometimes after lunch. It's this weather, you see. Much too warm for me."

I give her a brief smile and knock gently on Dad's door. It will do no good to pound on it. There is no answer so I knock again, harder. Still nothing. And no sound from inside. I turn to the woman and she must see the despair in my eyes because she smiles and says, "Would you like the spare key?"

Confused, I frown at her. She must be mistaken.

"Your dad gave it to me once. Years ago. Asked me to look after it in case of emergencies. I'd forgotten I had it until now."

I don't know whether to laugh or cry. The idea of Dad giving his neighbour a spare key seems unbelievable. He doesn't even trust me or Jenny to have one. He must have given it to her when he was having a clear day. But whatever the case, I am grateful for it now.

"I'll just go and find it," the woman says, leaving her door ajar as she disappears inside her flat.

The seconds tick by and begin to feel like hours. As each one passes, my anxiety increases. I try to tell myself he is asleep, but I know he only sleeps lightly so would have woken by now. Even our voices would have been enough to rouse him.

Dad's neighbour reappears, jingling the key in the air, proud of herself for being able to help me. It is all I can do not to grab it from her. "Thanks. I really appreciate your help."

"Do you want me to come in there with you?" I know why she is asking but shake my head. Whatever it is, I will deal with it alone.

"No, but thanks. I'll be fine. He's probably just gone out or something."

She doesn't look convinced. She must have lived next door to Dad long enough to know how unlikely this is. I wonder what else she knows about him. Whether she has worked him out.

"Well, just knock if you need anything."

The second she closes her door I thrust the key in the lock of Dad's, feeling strange because I have never once opened it myself. Inside, the usual stale air assaults me, but it is too dark for this time of day. I soon see why. In the living room, the curtains are drawn and there is no sign of Dad. He's not in the kitchen either but the blinds are pulled down, the slivers of light through the gaps casting bright orange lines onto the wall.

The bathroom door is wide open so I can immediately see he's not in there. That leaves only the bedroom to check.

With my stomach churning, I knock on the door, just in case he is asleep. When he doesn't answer, I open it slowly and peer inside, squeezing my eyes shut to start with. But when I force them open I am staring into more darkness, at Dad's empty bed. Unmade, with the duvet half-hanging on the floor.

You were convinced he was lying here dead, weren't you? Like Rhys. It's what you deserve.

Back in the kitchen, I dump Dad's shopping on the worktop then rush outside to escape the stagnant air. When I've calmed down I realise that, although he isn't here and I have no way of knowing where he might be, finding his flat empty is better than the alternative.

Pulling out my mobile, I scroll through my contacts until I find Jenny's number. She answers immediately but says she hasn't seen Dad since yesterday. "He was fine, though," she adds, "so I'm sure he's just gone for a walk or something."

I check the park, just in case, but there is no sign of him there. Neither is he wandering up and down Alderman's Hill or the high street, which I walk up and down several times, carefully checking in shops on both sides of the road.

When I get back to the car, my mobile rings. I half-expect it to be Dad, even though he would never call me and I doubt he still has my number. But this is what my mind does to me. It is James so I let it ring out; if I speak to him at this moment he'll know something is wrong. I wait to see if he leaves a voicemail but my phone stays silent. It won't be important then.

I check Dad's flat one more time before I go, but it is still as empty as before. At least now I have a key.

By the time I set off it is nearly three p.m. and I have the North Circular to contend with. At least Dillon will be at home when Luke gets back from school, so I don't have to worry about the boys. And I will come back to Palmers Green tonight to check on Dad again. I can tell James I am going to see Debbie.

I drive home in a daze, thoughts of Dad coming to harm intruding into my head, refusing to budge, no matter how much I try to focus on the road. And when I pull into our road, I barely remember how I got here. All I know is I am very late, it's nearly five and James will be home soon. I grab the shopping bags from the boot and head inside. I don't even bother glancing next door to see if Mrs Simmons is watching.

Sometimes it's possible to see or feel life-changing moments before they happen. When this occurs they are easier to deal with because there is no element of surprise. Other times they creep up on you, ploughing into you with the force of an articulated lorry.

I hear James' voice coming from the living room and assume he is talking to the boys. Leaving the bags in the hallway, I place my keys on the phone table and open the living room door, ready to tell James about my plan to see Debbie tonight.

What I am not prepared for is to see Dad sitting on the sofa, cradling a mug of tea, nodding at James. They both turn to me and the ground falls away beneath my feet.

"What the hell, Callie?" James says. His eyes flash with anger and something else. Betrayal. He has pulled me away to the kitchen while Dad drinks his tea in the living room. At least he has spared me the humiliation of having to explain myself in front of my father. "I don't even know where to start. What to say. I don't

336

even want to look at you." But he does and his eyes burn into me.

Of all the things I could say, I should not speak the words I do. "I can explain." But how can I? There is no justification for the lies I have told James. There is no way to crawl from under this one. The least I can do is tell him the little I can. "He's ill, James," I continue. "I'm ashamed to say it, but I couldn't bring myself to tell you how bad it was."

And then I tell him about Dad, how he started off an ordinary and loving father, but then began a slow descent into mental illness. For the first time I allow myself to use the official term. The label Dad has been given. *Schizophrenia.* It rolls smoothly off my tongue, the sound too light to portray what it is.

It's hard to tell what James is thinking. He lets me speak without interrupting but flinches when I explain I've been visiting Dad every week. Doing his shopping and cleaning his flat. Being a daughter to him. It would be one thing if I had pretended even to myself that he didn't exist, but the fact he has been such a big part of my life the whole time I've known James only makes my deceit worse.

I finish by saying what I should have started with. The fact that I am sorry.

James shakes his head, still staring at me. He is probably wondering who he is married to. "But why lie? That makes no sense. Did you think I wouldn't help you with him? That I wouldn't want anything to do with him? What do you take me for?" He fires these questions at me but doesn't wait for a reply. He has already answered for himself. "Were you ever going to tell me?"

"I wanted to. So many times. But the more time went on, the more difficult it got. It's not that I didn't think you'd help me, or accept him –"

"Then what?"

"I didn't want to burden you. Or for you to think I'd end up…" I can't finish my sentence. Now I've said it out loud, to James, I realise how irrational it sounds, how far gone I must have been to believe this.

We both stare at each other, each of us realising the significance of my fear, and then James walks out without another word.

I should get back to Dad, make sure he is okay, because this will be an even bigger shock to him. He must be having a good day otherwise how would he have made it here? In fact, I can't even think how he would have found my address, unless he looked through my bag while I was out of sight during one of my visits. I think it unlikely, but there is no other conclusion I can reach.

Forcing myself to move is not easy. I am rooted to the spot because I don't want to face Dad or James in the other room. It is only when Dillon and Luke appear that I manage to take a step forward.

"What's going on?" Luke asks, appearing in the doorway with his brother. "This weird man came and Dad sent us upstairs. Who is he?" Beside him, Dillon is silent but I am sure he is wondering the same thing.

"Oh, just someone I know. Why don't you go back up and I'll bring you some drinks in a minute?"

Neither of them says anything but they both move slowly to the door, Dillon staring back at me once Luke has disappeared. He knows I am lying.

Dad is smiling when I return to the living room. I didn't think to ask what James has told him about us, but it's too late now. "Caroline!" Dad calls, beckoning me over. I join him on the sofa, avoiding James' heavy stare. "This man's been telling me all about his photography. Sounds exciting. Was never any good at taking photos myself. Always managed to chop people's heads off, especially your mother's." He laughs.

"Dad, how about I drive you home now? I've done your shopping. It's at the flat."

"In Palmers Green," James says. So Dad has been here long enough for them to exchange these small details.

Dad slaps his knee. "Why are you trying to get me out? I'm happy here, just chatting to…sorry, what was your name again?"

I answer before James has a chance. "That's James. And I'm not trying to get you out, it's just that he's got work to get on with."

James rolls his eyes but he doesn't disagree. He obviously wants to question me more and knows he can't do it while Dad is here. He will also want to explain what's going on to the boys and I know he won't lie to them.

"James," Dad says, trying out his name.

I stand, hoping Dad will follow, but this is all new to me. I haven't seen him anywhere other than his flat or the park for years, so have no idea how he will react in a different environment. All I know is I need to get him home.

I turn to James, hoping he will notice my silent plea, and he pulls himself up and leans forward to shake Dad's hand. "Well, it was nice to meet you, Mr Byrne. Callie's right, I'd better get back to work, but I hope to see you soon."

Dad recoils from James and cowers against the back of the sofa. To his credit, James doesn't appear surprised or offended and he stands back to let Dad have some space.

"Come on, Dad, let's get home," I say, although his flat is not my home, and hardly a home to Dad either.

To my relief, he rises from his seat without any fuss and we head to the door. But then he turns around and fixes a cold stare on James. "I don't know about him, Caroline. Where's that nice boy you brought to the flat? Your boyfriend. Rhys? Yes, that was his name. Rhys."

CHAPTER THIRTY-SEVEN

Dad looks pleased with himself, sitting beside me in the car. He has no idea what he's done. "How did you find me?" I ask, although I suspect the answer.

"That nice boy, of course. He came to see me a while ago, and I told him how worried I was. That you'd been taken. He gave me your address and told me exactly how to get there." He stares straight ahead, as if what he has just said is part of an everyday conversation, nothing out of the ordinary. But then, it won't be for him.

And then he surprises me. "You're in trouble, aren't you? I don't know what's going on, but I know you need help."

I briefly turn to him. Is he offering me help? How can he be? And even if he is, there is no way I can burden him. "I love you, Dad," I say, and wait for a reply that doesn't come.

An hour and a half later I sit in the car outside Dad's flat. I have had time to prepare for this, to plan how I will keep my marriage together if James found out, but now the moment has come I know I can't face him. He will be sitting at home now, or rather pacing up and down, stewing over the knowledge that I have been with Rhys. And by now he will have worked out that I was with Rhys that night.

There is no way I can go back there.

I turn on the engine and head back onto the North Circular, away from Dad, wondering when I will see him again.

The drive through Acton and Hammersmith is a blur, and before long I am at the top of Putney Hill, facing the roundabout. Facing a choice. If I take the second exit I will be heading home. The third one will get me onto the A3 and away from London.

I have no idea what I will do until I find myself passing the Wimbledon exit. And then I am on the A3, ignoring the speed limit in my desperation to get away. I have nothing with me but my bag and the jeans and shirt I'm wearing. I don't even have a jacket. But still I keep driving. A speed camera flashes at me but I don't slow down. What difference will a speeding fine make when I am facing much worse?

My mobile rings and I ignore it. Whoever it is can't help me; it is too late for that. It rings again. Then three more times. I turn on the radio so I don't have to hear it.

As I drive I convince myself that if no car passes me, everything will be okay. James will stick by me and try to understand what has happened. We will be a family. I stay in the fast lane and when a yellow Nissan tries to overtake me, I cut in front of it. The man driving swerves into the middle lane, blaring his horn, and in the rear-view mirror I see him make an obscene gesture. This game is not only dangerous but pointless. Nothing will make things okay.

I pass a sign for Guildford and realise I have never been this way before. I have been abroad several times but in my own country have never ventured out of London. I laugh then, a loud cackling shriek that fills the car, and only stop when I think of Rhys and his plan to travel across America. And then I am crying, my view out of the windscreen blocked by a blur of tears.

And at once I know I must go back. I have to do right by Rhys.

I force my mind to focus once I've turned around and am heading back towards home. What will I say to James? How I can possibly explain what he has just found out? We both fell silent when Dad mentioned Rhys and when James looked at me for answers I still couldn't speak. I didn't want to insult him by telling him Dad is mistaken, rambling as he often does about things that don't make sense. There is no way Dad would know anything about Rhys unless they had met. So I said nothing, only that I would explain everything when I got back. And that was hours ago. I have no idea how he will have spent this time, but I can't put him through any more. I should make things easy for him and pack up my things the minute I get back, but I won't run away like a coward. And I don't want to leave him. The choice must be his.

When I get to the house I pull up outside but leave the engine running. Faced with what lies ahead, I freeze, unable to step outside. It is one thing to imagine doing the right thing, but actually going through with it is another matter. Could there still be a chance to salvage this? I don't have to tell James everything. There is always a way to keep things hidden. But I have done this for far too long now and it's eaten away at me. I need freedom.

The house is silent and bathed in darkness, making me wonder if James has left. It is possible he has taken the boys away, as far from me as he can. How could I blame him if this is the case?

But then he appears at the top of the stairs, and I take a deep breath. He descends slowly, clutching the banister, each step making a heavy clomp. Without a word he passes me and disappears into the kitchen. I don't know what this means, or what he wants, but I follow him in and head straight for the sink. I need a glass of water to stifle my growing nausea. There is a dirty glass on the side and I don't know whose it is but I grab it and fill it with tap water.

Someone has left the patio light on outside and a dull, warm glow seeps into the dark kitchen. It is better this way. I don't want James to see me under the harsh light.

Still ignoring me, he opens the cupboard, pulling out a bottle of whisky and pouring himself a large glass. It is more than a double but I am in no position to comment. He sits at the table and when I join him, making sure I take the opposite chair instead of the one beside him, he buries his head in his hands. His eyes are bloodshot when he finally looks up, his cheeks stained with tears.

"Tell me everything," he says, staring into his glass. "No more lies. I just want to hear the truth, whatever it is." He has had hours to think about this while I took Dad home, so he will be sure of what he wants. I never expected James to want details, I thought he would avoid them at all costs.

"Are you sure?" I ask. I am strangely calm now. "Because once you know, you can never un-know."

"Just tell me."

"Where are Dillon and Luke?" I ask, stalling for time.

"I took them to Emma's. I don't want them to be here. There's no way I can let them hear this. Now just fucking tell me."

This is a day of firsts: the first time Dad has been to this house, the first time James has set eyes on him, the first time he has sworn at me. And the first time he will hear that his wife has blood on her hands.

As we sit in the semidarkness, I tell James everything. And with every word I can feel a piece of him crumbling. He is just another casualty of my actions. But it stops now. When I get to Rhys' last night, I can't give him details, my brain won't allow it, and he lets out a sigh. I want to believe he is relieved that I have spared him, but I cannot read him at the moment.

By the time I've finished we are both crying and I am shaking as well. But I feel as if I am lighter, that just by speaking I have lifted a heavy burden, even if only slightly. But then I realise that all I have done is make this James' problem too. Now he also has to live with what I have done, to carry the heavy weight. The lies are better after all; how could I have thought otherwise? I feel my gut twist with panic and I sink to the floor in a crumpled heap, just like Eva Marshall did the night she was here.

I will James to help me up, but he leaves me where I am. He turns away and stares through the patio door. I don't know what I expected to happen once I'd told him, but it wasn't this. I thought there would be shouting and screaming, that he'd grab me and force me out of his house. Because it is just that, after all. His house. It was never mine. I did not expect silence and tears. But there is no rulebook for what to do when your wife confesses to killing someone, is there? James is only doing his best to cope with what I have told him.

When he turns back to me, his expression has changed. His tears have dried and his face is softer. There is something there, something I can cling to, and buoyed by this, I pick myself up and sit on the chair again. He doesn't flinch or move away from me. This is promising.

We sit like this for too long and all the time he doesn't speak I let myself believe we will find a way through this together. I have no idea what that could be, but two are stronger than one.

He looks at his watch – the one Lauren gave him all those years ago that he can't bear to be without – and then slowly reaches for my hand. "I can't process

346

this," he says, finally. "Any of it. I don't know what the fuck –"

And then I say it, over and over, as if I am a malfunctioning machine. *Sorry, sorry, sorry.* The words begin to roll into one until finally they are just a sound. A sound without a meaning. And then I am screaming it, shouting it, throwing the words at James because he won't believe me. Or won't let himself.

"Callie, calm down," he says, placing his hands on my shoulders to stop me shaking. Is this it? Has it finally happened?

I grab hold of his arms and am shocked to feel how cold his skin is. "Please, James. Please…" I don't know what I am begging for but I can't stop the words.

He pulls away. "What the fuck do you want? What do you want from me?" Then he kicks his chair, so hard it slams against the patio door. I reel back and am finally calm, but my breathing doesn't slow. I watch as he flings open the door and rushes outside, pacing up and down the garden.

I don't follow him immediately. He needs time to absorb everything. It's taken me long enough to do that myself, and I've had so much longer to adapt than I'm giving him. It's possible that tomorrow he will have got his head around this, and we will plan the next steps together.

You are losing it, Callie. Can't you see what's staring you in the face?

Outside, James sits on the step leading up to the lawn. Only when I'm sure I have pulled myself together do I join him. He flinches when my leg touches his as I sit down, but I ignore his reaction.

"Listen," I say. "It will all be okay. We'll get through this together. Like a family is supposed to."

You are insane. How can you possibly believe that?

He snorts. "I loved you," he says. "I did. But you never quite believed it, did you? That's what this is all about. Everything. It's because you had no faith in me, or yourself."

I turn away from him.

"If you'd believed in us, you would have known that even if you got sick like your dad, I would never turn my back on you."

I don't want to hear these words. I want him to yell and swear again. I need his anger.

"I keep wanting to ask you how you could do that…to Rhys, but it seems such a stupid question. I don't know…a cliché or something."

But he is wrong. It is an important question, and one I need to answer, for both our sakes. "I suppose I just don't know myself. That's all I can say. I just don't know what I'm capable of."

I don't know whether this helps James but he sighs and stands up. "Let's go back inside. I need another drink and I think you could do with one too."

This is promising and I agree, following him inside. As I close the door, I look outside and half expect to see Jazzy appear from the shed. This is the thing: once someone has been in your life, they will always be there, whether in the shadows or somewhere closer. Lauren,

Rhys. It is only now I fully understand how difficult it's been for James and the boys to move on.

We take our drinks to the living room and sit on the sofa, but it feels too civilised after everything I have done. Too normal. I feel as if we are bad actors in a terrible movie, unsure how to portray emotion and get across the severity of our situation. Of course we don't speak – it is safer just to focus on drinking our whiskys – and when I catch him looking at me he turns away.

When we've finished, he takes our glasses to the kitchen. I wait for him to reappear, but several minutes pass and he doesn't.

The doorbell rings before he has come back. Numb, I pull myself from the sofa but then I hear James' footsteps moving towards the door.

I strain to listen – the living room door is shut – and although I can't hear what's being said, I don't recognise the other two voices. Then the front door closes and James comes back in, looking at me with a blank expression.

Behind him are two police officers.

"Caroline Harwell?" one of them asks. I almost shake my head. It feels strange to hear my given name from anyone's lips but Dad's. "We need you to come to the station with us."

I stare at him, unable to digest what he's saying. He is young. Too young to have a job with such responsibility, surely? And the other one's skin is as white as paper, almost translucent. I wonder if I'm hallucinating and it is only James standing before me. I squeeze my eyes shut but when I open them again, the two officers are still there, moving closer towards me.

They haven't explained whether they are arresting me or asking me to go with them voluntarily, but it makes no difference. I move towards the door and smile at the younger officer, but he doesn't return it. They follow behind me and as we walk past James, I notice he is not looking at me, or them; he only stares at the floor.

Perhaps I should hate him at this moment for what he has done, but how can I? He is protecting his sons. At least he has given me the chance to explain.

Outside, I turn back to look at the house, trying to memorise every detail of the place I have hated for almost a year. I am sure that, whatever happens in the next few hours, I won't see it again. I even look next door and see Mrs Simmons by her window, holding the curtain away from her so she can have a good look at the spectacle next door. The officers usher me into the back of the car, but I don't look away or hang my head in shame. Let her make of this what she will.

As we drive off, I feel as if I'm in a taxi. I let myself believe this, pretending I'm on the way to the airport. It is our honeymoon again and we will soon be enveloped by glorious heat in Barbados.

It is a surprise when my mobile vibrates in my pocket. I thought I had left everything at the house and deliberately didn't ask if I could bring my bag. They will only take my belongings once I am at the police station so there seemed little point grabbing anything. I pull the phone from my jeans and stare at the screen, willing it to be a message from James. But it is Max. He says he is worried he hasn't heard from me and hopes I'm okay. I read it a couple of times but don't reply. Instead, I switch off the phone and drop it to the floor, kicking it under the slip mat. They will find it eventually and can do with it what they wish.

I have no need for a phone now.

CHAPTER THIRTY-EIGHT

Now

DS Connolly leans forward and stops the tape. "Interview terminated at…five twenty a.m." The click signals it's over, or at least my part is. Now it is a waiting game. Once again someone knocks on the door and the detective jumps up, seemingly glad to escape from my story. To escape from me.

I don't think he expected me to be so open. I have told them more than they need to know and maybe he doesn't know what to do with so much information.

Would it have been enough to simply say that I killed Rhys, and tell them how exactly his head came to be smashed against the Marshalls' coffee table? But that would go no way to helping them understand, and surely that's what they want? They are only human, and it is our natural instinct to want to know *why*.

And now I am left alone again with DC Barnes. She stares at her notes, her shoulders hunched, and I will her to look at me, to say something, just for the company. Even if she only opened her mouth to tell me how despicable I am, it would be better than this silence.

But she doesn't move until DS Connolly comes back, relaxing her shoulders as he sits down and whispers to her, indicating something on the paper he has brought back with him. Then he turns to me and there is no trace of the smile I saw earlier. I will have to get used to this; it's how everyone will look at me from now on.

"The carpet fibres we found at the crime scene are a match for your carpet." He delivers this news as if he expected a different result. Surely after everything I've said it can't be a shock to him.

I don't know how he feels about it but I am glad to hear this. It means this is the end and I am starting a new phase of my life.

"Do you want to add anything?" He stares at me and again I wonder if he is hoping I will suddenly deny it all, tell them it's been a horrible mistake and I need to be sectioned.

But I shake my head, because of course there is nothing else to say.

They both stand up and I notice DC Barnes is almost as tall as DS Connolly. She makes me think of Tabitha, the woman James should have ended up with. Perhaps he still will; life has a funny way of turning out. "Someone will come and take you to a cell until the next available court," she says. "We'll also assign you a solicitor as you don't have one."

I fall asleep as soon as I am alone in my cell. But within a couple of hours I am woken by someone telling me my solicitor has arrived.

His name is John Samuels and he is in his late fifties with thinning hair and narrow, determined eyes. Even though he tells me sternly that I shouldn't have spoken to the police without him being there, I immediately like him. He seems like the kind of man who has no time for pleasantries or small talk, only business. The kind of man who doesn't have a life outside his job.

They have given us an interview room so we can talk privately, and even provided us with cups of tea. I drink the tasteless liquid and go through my story again. It is not as detailed this time – I am too exhausted to repeat myself – but by the end of it he has all the information he will need. He doesn't judge me like DS Connolly did in the end, but gets straight to business, telling me how things will play out. I am only half-listening. What I think about while he is talking is how strange it is that a person can commit such a heinous crime and still have someone on her side, a wall to lean on. It is more than anyone deserves.

I have been to court and pleaded guilty. Mr Samuels is talking to me but once again I am only half-listening. The only information that sticks in my head is that I will be remanded to prison until my trial, which could take up to a year. It sounds so serious, much worse than *going* to prison. But for now I have to stay in this court cell. What am I supposed to do here? I don't have anything but my mind to keep me occupied, and that is a dangerous thing.

Before he leaves, he tells me that James is outside and wants to speak to me. He must sense my unease because he quickly adds that I don't have to, it is entirely my decision. But I don't have the energy to dwell on it too long so I nod, unsure whether it is a good or bad idea to see him. What will we say to each other?

Mr Samuels says goodbye and leaves me alone to wait for James. The second he has gone I regret not asking him more questions, playing out the conversation so I have the company of someone I haven't hurt for longer.

I wait but nobody comes. I can't tell how much time has passed since he left, but it is long enough for James to have appeared. But just as I convince myself Mr Samuels must have been mistaken, a figure appears at the door. I look up but it takes me a moment to realise it's not James standing there, because they are almost the same height.

Dillon.

This is far worse. I have not prepared myself for this confrontation. I didn't think James would let either of the boys anywhere near me. But here Dillon is, lingering by the door as if afraid to come nearer.

"Dillon? What are you –"

"Sorry…Dad changed his mind and wouldn't come. Is it okay for me to be here instead?" My heart softens because he is acting as if he is invading my privacy, intruding.

"Course, sit down."

He does as I suggest and pulls out the chair John Samuels sat in. I should feel more nervous now that I am facing Dillon, but I am strangely calm. He will want answers and I owe it to him to provide them.

"Does your dad know you're here?"

He shakes his head. "He went for some fresh air and I begged that man… your solicitor…to let me talk to you."

So we only have limited time before James realises he has snuck in and demands they get Dillon away from me.

"Why?" he says, his eyes brimming with tears. "Why?"

But there is no time for this. "Dillon, listen carefully. I need you to tell me again what happened. Everything this time. Every detail you can remember. I need to be clear about it all. It's really important. Don't leave anything out. Even things you didn't mention before."

He hesitates for a moment but seems to understand why I need to hear it again. And when he speaks this time, I am fully prepared. I need to picture it, to feel as if I was there with him.

"It was early that afternoon and I wanted to call Rhys. I don't know why, I just missed him, I guess. I used a payphone. I couldn't remember his mobile number but knew his home one.

"He was so happy to hear from me but asked what the hell I thought I was playing at, running away. He said you were all worried and I should call you. Well, that was the last thing I wanted to do. I said no way, and that you were probably happy I was gone and then he went all quiet." Dillon stops and takes a deep breath.

"Then he said he had to show me something urgent and begged me to come over. He promised it wasn't a set up or anything and I believed him because…well, friends don't do that to each other, do they?" He looks at me as if expecting an answer to this question, but I urge him to continue. Time is running out.

"So I went there. Turned up at seven o'clock like he asked, and it was fine. Nobody was there to drag me back home. Then he started drinking his dad's gin and…and we were laughing about that. He offered me some but I didn't want any. I almost forgot he'd said he had to show me something."

My stomach is in knots. I know too well what comes next.

"He made me promise that whatever happened at eight o'clock, whatever I saw or heard, I would keep quiet, stay hidden and not say a word until he told me it was okay. He said I needed to hear every word or I wouldn't get the whole picture. At first I thought it was just the alcohol making him a bit crazy, but he was serious. Rhys doesn't fuck around. Didn't…"

He stops talking for a moment, as if paying a silent respect to his friend.

"When the doorbell went he told me to get behind the sofa quick, so I did. It was kind of exciting. I didn't know what was going on. But then I heard your voice."

Shame floods through me and I look away. I don't need him to repeat the conversation I had with Rhys; it is deeply etched in my head. "And afterwards? What happened after I'd gone?"

"I waited till I'd heard the front door shut then came out. I can't describe how I felt. Numb. Angry. I hated you. More than I ever had before. It made me sick to think what you'd done to Dad. But I hated Rhys even more. Don't know why. I've thought about it every day but still don't understand it. Maybe it's because at least you were trying to end it." He is crying now, reliving that night will be causing him unbearable pain but we have to do this.

I too have thought about this a lot. It should have been me Dillon hated the most. None of this was Rhys' fault. "He was supposed to be your friend," I say. "You didn't care what I did to you because you never believed I loved you in the first place. But Rhys…"

He nods, digging in his pocket for something. I assume he is looking for a tissue but his hand comes out empty. He looks around the room and seems surprised there is nothing in here but empty plastic cups. He uses his sleeve to wipe his face. "Yeah. Maybe."

I glance at the door and he takes this as a sign to carry on. He must realise James will be back inside soon and looking for him.

"After you left, we argued. He said he loved you and you'd find a way to be together. I just wanted to hurt him, to knock the smile off his face because it lit up when he talked about you. I was so angry I just went for him. I shoved him and he fell backwards. Against the coffee table. And then…I grabbed his head and rammed it against the marble. I couldn't stop…" The rest of Dillon's words are lost in the midst of his sobs. "I ran then. Just ran. I didn't even want to go home but I knew I had to. I was almost there when I realised I'd have to go back to Rhys' and make it look like a burglary." His whole body starts to shake and he buries his head in his hands, gasping with sobs.

"It's okay," I say. But it's not, is it? He will have to live forever with what he has done. His guilt will be bottled up, and he'll never be able to tell another soul about it. I can take the blame for him but I can't erase his actions or his memories. I want to hug him but I can't risk the officer outside coming in. He is already watching us through the small window. But I reach for his hand and he lets me take it. This is the first time we have had any physical contact. It still surprises me that Dillon doesn't hate me. I can't explain it and neither can he, but I suspect it is because I am the only person he could turn to. He needed me. Finally.

"What happens now?" he asks, when his tears begin to ebb.

"Say nothing. Do nothing. Just let things be. You'll find a way to cope. Carry on with your exams. Do well for your dad. And your mum." This is the first time I have referred to Lauren without feeling negative.

He shakes his head. "But why are you doing this? What about you? You can't do this."

"Yes, I can. It's already done. You've got your future to think about. That's all that matters."

"But Dad hates you…he thinks –"

"And that is what he'll always have to think. Promise me, Dillon. Promise you won't say anything. Ever. It might hurt him to think I've done this, but knowing you did would kill him."

He says something then, but again I can't tell what because he is crying so hard. Eventually he nods his agreement.

"I just want one thing in return." He looks at me and I see fear in his eyes. He is afraid of what I will ask. "I need you to make sure my father's okay."

He rubs his eyes. "Dad told me about him. I'm sorry. I'm sorry for all of this."

"Will you do this for me?"

Nodding, he explains that James is already planning a visit to him later today. Hearing this, I can finally exhale. Dad is a sacrifice I've had to make for Dillon, but at least now I know he will be looked after. I tell Dillon it won't be easy and guide him through a list of things to avoid saying and doing.

"That man…your solicitor…he'll sort this out, won't he? He'll get you out of here?"

"He'll do what he can," I say.

The officer outside knocks on the door, signalling our time is up. I watch Dillon stand up, red-eyed and still shaking, and walk to the door. He turns back before he steps out of the room, offering me a weak smile. Earlier he asked me what happens next, but the truth is I have no idea. All I know is that I have got what I wished for.

I am finally a mother.

Message from Kathryn Croft

Thank you for reading *The Stranger Within*. Your support is much appreciated. I hope you enjoyed the book, and if you did, would be grateful if you could take a few moments to leave a quick review on Amazon.

I love hearing from readers so please let me know what you thought via Twitter or my Facebook page. You can even contact me directly through my website.

You may also be interested in my debut novel, *Behind Closed Doors*, which can also be found on Amazon.

Thank you!

Kathryn x

Acknowledgements

Once again, this book was a culmination of the invaluable advice and support of some amazing people. Therefore, a huge thank you to the following:

My wonderful agent, Madeleine Milburn; I am extremely proud to be one of her authors; my editor, Ellen Macdonald-Kramer for her amazing insights and all the time, effort and skill she put into helping this book work; Claire Bord, for the excellent editorial work she did on this novel; my friend, Jonny Garland, for fantastic advice, without which I would have been lost; Christa Holland, for an amazing cover design.

A special thank you as always to all my family and friends, I couldn't have done this without them and I am truly blessed to have them in my life.

Author Biography

Kathryn Croft has a BA Honours Degree in Media Arts with English Literature and before writing full-time spent six years teaching secondary school English. Her first novel, BEHIND CLOSED DOORS, reached No.1 in the UK Amazon Kindle psychological thriller chart. Kathryn is now hard at work on her next psychological suspense novel.

www.kathryncroft.com

60142998R00221

Made in the USA
Lexington, KY
28 January 2017